CHARMED BY THE PAST

SPIRITS THROUGH TIME

AIMEE ROBINSON

To Ben

CHAPTER 1

S arah was in trouble. She walked a delicate tightrope without a safety net. The edges were browning, a clear indication that the breaded chicken cutlet sizzling in the hot oil was ready to flip. But, oh, she had been wrong before, and history is doomed to repeat itself lest one learn from it. Too many times she had served herself her favorite entree, the coating still glistening with tiny bubbles of hotter-than-hell oil. Based on appearances, sitting alongside its companionable vegetables, it had been a perfect specimen of her happy, standard dinner for one that had come to be her norm. Looks could be sooooo deceiving, though. All it took was one slice of the knife to unmask the traitor within: pink, raw chicken breast.

She squatted down on her haunches a bit and sized up the chicken at eye level. Had she gotten the thickness right? That had often been her downfall. But, no, it looked to be within that quarter-inch zone she deemed an acceptable density for pan-frying.

Next, the oil. Was it too hot? She inhaled deeply through her nose, trying to assess for any smells of burnt or rancid fat, anything to indicate an improper fry. Nothing but deliciousness wafted her way. Okay, it was go time.

All the framework accounted for, she took her thin metal spatula and gently wedged it between the chicken and the edge of the pan.

Good slip, good color. Systems were a go for takeoff. With a deft hand, she gingerly lifted the breast up and over, bringing its uncooked side to nestle into the hot oil bath. A few errant breadcrumbs immediately popped and sizzled on contact. The sensory satisfaction was deeply encouraging, so she continued breading and frying the rest of the chicken for leftovers.

A ping sounded from Sarah's open laptop perched on the breakfast bar in her kitchen.

"Oh, really? Right now? Okay, okay..."

With one hand holding raw chicken and the other looking like the club fist of the Thing from *The Fantastic Four* thanks to her fried chicken dredging station, Sarah found herself, not for the first time, wishing she had a virtual assistant. "Alexa, please read my new e-mail."

Did Alexa even do that? Hell if she knew, but as she stood there, elbows-deep in Sunday night dinner, that particular feature would have come in super handy.

Sarah finished breading the final chicken cutlet, threw it in the pan of hot oil, and quickly washed her hands. While drying them on her "Don't worry, dishes. No one is doing me, either" kitchen towel, she walked toward her laptop to read the new e-mail. The subject read, "HomeAway.com Reservation Confirmation."

"Oh, excellent! The family reunion's a go!" Sarah said with an ear-to-ear smile.

After a year of planning, she had finally convinced the rest of the Johansson family that, yes, it was important to see each other at more than just weddings and funerals. And while the other Johansson progeny didn't exactly share her level of enthusiasm, they had all finally come to an agreement that a long weekend at the Jersey Shore next June would not be such a terrible way to pass a few summer days.

After the feeling of excitement subsided, Sarah realized she had just cleared the first hurdle, but an entire track of new ones lined up in front of her.

"Shit. The family reunion's a go," she grumbled, wiping the back of her chicken-greasy wrist against her forehead, catching a few wisps of hair in the process. They didn't call it dirty blond for nothing, right?

Sarah found herself in the principal role of event planner, creative director, and concierge for a greenlighted family history project, a family reunion, and a lot of promises to deliver on. As part of the enticement she had to offer up to her brother's family, as well as her three cousins and their families, she promised fun in the sun suitable for all ages, an interactive Jeopardy game based on family history and trivia (and she was still kicking her overactive imagination for coming up with that one), and swore up and down that she'd be able to find a shore house large enough for thirteen adults and ten children. And as the only adult cousin who wasn't married with kids, she had to bring her A game. No way could the inadequate singleton of the family overpromise and underdeliver.

So, yes, the house would include individual rooms for all the cousins. No, Jeremy's children would not have to sleep in a common area. Yes, even though the house was three properties in from the beach, there was a pool nearby offering day passes (because that was a priority when looking for a shore house). Yes, there were restaurants within walking distance because people didn't want to cook. Yes, there was a grocery store close by because people also *wanted* to cook.

And on and on and on. After months of searching VRBO, Airbnb, and straight-up word of mouth from her shore-going friends, she'd finally found the perfect house to rent on Long Beach Island.

Closing her laptop, Sarah walked over to her stove to tend to her chicken. With a quick grab of her tongs, she managed to save a breaded cutlet and keep it "golden, brown, and delicious," before heading into "charred, petrified, and calling for pizza delivery...again" territory. Plopping a cutlet on a plate, Sarah killed the heat on the stove, took the green beans out of the oven, served herself a hefty portion, and walked over to the fridge to grab some Frank's RedHot. Whether tender or dry, Frank's always belonged with pan-fried anything.

Sarah grabbed her partially consumed dirty martini and threw another olive on the skewer before she grabbed her dinner and sat down for another Sunday supper alone in her condo. At thirty-one, the routine was old, but circumstances being what they were, not a lot of change had happened in that department.

Most of her daylight hours were spent writing. But not the fun, creative type of writing. No, her writing was more of a pain in the ass. Literally. After ten years of climbing the journalism ladder, she was still firmly stuck in the not-so-grandiose job of assistant editor for a pain management magazine in an industry that no longer valued print publications. Yay. While Sarah spent her days interviewing doctors over the endless debate of which treatments did and didn't work for fibromyalgia (and, likewise, also having to endure the endless complaints from MDs about how PhDs weren't real doctors), her personal life needed its own form of pain management.

The last time Sarah had spent any considerable time in the presence of a man who wasn't her colleague or family was at the last medical conference she covered six months ago in Las Vegas. Sarah was a natural-born introvert, so networking had the same amount of appeal to her as colonoscopy prep. She hated the schmoozing that came with her job. After a day on the conference floor and attending seminars, she always looked forward to two things: room service and her Kindle. But at one particular conference, her editor had insisted she mingle. And when you'd been a damn assistant editor for ten years without so much as a glance from upper management acknowledging you could be more, well, you did what you were told.

During that particular evening, Sarah had caught the eye of an attractive drug rep in his mid-thirties who also primarily worked in her home state of New Jersey. The two met for drinks, and halfway through her dirty martini, her false confidence had started to kick in. Their conversation went from using Botox as a treatment for chronic migraines to evening plans after the drug rep's corporate-sponsored cocktail party.

Fast forward to later that evening, Sarah had exited the bathroom of the hotel lobby bar after a quick refresh and, in the process, noticed the same drug rep had just escorted a cocktail waitress out of the hotel onto the Vegas Strip. Sadly, as this wasn't a new occurrence for her, Sarah had called it a night and regretted the two hours she *could* have spent reading her Kindle while having *90 Day Fiancé* on in the background.

Sarah gathered her hair into a top knot, prepared to dive into dinner, and, not for the first time, wondered how she got to where she was and why the hell she couldn't seem to move forward with her life. Her job was a drag and getting her nowhere, and for a singleton going nowhere fast, her thirties proved to be a disheartening mountain to climb. Oh, sure. If anyone questioned her unmarried status, she emphatically responded with the "haven't found the right person" line or the "I'm focusing on my career" explanation. And while both of those were true to an extent, they were all surface fluff thrown out there to appease the masses.

In reality, she wasn't married because all the men she'd dated were either not interested or further along in their careers than she was, and that just stung. Sarah had a plan for her thirties, which involved owning real estate (check), married (nope), and—at the very least—a mid- to top-level department editor job (big, fat nope). How could she get serious with someone when they weren't on equal footing professionally to start out?

She speared a green bean with her fork, her mind on the tasks at hand. Tomorrow, she'd start to dive into that box of photos her Aunt Marie sent. She hoped to find some gems in there, maybe a few poignant black and whites of her mom and aunt as kids or a few summer vacation photos of all the cousins chilling on Sebago lake in inner tubes. Anything she could throw into her interactive Jeopardy game to help flesh out the payoffs she'd promised her family. She needed to ensure they enjoyed the reunion. Needed the validation that the lone cousin who *didn't* send out the kid-filled Christmas card photo each year still mattered.

After dinner, Sarah sank down into her couch, Roku remote in hand, and propped her feet up on the still-sealed box of photos, ready to commence with yet another Sunday night routine of killing two hours before she went to bed by herself.

Boy, this routine was old.

CHAPTER 2

"Did you know wombats have cube-shaped poop?"

The soft tapping across Sarah's keyboard stalled out. A line of D's ended her sentence when her middle finger dug into the keys. She swiveled in her chair toward the familiar voice of her colleague Tracy.

"I'm sorry," Sarah said. "What?"

"It's true. Wombats poop out these little cubed pellets." Tracy, another medical writer, worked a few cubicles down, but had largely been assigned the endocrinology beat in recent months. Their assignments hadn't crossed over much since, and Sarah missed her at the pain management conferences. Tracy would always insist they weasel into the front row of all the sports medicine seminars. More often than not, the pain docs in that field were easy on the eyes. Girl always had Sarah's back. She definitely didn't hate the conferences when Tracy was in attendance.

"Tracy, I'm going to need a bit more information here."

"Oh, no, you don't. I was just trying to get your attention so you'd pry your nose away from your screen," Tracy said as she walked around and began rummaging through one of Sarah's bottom desk drawers. "I know the signs when you're stressed. Your shoulders were hiked all the way up under your ears. You only do that when you've got a problem you can't figure out. Now, where the hell are your damn Oreos? Did you not buy more?"

"I don't have a problem." Sarah sighed, rubbing the back of her neck. "Just working through some tough edits. And I've only got the double stuff ones this time."

Tracey popped her head up, her thick mass of curls flipping back. One hand was cocked on her hip while the other held a mostly eaten pack of Oreos. The glare she gave Sarah could cut glass. "First off, the Oreo on its own is a perfect damn cookie. No need to be throwing your hard-earned money after more fake cream. The entire cookie-to-filling ratio is so far gone on those. Oh, I'll eat them!" she said as Sarah made a grab for the pack in Tracy's hand. "But I won't be happy about it. Second, your first drafts are always solid. What the hell could Nikki be picking apart now?"

Sarah huffed. "I missed an interview with Dr. Mendelsohn, and a writer for another pain website got it instead. I tried to fill in the gaps as best I could about the new opioid laws in California, but without Mendelsohn's comments, it fell short. Nikki called me out on it. I was just in her office for twenty minutes hearing all about how that was to be the big story for the week. She wasn't happy. Then she took the opportunity to shred up the rest of the draft. Little nitpicky stuff, too. Things she normally doesn't even concern herself with. You know, stuff that's always caught by the copy editors. I swear, I didn't even think Nikki knew what a dangling modifier was, but apparently, I have a lot of them."

"Now you listen to me, chica," Tracy said with an Oreo leveraged at Sarah's face. "You're a damn good writer. Nikki wouldn't know grammar if it crawled inside her and got her off."

"Tracy!"

"Oh, hush. She's not even in the office. I saw her leave for lunch already. And she knows how hard it is to land some of these pain docs for interviews. Heck, most of them only show up to give their seminar and then bolt right after. Unless the company's willing to take them out to dinner and cover their hotel and transportation, they don't like to talk. Besides, that woman has three kids at the house, all preteens and teenagers racking up Uber bills, and a husband who's away more than he's home. The woman is stress personified."

Sarah leaned back in her chair and just stared up at the ceiling. She knew everything Tracy said was justified, but it didn't change how things had played out. "I just don't think I'm good enough for her. Nikki clearly has expectations I'm not living up to."

"Girl, don't let that woman, or this place, make you think you're not enough of anything. They can tear down one of your stories, sure, but those are just words on a page, not you," Tracy said as she tossed the empty cookie packaging into the wastepaper basket before walking away. "And if Nikki thinks dangling modifiers at work are rough, just wait until all three of those kids start going through their SAT prep and testing. 'Oh, Mommy, you're an editor. Can you help?' Ha!"

The chuckle that vibrated through Sarah was welcome, but short-lived. Despite Tracy's well-intentioned girl talk, the truth flashed across Sarah's screen in every comment and strikethrough. She was far from where she needed to be.

Head down, she pounded those keys, hoping to push her boulder higher up the hill.

"Mother*fucker!*" Sarah screamed again as she caught herself on the edge of her coffee table after yet another too-damn-heavy photo album slipped from her hands and landed on her pinky toe. When her Aunt Marie said she'd "send over some photos," apparently, that meant archival leather-bound tomes of every single Polaroid, camera cartridge duplicate, and passport photo that ever crossed her idle scrapbooking hands. And not only Sarah but her poor toe, for the second time in twenty minutes, also suffered under the heft of this undertaking.

Sarah parked it on the couch, grabbed the balled-up kitchen towel of ice, and started in on the triage and rehab. After a day of sitting through meetings that were better served as e-mails, Sarah had looked forward to diving into the big box of history and had hoped to settle into a relaxing night of some good old-fashioned picture flipping.

There was just so much history she found herself immersed in over the last year, she honestly wondered how she would make heads or tails of it and present things in a way her family would care about.

Even though the Johanssons were spread out throughout the East Coast now, Sarah was fascinated to learn that both of her main family lines started their progeny in one location: Baltimore, Maryland. She had uncovered stories of divorce in local newspaper archives, seen old wedding announcements, and even found burial records of babies who never made it out of infancy. The most tragic, and most interesting in her book, was the story of her great-grandfather, Ramon Mendez.

During World War I, Ramon had come to the United States from Aguadilla, Puerto Rico, to study medicine at the Martinsville University of Science and Medicine in Baltimore. While there, he met his future wife, Helen Schneider, a clerk in the university's hospital at the time. Following graduation, the two of them married and Helen found herself pregnant with their daughter shortly after. Sadly, Ramon died after he contracted typhoid fever from a patient and never got to meet his daughter. He was only twenty-six years old. And what was even more astonishing was that Helen never remarried. She became a wife, mother, and widow all within eighteen months, and even though she would eventually live to be ninety-two years old, she never remarried and never had any more children.

While elevating her slightly-less-swollen-though-still-tingly foot on a pillow, Sarah cracked open the navy-blue cover of the first photo album. As she did so, the back cover resting on her legging-clad thighs slipped a bit, and an envelope fell out and landed on the floor. Sarah leaned down to pick it up, though trying to do so without moving her lower half presented a problem and caused her to tweak her back in the process.

"Argh!" she screamed, throwing her hand to her lower back. "Why is nothing easy?"

Trying again, Sarah leaned down and finally reached far enough to pick up the envelope off the floor. She opened it, still supporting herself on her elbow, and pulled out an old sepia-tone portrait of a young man who couldn't be more than twenty-one or so, with dark hair and dark eyes, staring straight at the camera. His reserved grin suggested this photo may have been for a planned purpose, such as a program or yearbook.

Sarah turned the photo over, and to her surprised delight, there was an inscription.

Ramon Mendez - 1919 - Martinsville University.

"Huh," Sarah breathed out through her contorted position as she examined the photo more closely. He sat on the front steps that led up to a large building. "Go figure. This was probably taken the year he graduated from medical school. Maybe right before he met Helen. I wonder what building that is."

As Sarah squinted at the background of the photo, she noticed a residue come off on her fingertips. It had a pale greenish tint to it, similar to the Statue of Liberty's coloring, but it almost had the feel of powder foundation.

"What the hell?"

Sarah brought her fingers to her nose to see whether she could identify the residue. She took one slow inhale through her nostrils. The scent, if you could call it that, snaked its way through her nasal passages and invaded itself like ivy winding up an old building. Her eyes began tearing up shortly before dry coughs wracked her body. Coughs turned to heaves, and the force of her exertion unsettled her delicate balancing act on the couch. She tumbled headfirst toward the carpet, but the corner of the glass coffee table blocked her smooth landing and bludgeoned her left temple in the process. The glass shattered under the impact, and Sarah landed facedown on the carpet.

Her coughing fits had begun to decrease in intensity, right as the metallic tang of copper entered her nose and filled her mouth. A great weight settled over Sarah, slowing down her breathing and forcing her eyes to get heavy. The last thing she remembered seeing was Ramon's photo still clutched in her right hand as a trickle of blood snaked down her wrist.

Tequila.

Cheap tequila.

Cheap tequila mixed with every other type of cellar-dweller distilled spirit a college student would throw together with fruit punch and dump in a cooler with ice.

The icepick-through-her-temple pain reminded her a lot of that. She needed to move. Get up and assess what the heck just happened. But moving seemed like the last thing her body was capable of. Behind closed eyelids, her on-fire brain did a systems check on her body.

Left temple throbbing on top of a hard, rough surface, with her neck cranked all the way to the right. Check.

Aggressive nausea a microsecond away from turning into full-blown vomiting. Check.

Mild aches in her foot and lower back. Check.

Lukewarm viscous liquid crawling across her cheek and trickling over her eyelashes. Not good.

Sarah groaned on the next exhale so as not to add her own vomit to the pool of whatever she lay in and inched her knees up under herself. Gradually, she lifted her head off what she assumed was the flooring under her living room carpet and cracked open her eyes. She blinked away the fluid impairing her vision and wiped her wrist across her face. When she pulled her arm down and finally saw the bright red smear of blood that painted her forearm, the boiling nausea kettle that was her stomach finally started to whistle. Crossing her arms over her stomach, she turned to the side and heaved up every-thing she had eaten that day.

Once the vomiting subsided, Sarah wiped her mouth on the back of her sleeve and panted heavily as she crawled back against the nearest wall and finally looked around the room.

Except it wasn't her living room.

Instead, she was face to face with a brick wall. Sarah squinted her eyes, quickly shook her head to clear the mental fog, and peered up and around. She was sandwiched in between two walls, and her butt rested in a puddle on the ground of a dank alleyway.

"What the..." Sarah breathed out, looking to her left. The opening of the alley led out to a street. There, a man and a woman walked by, with the woman's arm snaked around the man's elbow. Both were wearing heavy wool coats down to their ankles, which wasn't unusual for February. What was different, though, was the wide-brimmed hat the woman wore. Like something out of an old black-and-white movie. The style was off. And so was the cobblestone road. But if she were honest with herself, sitting in her own vomit puddle in a back alley when she should have been in her cozy living room was the most *off* thing about her situation.

A nagging feeling tickled the back of her brain. Maybe it was the blow to the head, which, thankfully, had mostly stopped bleeding, but she just couldn't shake what was in front of her. The last thing she remembered was lying on her couch and bending over to pick up a photo before she whacked her head and fell ass over tea kettle into sketchy alley land.

On shaky legs, and with a laser-trained eye toward the street at the alley's opening, Sarah slowly got to her feet. The pain and nausea started to ebb, which was good. Those things needed to get out of the friggin' way so her rising anxiety could take over and settle in. Jesus Christ, what the heck was going on? How hard had she hit her head?

She held out her left hand to balance herself on the brick wall and hesitantly began to walk toward the street. Cold dampness hit the bottom of her socked foot, and when she looked down, she saw something she recognized. Floating on top of the small puddle next to her foot was the small sepia-tone photo of Ramon Mendez...the same photo she had bent over to grab in her living room when this whole mess started.

She hunched down to pick it up and stared at the picture again. Ramon still sat on those grand stone steps in front of that large building, but something looked more familiar now. The dark wool coat he wore in the photo looked eerily similar to the coat the man wore from that couple who walked past the alley.

The anxiety started to rise more in Sarah's gut as she crept toward the opening of the alley. At least she wasn't totally alone. The butterflies in her stomach were still there as they practically flew all the way up her esophagus. As she broke through the dank, confined space that spat her out onto a bright street, she knew things were wrong. Very, very wrong.

Across the street, staring her straight in the face, was the exact same staircase as the one Ramon sat on in the picture she held. Not as in *roughly* the same staircase, only more weathered and updated with ADA-approved railings. No, the *exact* same staircase, down to the stone pillars that towered up each side, and the same unevenness of the landing.

Sarah's tongue felt like cotton, and heat began to creep up into her cheeks as anxiety clawed at her chest. There, across the top of the stone entryway, the words carved into its facade amplified her panic: *Martinsville University of Science and Medicine.* When she dragged her eyes down to the photo in her hand, the same exact words appeared above the doorway of the building Ramon sat in front of.

If those butterflies in her stomach weren't busy before, they had quickly gotten their act together. Her insides were on a full Mach-speed blender blitz, and her head wasn't much better.

What was she seeing? Her brain had trouble making sense of the imagery, like a color-blind dog in a field of green grass that would only ever see it as yellow grass.

Sarah's signals must have crossed somehow, the knock to her head having done a bigger number on herself than she originally thought. Yes, a simple concussion or some such thing.

Having settled on a potentially workable explanation, Sarah released some of her tension through a nervous exhale. Her eyes left the photo in her hand and traveled back toward the building in front of her. At the base of the stairs, caught on the metal railing, was a piece of newsprint wrapped around the metal obstruction.

The butterflies came back with a vengeance. Sarah couldn't recall the last time she had seen a newspaper *period*, let alone floating along a city sidewalk. As her chest began to rise and fall in time with her elevated heart rate, her feet slowly carried her over to the newspaper. Squatting down, she freed the paper and unfolded it...right before her stomach completely bottomed out.

The Evening Sun was stamped across the top like any proper newspaper heading, but the font and column widths were all wrong. There was no automatic typesetting, no standardized spacing between the lines of text. Words in articles butted up against each other and there were no clean lines separating the few images from the rest of the text. Confused, she looked up at the header again. Beneath the paper's name, the issue's date appeared in small, capital letters: Thursday, February 14, 1919.

She had no explanation, no logical reason for what she saw, but the building, the clothes on the couple walking past her, the paper…

Sarah looked down at the photo in her hand again before she assessed the building in front of her one more time.

Nope, the denial wasn't working. Sarah *knew* she stared up at the exact building from the picture in her hand. In the exact same time period the picture was taken…103 years ago.

Shit.

CHAPTER 3

When Sarah was sixteen years old, she had taken a course to become an emergency medical technician. For the next eight years, she rode for her hometown volunteer rescue squad. The adrenaline that pulsed through her each time the bell rang at the squad house was intense. What was even more intense was how, over the years, in the face of truly terrible emergency calls, she'd learned to think quickly on her feet and go go go. Her body had been trained to react to emergencies, even when her logical brain needed some more time to process the situation.

Sarah found herself in such a situation, and thank God her brain got with the program, tamped down her hysteria, and started coming up with a damn plan. That was all the jarring she needed to start unraveling her circumstances.

First, scene safety.

Where could she go that was safe enough so she could stop and think for a moment? The alley wasn't an option. Maybe a park bench?

"Miss, are you all right?"

Her forward-moving action planning skidded to a halt on her next breath. Sarah jerked her head to the left and came face to face with a somewhat panicked elderly man no taller than herself. He had white hair that peeked out underneath his brown bowler hat, more of that same trend-right wool coat apparently. He leaned heavily on a wooden cane, the end of which was rooted in a notch between two of the street's cobblestones. He squinted at her with a mix of concern and curiosity.

It was at that moment Sarah finally took stock of her appearance. To put it the politest way possible, she was a friggin' mess. Sarah immediately threw her hand up toward her forehead and remembered the gash there. When she pulled her hand away, she didn't see any fresh blood, thank goodness, but there was plenty of the dried stuff to cause alarm. As she looked farther down, she got the larger picture of what this man saw: more blood stains, dried vomit on her cardigan, dank socks, no shoes. She looked like an attempted murder victim.

"Miss, do you need to see a doctor? Have you been attacked?" the man prodded, his voice laced with real concern this time as he took in more of her appearance and attire.

Of course. The hospital!

"Um, yes, sir. I think I should go to the hospital," she forced out on a whisper, realizing she spoke that more to herself than to the gentleman as she eyed the door at the top of the stone steps. If she could get inside, she could find a restroom, clean herself up, and assess her next steps. "Yes, sir. I'd like that." Best to call him "sir." That was more believable, right?

"Of course, my dear. Let's get you inside right away," he said hurriedly as he grabbed the inside of her elbow with his thick-gloved hand and cautiously began leading her up the steps to the hospital entrance, cane in tow. Sarah felt a slight pang of guilt, as this man clearly struggled just to get himself up the steps with his cane, let alone do so while attempting to aid her. "Where is your husband?" he asked.

Sarah was so focused on the climb up the steps, her attention wasn't on his words. Did he just ask about a husband? "I'm sorry, what?" Sarah replied as she crossed the threshold and received the biggest shock to her system yet.

If she had any doubt left she was no longer in her present time, that got squashed really quick. As she looked around the inside of the hospital, a sea of white moved at a subway-rat-scurrying pace. Who she presumed were doctors and nurses were dressed head to toe in white gowns, with white shoes, white surgical hats and nursing hats, and even some in white masks. A nurse hurried in front of Sarah's path, pushing a wooden cart with various medical supplies on top, none of which Sarah could immediately discern. The base of the cart, though, was neatly stacked with white cotton sheets, blankets, and towels. The nurse rushed the cart to a large auditorium-like room off to the left.

As Sarah craned her neck to peek over the gentleman's shoulder for a better view of the room, she almost got her head lopped off by another nurse who whizzed past her, arms laden with more supplies. Geez, what was going on?

"Ma'am, wait here one moment and I'll find a doctor to assist you. Here, settle yourself down right here until I return," the gentleman said to Sarah as he guided her over to a small wooden stool in the corner of what Sarah could only think of as the 1919-equivalent of an emergency room. "What is your husband's name? I shall call on him immediately," the man prodded through exhausted breaths. The small effort walking up the few stone steps outside had, in fact, been more exertion than the man was used to.

"Oh, thank you," Sarah said as she accepted his offer to sit. "And I don't have a husband."

"No husband, eh? Well, my dear, not to worry. The doctor can speak with your father, then. Not to worry, not to worry..." the man mumbled to himself as he slowly walked off, leaning heavily on his cane, toward a large receiving desk staffed with several nurses.

Sarah tried to wrack her brain with what she knew of the post-World War I era in Baltimore, but it wasn't much. If she had to land herself in a different time and place, she could think of a lot more desirable locations and decades. Desirable wasn't even the right word. Anything more closely related to her sphere of knowledge more aptly covered it. So, you know, New Jersey, basically. Well-traveled she was not.

But as she sat there and watched the elderly man wait patiently to speak with the bustling nurses at the desk, a prickly feeling snaked up the back of her neck again. Something told her the fewer people who saw her, the better. Hell, she didn't even know how this had happened. Or why it happened. Or how she was expected to go to the bathroom in 1919. They had toilets, right?

Of course, they did.

Right?

Without thinking too much, Sarah quickly scanned the emergency room and noticed a less crowded hallway immediately off to her right. She hoped that, perhaps, there may be a bathroom there. Or, at the very least, a quiet place to think. She desperately needed to think. Eyeing the old man one last time, Sarah stood up and sprinted toward the hallway, her socks leaving wet impressions on the hardwood floor.

So much for being inconspicuous. All she was missing were road flares.

As she proceeded down the hall, she passed more wooden carts laden with linens, but no clear bathroom. *C'mon, show me a sign on a door that says ladies, dammit!*

She hadn't yet run into any other people, but she figured her wing and a prayer were on borrowed time at that point. Crossing down another hallway at her new pace of sprint-shuffle-sprint, she eenie-meenie-miney-moed one of the doors to her right, put her ear up to the wood to listen for she had no idea what, turned the knob, slipped in, and clicked the door shut behind her.

"If that's how the new nurses here are dressing, then you deserve to be in this damn bed more than I do," a gruff, gravelly voice barked out from several feet behind her.

Sarah spun on a dime and slammed her back flat up against the door. Unfortunately for her, the room she had chosen was not, in fact, a bathroom, as she had hoped. No, she had wandered her panic-stricken tush into what was obviously a patient's private room.

Shit. Shit. Shit.

"Um, I'm so sorry. I...uh..." No words. There was straight up no words to explain things. No synapses fired. No spark plugs engaged.

Just a whole lot of crickets began chirping in her head. For lack of anything better to do, Sarah just planted her feet to the floor and stared at the man in the bed.

The back of the room was fortunate enough to be on an outside wall, allowing some late afternoon daylight to seep in through the sole window. What little light there was landed on the end of a single bed, the headboard of which was up against the wall immediately to Sarah's right. The bed's occupant, whom Sarah automatically now thought of as Grumpy, barely fit on that poor hospital bed's metal frame and rice-cake-thin mattress. At the end of the bed, two socked feet overhung the edge underneath what looked to be a scratchy wool blanket. The linens were hardly large enough to drape over the man's lap, the edge of the sheet stopping just at his abdomen.

As she looked more closely, Sarah took in the white linen button-down shirt the man wore. Held in place by two loose black suspenders, the shirt gaped wide open at the collar and revealed a peek at his thick, dark chest hair, which crept down lower beneath his top. Though the shirt was generously sized, the shape of the man's arms pushed its limits. Heck, the size of the man himself pushed the limits of the damn bed frame. The man kept his dark hair on the longer side, so it just kissed the tops of his wide shoulders, and his hair looked much softer than the coarseness his beard and mustache would suggest. His brow was angled down, shrouding his narrowed dark eyes as they bore right into her own.

Sarah had made a huge mistake when she chose this room. She had made a huge mistake when she left the old gentleman's side. It was a huge mistake she was even where she was. The weight of her situation crashed down onto her shaking shoulders and forced her to slide down the length of the door and land on the floor. Despite the stranger staring at her, she curled her knees up to her chest, wrapped her arms around them, ducked her head down, and let everything go.

The sobs that tore out of Sarah's throat couldn't have been held back by the Hoover Dam. But wait, that hadn't even been built yet, had it?

She was done. Just done. It had all been too much too soon. Sarah felt as if she were out of answers and out of options. When she had been back in her condo, the evening had just begun. Here, it was late afternoon, and she had no idea what she would do. She was a mess. She needed to get clean and dry, find shelter, food, but her brain just couldn't get its act together. In a moment of desperation, after she was all cried out, she did the only thing that came to mind.

"I need help," Sarah said as she lifted her head slightly and stared into her folded forearms with glazed-over eyes, refusing to look at the man. After a minute of silence, she braved his gaze and looked straight at him, repeating her plea.

"I need help, sir. I know what I look like, and I can't offer much in the way of an explanation right now for my appearance, or why I accidentally stumbled into your room...and I assure you it *was* an accident...but I need to get clean and dry right now. That needs to be the first step," she nervously acknowledged. The words just tumbled out of her. She didn't realize how long it had been since she had *really* spoken to someone.

"I promise to be on my way as soon as possible, but at this moment, is there anything you can do to help me?" Sarah knew she was taking a risk. Hell, everything she'd done up until now had been a risk. And once she finished laying it all out there for him, the ball was officially in the man's court. She just sat there, never took her eyes off of his, and waited.

Your move, Grumpy.

The man continued to stare at her. Oh, sure, he did several once-overs of her vomit-stained clothes and blood-stained face, but didn't say anything. After an uncomfortable stretch of silence, Sarah wondered whether she should repeat her plea or just get up and leave to take her chances elsewhere. The only indication the man had even heard what she said was the slight tick in his jaw when he homed in on the gash on her left temple. The fingers of his right hand began to creep slowly toward the edge of his blanket, balling the fabric into his fist.

Sarah watched the man's eyes as they traveled studiously over her face, hair, and clothes (and her very obvious non-1900s black leggings). In the span of the mere moments that man assessed her, she couldn't explain anything further because there was nothing else to explain. He served as a witness to the inexplicable. And in the space of those two thoughts, Sarah silently hoped for trust. Trust that his next actions wouldn't lead to more panic and fear on her part, and trust toward him that what he saw was, indeed, real.

Before she could examine things further, the man sharply tilted his bearded chin toward a door to his left in the corner of the room without ever taking his eyes off hers. "Bathroom," he snipped out.

That was all Sarah needed to hear before she scrambled to her feet and quickly closed the bathroom door behind her. Later, she would thank the man for trusting her when he had no reason to do so otherwise. Later, when the blood and tears were washed away down the drain, she'd more clearly assess her situation. Later, when she could stop moving for a moment and just breathe without panic seizing her muscles, she'd figure out what story she would tell the man who had just acknowledged her inexplicable difference without saying a word.

But in that moment, all Sarah did was sit on the cold white tile floor as she stared up at the bare lightbulb hanging over the sink until her eyes burned. Maybe staring into the light would lead her to a better outcome than the traumatic darkness that had brought her here.

After two more minutes on the floor, Sarah steeled her spine, rose to her feet, and turned on the faucet at the enameled sink.

One step at a time.

CHAPTER 4

"I sure hope you know what you're doing. This trick you're pulling is a once-in-an-afterlife arrangement. You're barely a hundred years into your tenure. You sure throwing your ace out like that so early is a good idea?"

Ramon stood across the street from the hospital's entrance with his friend and former Martinsville classmate Johnny Gates. Ramon's eyes tracked Sarah's movement up the stone steps, her arm hanging on to her elderly escort. When the heel of her socked foot finally crossed the hospital's threshold, he breathed a sigh of relief and turned to his friend.

Johnny leaned against a lamp pole, white tendrils of vapor dancing around his body. Over his shoulder, a couple walked past him on the sidewalk, but didn't look his way. The face of his old friend was a great comfort, despite the cocked eyebrow and crossed arms. Johnny had been Ramon's right-hand man ever since they sat next to each other in their freshman anatomy course at Martinsville. He had offered Ramon, who had still been perfecting his English back then, a cigarette after class.

Beyond grateful for the small offer and what it could grow into, Ramon had exchanged the favor by sharing his coconut candies from Puerto Rico. Their friendship grew from there, with Ramon eventually asking Johnny to be his best man at his wedding. A short time later, Ramon died from contracting typhoid fever from a patient. Five years following, Johnny died as well after he was injured in a streetcar accident.

The two now stood outside the hospital Sarah just walked into. The winter wind would have been bracing for any living being, but neither spirit felt the cold. Ramon waved his hand in Johnny's direction, dismissing his friend's concern. The white mist floated around his limb like a second skin.

"Yes, I'm sure. I've been watching Sarah for some time now. She's been an absolute joy to observe. I can't even begin to tell you how much she's uncovered about my family. I hadn't even known my ancestors originally hailed from Spain."

Johnny scoffed at the statement. "I'm sorry, but I'm going to need to hear a lot more than admiration for her research to convince me your hairbrained plan is a good one."

Ramon's plan *was* a good one. As a spirit, even though he was gone from the mortal plain, he could still visit and watch over those he left behind. Time travel for a spirit was as effortless as breathing was for a living thing. Likewise, in the spirit world, it was an occasional treat for one well-intentioned afterlifer to share their gift of time travel with the living. Every now and then, Ramon heard tales of spirits sending the living through time. In fact, a variety of explanations had been manifested in the living world to account for the occasional disappearance. Crop circles and standing stones were a few of his favorites. But whenever he heard of spirits sending the living through, the trip was always permanent and never done often.

Until Ramon dug further.

The mechanics of it were a bit complicated, but through his observations of other spirits, he learned about the ability to send the living through time *temporarily*. All spirits left behind an essence of light green dust when they were in the mortal plain. And because they couldn't avoid leaving physical evidence of their wanderings, they didn't often visit. Or if they did, the visits were incredibly brief.

But Ramon had found a loophole in that green essence. By breathing in the essence, not just merely touching it, the living

23

being would be tied to his spirit. The dust would be imbued with the necessary forces to send an individual to a time of his choosing. But like all things in this world, nothing lasted forever. The ability was short-lived. And when his essence started to wane, seeping from the person's body, they would be pulled back to their time. The temporary trick could be done only once, and never repeated.

"Have you seen how much she doubts herself?" Ramon asked, more to himself than his friend as he stared back at the hospital. "The girl is like a duck in a small pond, flippers flailing beneath the surface of the water but never propelling her beyond the small confines of the same muddy embankments. She needs someone to open her eyes so she can see what's right in front of her."

"And what makes you think this little jaunt through the past is going to help her see herself clearly?"

The corner of Ramon's lips lifted at his friend's question. "Because no one knows their true mettle until they're tested. And there's one heck of a challenge lying in that hospital."

It had been a long time since anything had truly surprised Jacob Bellamy. It was a little refreshing to know he was still capable of the emotion. Though the fact that it was triggered by an abused and confused woman who happened to wander into his room at the hospital perhaps spoke volumes about what got a rise out of him these days.

Jacob had been confined to this hospital for the better part of two weeks now, and to say he was tired of his room with a view was an understatement. But then, he was tired of so much in general. War could do that to a man. When the armistice was reached on November 11th, just three months ago, ending the Great War, Jacob hadn't felt the relief he thought he would after more than a year of fighting. After all, an arbitrary date on a calendar didn't mean anything for the men he saw bayoneted and shot in the name of God and country.

Because why have just one type of weapon the enemy can level at you when two are so much more effective?

His latest stint in the hospital was to be his final leg of "healing" in the post-war rat race before he could head back to his farm and retire. How Jacob was expected to heal from an injury that was all in his head he sure as hell didn't know, but that's what the long, white coats were for, he supposed. Still, the damn night terrors hadn't eased up, and it was kind of hard to obey doctor's orders to rest when Jacob's last decent night's sleep had been before the draft.

Which he just narrowly qualified for. Being at the older end of the age limit, he was drafted about a year and a half shy of not having the war be his problem.

Lucky him.

He was lost in the cycle of attempted mental repair that threatened never to come, and the broken woman who landed herself a spot on the floor in his hospital room presented the perfect puzzle for his addled brain to mull over.

And what a puzzle she was. When the woman slid to the floor in front of him and let out those wails, he hadn't had a clue how to respond. She reminded him of a deer he and his younger brother, Isaac, had come across on a hunt several years back. There had been a group of deer making a mess of their crops, and when he and Isaac finally homed in on them one day, Isaac landed the shot that took down the smallest of the pests.

When the two of them started to pack up and make their way toward the kill, Jacob was halted by the whining he heard coming from one of the other deer. He couldn't see her very well through the trees, and she had taken off shortly after he and Isaac moved in, but the whimper had stayed with him. It was the first time he registered the sound of agony coming from an animal that *wasn't* dying. It was clear they had just taken down the doe's fawn.

So when this woman began to break down in Jacob's room, he had no choice but to pay attention. It was a muscle-memory reaction he had to that kind of sound. But then, when he started to look more closely at the details—dried blood caking her dirty blond hair; all manner of filth on her clothing; and odd trousers that appeared to be women's stockings, only thicker and more opaque, but with no skirt to cover her body—it was clear she had a story.

What was also clear, unfortunately, was just how long it had been since Jacob had spent any time in a woman's presence who *wasn't* a prodding nurse. The girl was a wreck, in every sense of the word, but when she'd lifted her head, landed her glassy hazel eyes square at him, and held steady as if she were standing in the middle of a tornado and had just demanded the damn thing to stop spinning, Jacob froze. His thoughts had derailed, and he had to remind himself of the mechanics of breathing. After a few breathless heartbeats, his lungs got with the program and he nodded his chin toward the private bathroom in his suite.

That had been about twenty minutes ago, and the woman hadn't yet emerged. What would he say to her? Demand an answer as to why she'd barged into his room uninvited? Though she clearly needed help more than accusation. Should he go in and check on her? Would she even welcome that? If she had sustained her injuries at the hand of a man, he doubted she'd allow him anywhere near her. But then again, she hadn't cowered at all when she asked for his help, and Jacob was a larger man than most. On the contrary, her stare and request brooked no argument. Intimidated she was not.

As Jacob mulled over how to handle his surprise visitor, the door to the bathroom slowly creaked open. After a brief moment, the woman calmly walked out, closed the door behind her, and just stood there. Her right hand was still behind her back, resting on the doorknob as if it were her lifeline.

"My apologies for how crudely I addressed you earlier," Jacob stammered after he cleared his throat. He wasn't used to tap-dancing in a conversation, and it was clear the discussion that was about to follow had to be handled in a delicate manner. Was she as nervous as he was? And what the hell did he have to be nervous about at all, exactly?

Extending his hand toward a wooden chair directly across from the foot of his bed, he said, "Please, won't you have a seat?"

The woman eyed the piece of furniture as if it were the dunce chair in the principal's office at school. Her elbow-length hair was damp, though no longer blood-stained. The gash above her left eye was still there and looked to be about an inch long. She wore a knee-length, long-sleeved dark green sweater that was open all down the font. It had no method of closure, as far as he saw. Beneath the sweater, she wore a form-fitting navy-blue shirt that showed off much of her neckline, though the garment appeared much more casual in nature despite the plunging style.

The most peculiar aspect of her attire, however, remained her trousers. Jacob thought of them as undergarments, and this propelled his earlier unspoken theory that she had been attacked or brutalized in some fashion. The shape of her legs was on full display, with the rest of her only being covered by the length of her sweater. Her socks looked similar to his own, though hers seemed much thicker and he wondered how she'd be able to fit her feet into the fashionable boots he'd seen women wear. The last thing he noticed was the damp patches of fabric all along her outfit. Clearly, she had attempted to rinse out the remnants of her ordeal, whatever that was.

The woman took one more deep inhale through her nose and exhaled through her slightly open lips before she walked over to the chair, her eyes never leaving his own. Did she think he would hurt her? Or was she afraid of the questions he'd ask? And he *would* ask questions.

Once she was seated across from him, Jacob was unsure how to proceed, exactly. *Best to start at the beginning, I guess.*

"What is your name, miss?" Jacob asked.

After another deep breath, she answered him. "My name is Sarah Johansson, sir. Thank you for letting me use your bathroom and for not alerting people of my intrusion." Her gratitude was acknowledged with slightly downcast eyes.

Jacob waved her thanks away with his hand. He needed to know more and he doubted she'd thank him momentarily. With a gesture toward her forehead, he asked, "What happened there?"

"I fell and hit my head," Sarah replied quickly. It was clear she had rehearsed that line to herself.

"Miss Johansson," he articulated, "let me help us understand one another, if we are to proceed with this conversation." Jacob leveled his stare at her as he leaned forward slightly in the bed. "I have seen grown men take a bullet through the head mid-sentence. I have seen boys barely old enough to shave choke out their last breaths amidst unseen mustard gas clouds. Please excuse me if my tolerance for banter isn't something you're used to. Now, tell me what happened and why you are in my hospital room."

Jacob had no idea why he was so forward with her. He had no intention of scaring her, as she clearly had just gone through an ordeal. But he wanted answers, and if there was one thing he had learned in war, it was that strength begot strength. With that, he crossed his arms in front of him, stared directly into her eyes, leaned back on his pillow, and waited.

As a girl, Sarah always got teased for how much she talked to herself. And it wasn't just talking. When she was alone in her room, she'd have full conversations with herself while she faced off with her reflection in the full-frontal mirror. She'd practice her monologues for drama class, rehearse a difficult talk she planned to have with her best friend about losing one's virginity, and generally work through the myriad pros and cons lists of life she'd made throughout the years. And then one couldn't forget the full-bore singing to herself in the car when Britney Spears' "Baby One More Time" came on the radio.

Needless to say, before she emerged to face the man in the bed again, she took her damn time in that bathroom and talked things out with herself as much as she could. After she ran through every single possible scenario of what happened, her mind still kept drawing her back to one final conclusion: She was not in 2021 any longer. And, boy, did that fact just sucker punch her right between the ribs. She had never been a spiritual person, nor had she ever really given much thought to anything otherworldly, but, damn, was she a convert now.

It took her all of five minutes to clean herself up, but the rest of her time in that bathroom she'd spent sitting on the tile floor in silence. That man in the bed was *intense*. She had no idea what led her to be so forthcoming with the honesty, especially given the current situation. Jesus Christ, what the hell was she going to say to him? What could she say to anyone from this time, really? She had miraculously managed to muddle her way through things thus far, but that couldn't last much longer.

The biggest question she kept asking herself was whether she should tell the truth and what kind of hot water that would land her in. From every Hollywood time travel fantasy she had ever seen, it was a giant no-no to reveal the truth about where the time traveler came from. The truth meant you were something different. The truth meant you were something dangerous. The truth meant you were deadly, and, yeah...kill the witch and all that.

But she was hardly in ancient times here, thank goodness. There were people still alive in her own time who *might* be alive now, for crying out loud, though that was a stretch. And when she chose to stare down Grumpy with her not-so-silent plea for help, he hadn't flinched. Of all the things Sarah couldn't comprehend about her current situation, his reaction to her quasi-confession was perhaps the most jarring.

Why had he offered to help her? She looked like roadkill and had just burst into his private room smelling like a sewer rat. But yet, he still helped her. Why? It didn't matter at this point. She was out of time and out of ideas.

On one final deep breath, she jumped out of the frying pan and into the fryer.

CHAPTER 5

"I fell and hit my head," Sarah repeated for no one's benefit. Before she even finished getting the end of her sentence out, the severe eye roll emanating across the way from her newfound roomie gave her an inkling of which direction her story should *not* go.

"Miss Johansson," the man interrupted, "I'll stop you there."

"No, let me finish!" she hurried out. "Yes, I fell and hit my head. And I can freely tell you what I did before then. But after that, it's honestly a blur." Sarah was surprised to realize that, yes, she really couldn't recall what had happened in the in-between. "I was in my living room, looking through old family records for a project I'm working on. I fell off the couch when I reached for something on the floor and struck my head on the edge of my glass coffee table. When I woke up, I was in this hospital."

"You found yourself in a hospital, alone, and in such a state of dishevelment one would think you had just been attacked? Who was the doctor who attended you?" Jacob pried. It was quite clear he wasn't buying what she was selling, but she had to keep trying.

"Uhh...erm...Dr. Carlson," Sarah stammered out.

"Dr. Carlson," Jacob parroted.

"Yes, I believe that was his name." Sarah never let her eyes leave his. She stared him down with as much conviction one would use to convince a flat-Earther that the Earth was, in fact, round. If she *acted* like she believed her own bullshit, the power of persuasion should take care of the rest. Or so she hoped.

The man continued to stare back at her. If Sarah thought her childhood see-who-blinks-first contests were intense, they had nothing on this man. They sat like that for a solid minute, with nothing further passing between them. Sarah actually had kind of hoped he'd speak more. His voice did something to her. His baritone vocals skated over her skin like treads over gravel, but in a soothing kind of way. Kind of like the pounding lull of a relaxing massage. The repeated vibrations were jarring but still managed to set her at ease...calming out the rough edges.

At that moment, Sarah decided to change course. "Look, Mr...." Sarah prompted.

"Jacob," the man provided. "Jacob Bellamy."

The surprise at being given his first name right off the bat, as that probably wasn't the custom in 1919, threw her a bit.

"Okay. Jacob. I don't exactly—"

"Corporal Bellamy, I just got your latest notes from Dr. Callihan and he's given you the all-clear to be discharged this afternoon...Oh, my! Miss, are you all right?" To Sarah's great misfortune, a nurse had chosen that particular moment to barge into Jacob's room and hand him his ticket out of there. Naturally, one look at Sarah and her mud-puddle-makeup-meets-wife-beater wardrobe cut the nurse short.

"I...uh...yes. I was just talking with Corporal Bellamy. And it looks worse than it is," Sarah said as she nonchalantly waved toward her forehead. "I'm fine." She had to have known the nurse wouldn't have stopped at that.

"But, miss, what are you doing here? This is a private room. Have you been checked in elsewhere?"

To Sarah's immense surprise, before she was left to trip over her own tongue, Jacob interceded. "She's here at my request. Miss Johansson and I are childhood acquaintances. I heard she was in town and I called upon her for a brief visit before she leaves Baltimore."

Jacob could have knocked both Sarah and the nurse over with a feather. Each woman knew that was a bold-faced lie, but neither was in a position to call the man out on it. In fact, he delivered the lie with utmost sincerity, his tone daring anyone within earshot to question him.

Sarah's fly catcher still hung open while the nurse began to hem and haw over the latest news her patient had just delivered.

"Yes, Corporal Bellamy. Of course. Well, uh, here are your discharge papers then," the nurse said as she slowly walked over to Jacob with her extended hand holding the papers. The entire time, the nurse didn't take her eyes off Sarah, and Sarah couldn't stop staring at Jacob in utter disbelief.

After the discharge instructions were briefly discussed between the nurse and Jacob, the nurse left the room. Not a nanosecond after the door clicked, Sarah rounded on him.

"What the heck was that?" she hissed through clenched teeth as she bolted upright out of her chair, arms out at her sides. She had more to say, but his raised hand and lowered eyes put a halt to her tirade.

"I believe you should thank me, Miss Johansson. I could have easily told the nurse of your intrusion, which would have brought all manner of attention your way. And while you have yet to fully answer my questions, I know undue attention is not what you'd appreciate at the moment. Am I correct?"

Well, shit. He had her there. The smug bastard.

Sarah eased down on the chair again as Jacob pulled back the covers draped over his lap and swung his legs over the edge of the mattress. He stood up to his full height and slowly walked over to the foot of the bed, rounded the edge, and sat down. The mattress, all at once being relieved of his great weight, depressed back down to its wafer-thin state after its short reprieve. Once resettled, Jacob rested his elbows on his knees and leaned over toward Sarah. There were only two feet of linoleum that separated them.

"Where do you live?" Jacob asked in a low voice, as if he knew the answer wasn't one for prying ears. The baby hairs at her temple danced slightly when he accented the W and H together, blowing out the question across her senses. She felt the closeness acutely.

"I don't live around here," Sarah answered honestly. Having Jacob so close to her orbit made her heart pound as if she were clearing hurdles in the Olympics.

Surely, he could hear the *thump thump thump*, right?

"You genuinely don't remember how you came to be in this hospital?" Jacob raised his left eyebrow at the question. For a man who had just given a bold-faced lie to a medical professional with as much nonchalance as one checks the time, he was incredulous as he sought out the truth.

And Sarah would give him the truth. At least, as much as she could give for the time being.

"No," she whispered. "I don't."

Her heartbeat thumped in her throat while she waited for his next move.

"Do you have a husband?"

At that, Sarah smiled. She should have been shocked by the question, but as this was the second time in as many hours that inquiry had been hurled her way, she let it land where it did. "No, I don't."

The corner of his lip turned up just so slightly that if Sarah wasn't intent on staring at his beard, she'd have missed it. Not that Sarah was staring intently or anything.

"May I ask how old you are?" Jacob continued.

"I'm thirty-one," Sarah said.

"Do you not live with your father then, unmarried as you are?" Jacob queried her.

Sarah treaded lightly on this next one, as she wasn't entirely sure of the customs but she had a pretty darn good sense that thirty-one-year-old single women typically did *not* have their own condos, let alone professional careers.

"I don't presently live with him, no."

Jacob sat up straight, rubbed his hands on his knees, and looked out toward the window where, in just a few short hours, the sun threatened its close of business for the day. As fun as it was to be verbally poked and prodded by a gorgeous man in a hospital bed, Sarah felt compelled to end the tête-à-tête at that moment. Night would be here before she knew it, and that realization froze her cold.

What would happen when the sun went down?

As if he read her thoughts, Jacob cleared his throat to grab her attention again. Apparently, he had noticed her mind drifting off as well. "The Northern Hotel. You know it." As in, not a question.

"I'm sorry, I don't. Should I? As I said, I'm not from around here." Sarah felt the need to clarify again, though she didn't know why. It wasn't as if she could expand on the subject in any great detail.

No, I'm not from around here. I actually permanently reside in New Jersey. Yes, not too far away distance-wise, but the time warp jet lag will kill you!

"After my discharge from this damn place, I have made arrangements to spend a few nights at the Northern Hotel in the city, not too far from here." He then stood to his full height in front of Sarah, who remained seated. He was still feet away from her, but for some reason, the disparity in their sizes unsettled her. His proximity was too close for comfort. His socked feet mere inches from her own proved too intimate in some regard. "If you need a room for the night, I can arrange one."

Sarah looked up at the behemoth before her and decided to follow him, at least to the hotel. If she had space to herself behind a door with a lock, she could spend a moment or two thinking about her next steps.

On a slight nod, Sarah accepted his offer.

The good news about being in the military was the lack of personal possessions that needed to be carted around. Standing next to the open door of his hospital room, he looked down at his one canvas bag that held all his belongings and thought how lean he'd lived the past year. Then his eyes wandered over to his guest, took in her appearance again, and felt like a clod for the casual thought he had about living lean when Sarah clearly had even less than that. God, he'd have to find her some clothes before he got to the hotel. And when had she suddenly become his charge?

Sarah stood off to the side, out of the view of the open doorway. Hesitant and unsure, she had wrapped herself in the large wool

34

hospital blanket from his bed. Fine for temporary modesty, but it would do no good outside the hospital in the February Baltimore streets.

Jacob walked over to the far side of his hospital bed and picked up his thick winter coat, which was draped across the nearby chair. Sarah's eyes were downcast, her body huddled beneath the blanket. If an explosion were to go off six inches away from her, he doubted she would even acknowledge the auditory intrusion. She seemed so lost in her own thoughts.

Slowly, so as not to startle her out of whatever mental story held her rapt attention, Jacob inched his way around the other side of the bed so he was standing behind her. With deft fingers, he gently hooked the tips of his fore and middle fingers under the edge of the blanket at the base of her collarbone.

"May I?" he asked. His breath skated across her skin, and he noticed the goosebumps that congregated in the wake of his words.

After a pregnant pause, Sarah seemed to acknowledge his presence and slipped off the rest of the blanket. She folded it up neatly and left it on the bed. Jacob then held open his coat for her, hoping she'd accept. The coat fell to mid-calf on him, but on her, it would no doubt brush the tops of the shoes Jacob had asked one of the nurses for. They were white nurse's work shoes, but the poor woman needed something more than socks in Baltimore's streets. They would have to do.

Sarah took his lead and two-armed it into his coat. As expected, the thing swallowed her up, but it couldn't be helped. At least she'd be warmer than she was.

"The hotel is only a few blocks away from the hospital, at the corner of Light and Redwood. The walk shouldn't take more than fifteen minutes," Jacob assured her as the two of them walked out of the hospital room.

Sarah shuffled next to him and nodded her response. As they made their way down the hall, two young doctors ambled toward them, heads bowed in conversation as they headed in the direction of the hallway Jacob and Sarah had just come from. Jacob turned slightly to get out of the way, and when Sarah raised her head to do the same, her feet slammed to a halt. Her neck craned around to look at one of the doctors who had just passed her.

"Miss Johansson, are you all right?" Jacob asked.

Sarah just stood there as she watched the pair of doctors walk down the hall and make a right-hand turn at the end of the vestibule, heading out of sight. After another few seconds of silence, Jacob said to hell with it and gently shook her by her shoulders in an effort to snap her back to attention.

"Sarah," Jacob roughly gritted out. "What happened? Can you hear me?"

At the mention of her name, Sarah's eyes found his again, but the words that ran from her mouth made absolutely no sense to him. "Ramon Mendez," Sarah breathed.

"What?"

"One of those doctors who just passed us, his name is Ramon Mendez. I know him."

"All right. Was he the doctor who examined you when you arrived here? I thought you said his name was Carlson."

"No," Sarah rushed out. "No, no, no. Ramon Mendez isn't my doctor...he's my great-grandfather."

CHAPTER 6

T he words had left Sarah's mouth before she could take them
back.

Of all the weird things that had happened to Sarah up until this
point, though, none had made sense. Absolutely none of them. Being
at a loss for explanations, frames of reference, and, hell, decent clothes
put a hazy film over her situation. So when she looked up in that
hospital hallway and saw the exact same face she remembered staring
at in a photograph right before this whole episode of *Bill and Ted's
Excellent Adventure* started, something finally clicked. Sort of.

That was Ramon Mendez. There was no doubt in her mind. If she
was correct, and the year was, in fact, 1919, then Ramon would have
been in his final year of medical school at Martinsville University. As
in, right now...and she just walked past him in the freaking hallway!

Ramon was here, and so was she, and that meant, if things were
due to follow the normal course of what she knew to happen next, his
future wife, Helen Schneider, was at the hospital somewhere as well.
Sarah recalled Helen worked as a clerk at the hospital, and that was
how they met.

"Sarah...Sarah!"

The throaty growl that barked out her name snapped her to attention. Jacob was next to her in the hallway. His large, weathered hands

dug into her upper arms, and his face contorted into a combination of frustration at not being heard and flat-out annoyance at having to repeat himself.

Oh, hey, look. Grumpy's back.

"I'm sorry, what?"

He quickly removed his hands and lowered them to his sides. "Sarah...apologies...Miss Johansson, are you all right?"

Seeing that man frazzled was the most endearing thing Sarah had witnessed in a while, and that fact was something she didn't want to examine too closely.

"Yes, I'm fine. I, uh, thought I recognized one of those doctors. That's all." After a brief pause, Sarah asked, "Did you want to head out now?"

Jacob hesitantly nodded at her response, then took one last look down the hallway they had just come from before he picked up his duffle bag again and led them down the corridor, through reception, and out the front entrance.

Leaving the hospital was a very different sensation than when she had arrived. Granted, it had only been a few hours, but instead of the pea soup fog that surrounded her circumstances when she'd landed here, now she had a connection...a thread to unravel...and the aid of someone who, hopefully, wouldn't arrange to have her thrown into the nearest loony bin this side of the Potomac.

Sarah stood, once again, at the top of the same stone steps that Ramon sat on in that photograph.

Oh, the photograph!

Without another thought, Sarah's hands flew to the oversized pocket on the left side of her cardigan. Her fingers dove to the bottom of the fabric and made contact with the bent edge of photograph paper. She pulled out the picture, and sure enough, Ramon Mendez was there staring her in the face. Before she could draw attention to the photo or anything else, she stuffed it back in her pocket and looked around at the Baltimore landscape.

As she fell in line next to Jacob and proceeded to walk down the sidewalk, Sarah huddled deeper into his coat. It wasn't actively snowing, but the ground was wet and slushy in some spots. She popped the collar of the coat up higher around her neck, and on the next inhale, a mix of the cold, crisp air and something else tickled her nose. She couldn't quite put her finger on it, but it reminded her of woodsy balsam and that metallic, sulfurous tang of gunpowder.

Though she had never fired a gun herself, she had been to enough small-town parades and sporting events where members of the armed forces honor guard fired off ceremonial weapons, the action leaving a cloud of smoke for any nearby spectators to suck down. But the smells didn't bother her. On the contrary, they soothed her a bit. Maybe it was because they were scents she easily identified from back home, or maybe they just settled her because she associated them with Jacob, as he was quickly becoming her lifeline here. Either way, she drew the coat in closer around her and slogged onward.

The two of them walked three more blocks, neither of them saying a word as the electric streetcars ran up and down the main drag. It reminded Sarah of the old trolleys in San Francisco, though without the hills and with hardly anyone in them. She guessed it was an off-hour for travel being so late in the afternoon.

"Let's stop in here for a moment," Jacob said, shaking Sarah from her thoughts.

She looked up at the building in front of them. It had the feel of a New York City department store with its store-front windows and clothing displays, though there was also a sign claiming, "Cooked bread and cheese with a soda pop: only 75 cents!" She figured out the soda pop portion of the sign, but the other thing was a head-scratcher. Regardless, it did remind her of how hungry she was.

"Sure, all right."

Once they entered the store, Jacob took her shoulder and guided her over to an eating area. It looked exactly like a diner, with red leather circular seats and the grill right behind the long counter. What *wasn't* like her diners were the racks of women's clothes three feet behind her. When she glanced around at the setup, she noticed a cart of paperback books and periodicals near the main entrance, along with shelves stacked with bottles of aspirin. It appeared to Sarah that Jacob had taken her to...a Wal-Mart.

"What can I get for you, miss?"

A man appeared before her beyond the counter, and the smell of grease on the cooktop reminded her that she needed to get on board the eating train pronto before she started gnawing off her fingernails. Sarah recalled the sign out front and figured it was best to just go with the flow. She knew what bread and cheese were and she could work with that.

Until she remembered she had no money.

Before she could parse out that situation, Jacob threw some coins on the counter and grabbed the seat next to her. "Order what you'd like. And after, you can pick out any clothing you need before we continue on to the hotel."

"You don't have to do that," Sarah began to argue, uncomfortable with the idea of being a charity case. But when he quickly shot her down with that grumpy glare of his, he reminded her of what her situation looked like, highlighting her lack of means and basic amenities.

"Look, I gather there are things you do not want to tell me," Jacob said as he came in close, ducking his head toward her ear. "And why I feel compelled to help an interloper such as yourself, I don't know. Christ knows I have my own life to get back to. But I am not so terrible of a bastard as to disregard your circumstances. For now, eat. Soon, you can rest. And once you have done that, tomorrow morning, you can then explain to me why you think you saw your great-grand-father at the hospital when that man was clearly no older than you or me."

Sarah pulled her head back slightly and turned toward Jacob, her breath rushing out on a swift exhale. The look in his eyes was menac-ing. He seemed like a guard dog unsure whether she was the mail carrier with a bone in her pocket or the bratty neighbor who kept throwing rocks at him over the fence. Either way, she was acutely reminded that she shouldn't assume to be among friends...even if that presumed friend was her all or nothing at the moment. And more to the point, he had heard what she said about Ramon. Crap.

Given their close proximity and the intensity of his threat, Sarah leaned even closer, their noses only a few inches apart. "Understood. But I need you to know one thing. And this is non-negotiable."

"What is that, Miss Johansson?" Jacob never budged from his position.

"I'm keeping the coat." With that, she turned on her stool and grabbed her knife and fork, ready to dive into whatever the cook brought over.

Grilled cheese. "Cooked bread and cheese" was a grilled cheese sandwich.

And that was absolutely perfect.

Jacob hadn't lied when he told Sarah he had his own life to get back to. Okay, maybe he'd exaggerated the significance of the life waiting for him back at the cabin on his family's farmland outside of Baltimore. If there was anything significant about it, it was significantly solitary. And that was exactly what Jacob needed.

Once he had gotten Sarah settled in her hotel room for the night, he had gone back to his own room to think and crash. He had questions. So many questions. Most of them were Sarah-focused. Only a few had anything to do with his actual discharge from the hospital and his release back out into society.

This had all been too much too soon for him. He wanted his seclusion, and in his mind, that was what he needed to work through his "shell shock," as they called it. The doctors had different names for it than what his brothers in the trenches called it, but names didn't really matter when "not right in the head" was the core problem.

When the morning came and the hour was finally a reasonable one for an insomniac to leave his room, he did so and made his way downstairs. Jacob grabbed a seat in the sitting area of the hotel lobby, accepted the offer of coffee from the hotel staff, and continued to brood. As he pulled the cup away from his mouth and stared down into the porcelain, the muddy color of the black coffee reminded him of the dirty clothes Sarah had on when she first burst into his hospital room. He should have called that damn woman's father or whoever was responsible for her the first chance he had. What the hell was he thinking taking her as a tagalong?

41

The truth was that he wasn't thinking. Much like his Army training taught him to be, at his core, Jacob was a reactionary. He never would have left a woman in her condition to fend for herself, but why he felt the need to *be* the one doing the helping instead of handing off her care to her next of kin as would have been most appropriate he had no clue. Boy, was she a spitfire, though. She was a renewed breath to him after more than a year of inhaling poisoned air and battling mental demons. And that was what unnerved him to no end.

When he woke up that morning, he had placed a request with the hotel lobby clerk to deliver a note to Sarah's room, asking her to join him for breakfast downstairs at eight a.m., during which they would discuss next steps, as it were. He needed to get out of the city proper, but he wouldn't do so without knowing she was attended to.

It was a little after seven forty-five a.m., and Jacob sat folded uncomfortably on the ornate lounge chair near the fireplace. Every time he heard heels on hardwood, he turned around to see whether she had arrived. His neck felt like a bottlecap at this point.

Another minute ticked by and when Jacob turned his head yet again, his stomach soured. A man in a tan trench coat and matching wide-brimmed hat entered the lobby from the main staircase. His face was pockmarked, and the shell of his left ear, which peeked out a tiny bit from under his hat, looked as if it had been in an accident and was partially torn off. Jacob remembered all too well when the man sustained that injury. Knowing how the man had chosen to live his life since then, Jacob wished like hell the whole damn ear had been blown off along with the man's stones.

In a move that was in no way discreet, but was put on for discretion's appearance, the man grabbed the front of his trousers between his legs and adjusted himself slightly, doing a small hop and wince in the process. Right then, a woman with ash-blond hair, a prominent decolletage, and noticeably no stockings descended the stairs. When she rounded the banister and saw the man, the two shared a brief look before she walked out of the hotel. Jacob noticed that she wore a wedding ring. The man did not.

The apparent recipient of the blonde's good favors then reached inside his lapel to his coat pocket, pulled out a cigarette, and held it between his pointer and index fingers at the ready on his way outside. Before he made it to the door, he caught Jacob's eye and stopped.

"Bellamy." The man snorted. "Didn't figure you'd patronize such an upscale establishment. What brings you to the finer side of life? They finally let you out of the padded room, I see."

Richard "Dick" Stevens and Jacob had both been in the same infantry regiment in the Army, and that was where the similarities ended. If the war hadn't halted when it did, Jacob was sure Dick would have gotten his head blown off for opening his fat mouth when he shouldn't have or screwing the wrong person's wife. The man always had an agenda, and his penchant for not taking orders, coupled with his attitude and lack of moral compass, made Dick a festering boil on the butt of Jacob's wartime nightmare.

"Stevens." Jacob nodded. "I can see you're still at it." At that, Jacob stood to his full height. If he had to continue a conversation with the bastard, at least he would do it towering over him by a good five inches. As a rule, Jacob loathed using his size as an intimidation tactic. That sort of practice was for weak men with even weaker vocabularies. But in this instance, he was glad to make an exception. "How's the ear?" Jacob said with a slight smirk he mostly kept to himself thanks to his beard.

"Oh, just fine, thanks. Had no trouble at all hearing that broad last night. Speaking of which, was it *just* your skull that got rocked? Rumors spread and all that," Dick said through a smile around his unlit cigarette. He cupped his hands around a match he had just lit and quickly brought it to the end of the butt. Two quick inhales later, Dick shook the match out, dropped it to the floor, and blew a plume of white smoke directly into Jacob's face.

Jacob wanted to punch the snigger right off the bastard's face, but he knew better. Hell, he wanted better. He was done. Don't engage. Be the bigger man. Well, he *was* the bigger man, but peace didn't always come so easily just because one took the high road. He was about to open his mouth to say something he'd no doubt regret when he saw Dick's face turn back toward the staircase.

The clicking of low heels drew both men's attention. Sarah had finally come down from her room. The outfit she had picked out at the five-and-dime was simple, just a high-waisted black pencil skirt that fell to her ankles and a white-and-blue, button-down pinstripe blouse tucked in at the waist. Her shoes were black low-heeled Mary Janes, and they clicked in time with Jacob's heartbeat as she made her way toward the men. She wore her blond hair straight and down over her shoulders, clearly forgoing the hat he had insisted she have. All at once, she looked out of place, yet right where she belonged.

Dick saw her approach, and before Jacob could intervene, Dick beat him to it and made his introduction. "Hello, miss. Jacob neglected to mention he had a companion this morning."

At that, Sarah's eyes bounced back and forth between the two men. "Oh, I'm sorry to intrude," she said, backing up. "I hadn't realized Jacob was meeting with someone."

"Not to worry at all, Miss…" Dick prodded.

"Johansson," Sarah added uneasily.

"Miss Johansson," Dick said as he grabbed her left hand and proceeded to bring it up to his mouth. "It is my true pleasure to meet you. I am Corporal Richard Stevens and served with your Jacob here in the same regiment." Dick gently kissed the back of Sarah's hand, though he chose to linger longer than appropriate.

"We have a breakfast engagement," Jacob interrupted and took Sarah's left hand into his own. Dick was left bent awkwardly at the waist with his cigarette still dangling between the fingers of his other hand. "Take care, Stevens," Jacob growled out through gritted teeth. With that, he escorted Sarah into the dining room, her hand still in his, and left his cup of black coffee on the table by the fire.

"I hope to see you again soon, Miss Johansson. I can't wait," Dick called back to her and took a long drag of his smoke.

As Dick's words died on the air, Jacob fought off the strong urge to turn around and sling that hot coffee at the man where it would do the most damage.

CHAPTER 7

It was good to see some things never change, Sarah thought, as Jacob led her away from the pissing contest she'd walked in on in the hotel lobby. With no frame of reference for the tension between the men, she decided to put it out of mind for now and focus on bigger things. Like how she had spent the night trying to figure out what the heck to tell Jacob about what he heard her say in the hospital hallway...because he definitely heard her mention the whole Ramon-is-my-great-grandfather thing.

Sarah and Jacob sat down at a dining table decked out with a white linen tablecloth and the standard-issue napkin-with-spoon-fork-knife. Her palms were already sweaty as she reached for the glass of water in front of her and began to chug, chug, chug. Out of the corner of her eye, she noticed Jacob stared at her, so she slammed the glass back down and paid extra attention to absolutely anything else in the room aside from his gaze.

"Miss Johansson..." Jacob began and cleared his throat.

"Look, before we start, I just want to thank you for everything you've done for me...and I do mean *everything*. The meals, clothes, hotel. I'm eternally grateful. As you've so acutely assessed, I've been without access to those immediate means. But I assure you, I can manage on my own."

"Oh, I have no doubt that you're fully capable, Miss Johansson."

"It's all right if you call me Sarah, you know. I'm not one for propriety in general."

Jacob's head quirked to the side at first, but then he shrugged at the comment as he put his napkin in his lap. "It makes no difference to me. Your name, the clothes, any of it. You were in need, end of story. Now, speaking of stories...where do you live? Answer honestly, please, Sarah. If there's one thing I've picked up on about you in our short time together, it's that your talent for lying is sorely lacking."

It was Sarah's turn to glare at Grumpy. The man wasn't wrong, but did he have to rub it in? Geez. Okay, time for the truth bombs she had rehearsed during her three a.m. run-through.

"I'm from New Jersey," she stated.

"How did you arrive in Baltimore? Did you travel by yourself?"

"I did travel by myself, yes." Technically not a lie.

"You did not have any baggage with you at the hospital," Jacob noted.

At some point, breakfast had arrived, though Sarah didn't remember ordering anything. Regardless, food was the furthest thing on her mind. Jacob, however, had no problem gorging himself as he dipped a toast point into the runny yolk of his sunny-side-up eggs. Sarah watched as a bread crumb landed in his beard and snuggled in between the fibers before he wiped it away with his napkin. For not the first time, she wondered what his beard felt like. Was it soft throughout? Or maybe a little scratchy at the ends? The daydream was a welcome distraction.

"What happened to you that brought you to the university's hospital in the first place?"

When she glanced down at her plate, her hand shook as she picked up a fork to push her potatoes around. She was too nervous to eat, so she put her fork down and began to tell her version of the story. She needed Jacob to believe her.

Here goes nothing.

"First, I need a promise from you. I'll tell you what I can, but you must swear to me you won't call any sort of authorities or tell anyone you've seen me. If you choose to disassociate with me when I'm finished, that's fine. I'll find a way to manage, and I'll be more than understanding. I know you have absolutely no reason in the world to trust me, but I need to know where we stand first."

Jacob had stopped eating when Sarah began to speak. The silence between them magnified the other sounds in the room: Porcelain cups clanked on saucers as patrons sipped their hot beverages, footsteps of waitstaff shuffled as they weaved in and out of tables, and the nervous tapping of Sarah's fingernails on the tablecloth marked time as she waited.

In the next heartbeat, Jacob reached across the table and covered her jittery hand with his larger one, calming her nerves. Sarah felt the rough edges of his skin on hers, the calluses on the joints. She wondered what his profession was before the war, as he obviously wasn't an early twentysomething plucked from his mother's kitchen table and plopped into the war via the draft. He looked to be close to her age, if not slightly older. If she were to guess, she figured he had worked with his hands to some regard. In that moment, she felt a pressing interest to learn more about him and just prayed he wouldn't do anything that would force her to turn tail.

"Sarah," he said as he wrapped her fingers more securely in his palm to steady them, "I swear to you on the souls of my beloved mother and father, and that of my baby brother, Isaac, I will protect your secrets and safety. May God strike me where I stand if I behave otherwise, though I have my doubts as to whether I even have his ear at all."

Sarah looked down at their stacked hands and then back up to Jacob. The enormity of what she was about to do had finally settled on her like a weighted blanket, and for whatever reason, she had been given an ally. The thought that she wasn't alone in this both soothed and unnerved her, causing her eyes to glass over slightly with unspoken emotions. With that knowledge, she released his hand, sat back in her chair, took a deep breath, and began.

When Sarah eased back into her seat, Jacob felt a little relief of his own. Whatever she had gone through, the reckoning he now forced upon her caused her great stress. It was true he would vow to see her privacy and safety protected, but not for the first time did he wonder just what the hell he had gotten himself into. So out of respect for her and to ensure the memories of his family were honored, he sat back, crossed his arms over his chest, and braced himself for whatever Sarah had to say.

"I told you I traveled here by myself and that I'm from New Jersey," Sarah started. "That's all true."

"All right," Jacob said with a nod.

Sarah took another deep breath before she proceeded. "It is also true that I don't remember how I got here, exactly. Before I found myself in Baltimore, I was sitting in the living room of my condo...uh...house, looking at old photographs of my family. You see, I had been in the process of planning a family reunion."

At this, Jacob cocked his head to the side. "Did you have a lot of family fighting in the war? Is that why you were working at reuniting them?"

"Not exactly, no." She took another pause before she went on. "For the rest of my story, I'm going to ask you to suspend disbelief for a moment because I don't understand things either. Where I come from, my family is spread out all over the East Coast. I have relatives in Maine and New Hampshire, all the way down to Western Pennsylvania and nearby here in Catonsville. We hadn't seen each other in a very long time, and my goal was to get us all together again as a family for a fun weekend. As part of this endeavor, I had volunteered to also present some research on our family history, hence why I went through old family photos and records."

"I understand. What does this have to do with your arrival?" Jacob had many nice qualities, his mother had always assured him, but patience was never one of them.

"I'm getting to that, Grumpy," Sarah grumbled back.

"Grumpy?" Jacob raised an eyebrow.

"Sorry, but I've noticed you can be a little on the moody side sometimes. Your scowl isn't as endearing as you think it is, you know."

"I'll do well to remember that the next time my privacy is invaded by a beautiful trespasser," Jacob shot back mostly in jest, the corner of his lips raised.

Sarah's fair cheeks showed a hint of blush at his comment, but she stayed her course. "Good. Smiles help, too. Just sayin'," she said with a slight grin, and the mood lightened between them. "But at any rate, I was lying on the couch in my living room when I noticed an envelope on the floor. I leaned over to open it. There was a photo inside, and while I examined the photo, I lost my balance and fell off the couch, hitting my head on the corner of my glass coffee table, hence the head wound."

Jacob's eyes quickly shot to her temple where the scrape was. The scrape was still red and angry, but looked to be healing. Her hair mostly covered it now. Later, he would examine the relief he felt at the simple cause of the wound. He had worried she had perhaps been a victim of a violent attack. He wasn't yet sure why that unnerved him so much, more so even than if he heard that had happened to anyone else.

"I fell on the floor, or...wait, no, that's not right." Sarah stopped to re-examine and stared off toward the wall as she wrestled with her memories. "No, there was something on the photo paper. A green residue or something. I remember being surprised it was there and then smelling it to see what it was. I got really sick after that, coughing, dizziness, nausea...that was how I lost my balance and fell. I remember seeing lots of blood before my eyes got heavy and I blacked out. When I woke up, I laid in an alley near the hospital."

When she paused her narrative, Sarah raised her eyes and locked straight onto his own, her throat going up and down on a nervous swallow. She was back to the scared take-no-bull woman who had barged into his hospital room yesterday.

Had it only been yesterday?

She was before him, once again, with everything to lose yet demanding to be heard and trusted. She would make a great Army general.

"You truly don't remember how you got from your house in New Jersey to that alley?"

"No," she said on a quiet, shaky breath.

Jacob made a grim line with his mouth as he started shaking his head in frustration. "I trust you, but your story doesn't make any sense. I will uphold your privacy, but I do demand honesty." Was she taking him for a fool?

"Wait, please!" she yelled as she began to rummage around at her waist and pulled out a folded piece of paper she had tucked under the waistband of her skirt. A few other patrons in the room raised their eyes to her. Sarah noticed and lowered her voice before she continued her plea. "I know what I'm saying sounds crazy. I asked you to suspend disbelief, remember?"

Jacob put his hands on the edge of the table and leaned forward, his voice a whisper. "Yes, you did, but what you've described is not—"

"Here! Look. This is the photo I looked at before everything went dark for me." She handed Jacob over a photograph no bigger than his palm. The image was of a young man he presumed was a doctor, sitting on the front steps of the hospital building Jacob knew all too well. The man in the photo looked vaguely familiar, but he couldn't place him.

"That man," Sarah went on, pointing her finger at what Jacob held in his hand. "The guy in the photo is the same doctor we passed in the hallway back at the hospital yesterday."

Yes, now that he looked at it, Jacob could recall the vague similarities. Though, if he were honest, he hadn't really gotten a good look at the man. One thing that bothered Jacob about the photo, though, was the paper. The photograph must have been taken recently since the building front looked exactly the same as what he knew. But the paper was so...old. The edges were weathered, and not from being folded in Sarah's waistband. No, the paper was also severely discolored. Yellow in tone, as if it had been sitting in a box for decades.

Looking for more answers, Jacob turned the photo over in his hand. There was writing on the back of the paper. As Jacob read it, his mouth fell open in shock as his brows knitted together. The inscription read "Ramon Mendez - 1919 - Martinsville University." But this photo couldn't have been taken more than a month ago. The man was still wearing his heavy winter coat in the photo and it was only

February, for God's sakes! But the age of the photograph paper itself told a different story.

"What is it that I'm seeing here?" Jacob rushed out on a low whisper as he held up the photo toward her. "Because I'm having a hard time comprehending..."

Sarah reached over and took the photo from Jacob's trembling fingers and set it down on the table before wrapping his hand in her own two. Amazing how this woman could turn the tables on him at his own game, even amid her own fear and anxiety.

"I have no cards left to play. What you're seeing is a photo of Ramon Mendez sitting on the steps of the Martinsville University of Science and Medicine in 1919, the same year he will graduate from its medical school...but that won't happen for another four months. I know this because the man in that photo, Ramon Mendez, is my great-grandfather. I have his yearbooks sitting on my bookshelf back at my home in New Jersey."

He couldn't believe what he heard. His brows furrowed down in confusion at her admission. Perhaps he should go back on his promise? Notify the hospital again of her condition? Clearly, she was not well. But then, how would he explain that? Then there was the photo... The squeeze on his hand brought his attention back to her.

"When I was in my living room yesterday holding that photo in my hand, the date was February sixth, twenty twenty-one...one hundred and two years *after* that photo was taken. I literally don't know anything about the hows and whys, but I do know that I saw my great-grandfather in that hallway yesterday, and I've always believed things happen for a reason. You demanded honesty from me, and I've freely given it. I'll also add that, in this moment, I'm scared, confused, and oddly determined to get to the bottom of things. Will you help me?"

What more was there to say? His spitfire looked at him from across the table with steel in her eyes, but yet her small fingers still trembled slightly around his own. Though he didn't, *couldn't*, comprehend the circumstances he'd found himself in, he was no stranger to a challenge. So, yes, he would listen to her, suspend his disbelief, and offer her aid in whatever form that took. When he looked inside himself just now, into that dark, cavernous hole that had eaten away at him throughout the past year, he didn't find it so daunting anymore. By some miracle, the prospect of taking on Sarah's burden seemed to shed light on his road ahead.

Sarah sat there holding her breath, her hands tense around his, the tips of her fingernails just beginning to leave little crescent indentations on his skin. She waited for his response, for his yay or nay.

Oh, hell.

"Yes," Jacob whispered. "I will help you." At his own admission, they both let out a heavy exhale of relief. "I don't understand any of this, but it seems you don't either. And I believe you. Against my better judgment, I believe you."

"Oh, thank God!" Sarah rushed out as she released his hands and brought hers to her face, rubbing away the stress lines that had formed on her forehead. "Thank you," she said as she lowered her hands to wipe her sweaty palms on her skirt. "Thank you. Just...thank you."

Her gratitude was the new spark that lit his beacon.

CHAPTER 8

Dick Stevens watched as Bellamy and Miss Johansson entered the dining area. He turned his head so his right ear, his good ear, faced the couple as they sat down. He was never one to turn down an opportunity to screw over Jacob Bellamy, especially not an opportunity as beautiful as Bellamy's apparent new interest, Miss Johansson. Sure, Bellamy was the last person Dick expected to see in the hotel lobby, but rumor had it the man's brains were so scrambled from the war, he'd voluntarily checked himself into the psych wing at Martinsville. Dick knew of no self-respecting man who would freely cop to mental issues, let alone a psychiatric breakdown. What a fucking pussy.

Speaking of pussy... that Miss Johansson certainly sparked his intrigue. He peeked sideways under the brim of his hat to get a better look at what captured Bellamy's attention. Her long dirty blond hair was what first caught his eye, as he didn't know many women who wore their hair like that. Most of the broads he saw wore their hair short in that bob style. And as he was always a man appreciative of having something long to grab onto, he smiled at the thought of wrapping the length of Miss Johansson's hair around his wrist.

He watched as Bellamy pulled out a chair for her at one of the tables. When she sank onto the cushion and Bellamy pushed her in,

Dick got an eyeful of how round her hips were. Even through her skirt, he could tell her generous ass hung over the sides of the narrow seat. Once she was seated, a member of the waitstaff walked in front of Dick's vantage point and cut short his musings.

Just thinking about the way her ass swayed in that skirt earlier as she walked across that hotel lobby floor made his cock hard. Envisioning the look on Bellamy's face when Dick took over the reins of that woman made him even harder.

God, he fucking hated that man. It was his damn fault Dick's face and ear resembled a crag in a mountain range, that the hearing in his left ear was so diminished he'd taken to walking on the left-hand side of the roads so the sounds of the streetcars would come in loud and clear. He'd had to learn that lesson the hard way, being dealt a few narrow misses when Dick had crossed the street from the right side going left and wandered right into the suckers. The electric brakes of the streetcars, once loud and arresting to his ear, now sounded like a barely simmering tea kettle in the kitchen when one was on the opposite end of the house.

He and Bellamy had come up together through the ranks of non-commissioned officers in Baltimore's 313th Infantry Regiment during the war. As a runner who carried messages between units, Dick had been at peak physical fitness with the desired stamina to push on through mile-long runs in the trenches. It was dangerous as hell, and everyone knew it was just a matter of when, not if, you got a shell to the head, but they'd relied on him. *Needed* him. And he'd been damn good at it, too, until Bellamy's bad intel one day sent him too close to enemy fire. Dick was, in kind, treated to a face full of shrapnel, a mangled left ear, and permanent disfigurement.

So, yeah, there was no love lost there. Dick had long desired to find a way to repay the favor, as it were. Seeing Bellamy again with Miss Johansson, he had just the idea of how to do it.

Heel-toeing it across the hotel's lobby floor, Dick walked up to the clerk at the front desk.

"Checking out, sir?" the attendant inquired as he reached for his guest ledger.

"Actually, there's been a change of plans. I'll be extending my stay a few more nights," Dick replied as he slid over the ashtray on the top of the counter and stamped out his cigarette, adding one more dead soldier to the pile.

Never in a million years would Sarah have bet money on Jacob believing her. Not only that, but the relief she felt at his offer to help was so profound, she hadn't realized how starved she was for trust and human connection...or how she had been holding her breath the entire time she waited on his answer.

"Are you really from another time, then? God, I can't believe I'm even asking that question," Jacob said as he shook his head, but there was a lilt to his voice when he mentioned it. The moment was brief, but not so brief that it skipped Sarah's notice. Clearly, he was unhinged a bit but was doing his best not to let it show.

"Is there another place we can talk about this? I'm just nervous about others hearing us." Sarah looked around the dining room, and even though no one paid her any mind that she saw, laying something this monumental and far-fetched out there in a public setting didn't sit well with her. She had already met her risky behavior quota for the day.

"Sure. We can go to my room." Jacob pushed his chair out and quickly rose to his full height, causing Sarah to crane her neck back to take in the view. He wore similar dark gray wool slacks to what she had seen him in the day before, and as she was at eye level with his waist (thank you very much), she quickly darted her eyes elsewhere and had them land on the hollow of his throat just below his Adam's apple. Why there she had no idea, but it seemed like neutral territory. Yup, total friggin' Switzerland.

Shaking off the distraction, Sarah rose out of her own chair, and the two proceeded toward the lobby's main staircase. As they climbed the stairs, Sarah threw a look over her shoulder once or twice to see whether that man from the lobby was nearby. Colonel Richard something. She couldn't recall his name immediately, but the man gave her the heebie-jeebies. Not to mention the last time any man had kissed her hand in that way was...never. A man had never kissed her hand that way or any way for that matter. She wasn't sure whether it was a custom of the time she now found herself in, but she knew a lecher when she saw one. And Colonel what's-his-nuts' behavior didn't throw up red flags so much as road flares. Best she not run into him again.

Jacob's room was on the same floor as the one she had stayed in, and only took two flights of steps to get there. Once Jacob unlocked the room and entered, he extended his hand out and indicated for her to have a seat in the wooden ornamental chair by the desk. Jacob had taken off his jacket, placed it on the coat hook near the door, and rolled up his sleeves to just below his elbows, showing off the thick tendons that snaked down his arms.

Once Sarah sat down, Jacob grabbed a seat across from her on the edge of the bed, his bare forearm propped up against the brass footboard. He looked nervous as he rested his forehead on his fingertips, examining Sarah as if she were no longer a human being but a mythical creature who would sprout wings and fly through the room at any moment.

"So, do you have an idea how to return—"

"I think I know why I'm here—"

The two spoke at the same time, neither hearing what the other said.

Jacob immediately gestured to her, his first two fingers extending in her direction. "Apologies. Please, you go first."

She gave him a small smile and nodded, determined to continue before she lost her nerve. "As I started to say, I think I know why I was sent here."

Jacob's eyebrows shot toward the ceiling, but after he let the words sink in, he gave her a nod to continue.

"I already told you that my great-grandfather, Ramon, earned his medical degree from Martinsville University and graduated...well...is due to graduate in June nineteen eighteen."

A pause. "Yes."

"Ramon met his wife, my great-grandmother, Helen, at

Martinsville that same year. She also worked at the hospital as a clerk, though in what department I don't know."

More nodding from Jacob. So far, it seemed that Sarah hadn't lost him yet. That was good. She sincerely hoped he'd stay with her as she took her next dive into crazy-hunch-land.

"Following Ramon's graduation, he and Helen married. After that, as you may expect, they got down to business doing what any newly married couple does. The result? Helen got pregnant with my grandmother, Ramona."

"Ramon named his daughter Ramona?" Jacob said with a raised eyebrow.

"Yes," Sarah said solemnly. "There was a reason for that. You see, soon after Helen found out she was pregnant, Ramon contracted typhoid fever from one of his patients. He died when he was only twenty-six years old, before Ramona was born. She never got to meet her father, and Helen went on to live to be ninety-two years old, never remarrying and never having more children."

Sarah decided to pause there and watched Jacob mull over the story for a moment, let things settle where they may.

"I've got to be honest, to hear you talk in the past and future tense together is dizzying," Jacob conceded. "I'm still having a hard time coming to terms with things, and I don't know what to believe. To talk about the past and future out loud as if they're one and the same, I feel like I'm two seconds away from being readmitted to Martinsville."

Her heart sank at the admission. Jacob leaned forward on the edge of the bed, braced his bent elbows on his knees, and lowered his head in his hands. His fingers snaked into his thick hair on either side of his skull and dug in, as if the pressure applied by his fingertips would dissipate some of the fog from the truth bombs Sarah had hit him with. She'd be lying to herself if she said she was no longer worried. Not that she hadn't been worried all along, but there had been a moment with Jacob down in the dining room when she felt in her bones like she wasn't the only crazy one. Misery loves company, right?

Abruptly, Jacob shot his head up to look at her. He was still bent over his knees, and his eyes looked a little bloodshot from the quick bottom-to-top movement. All at once, he locked down his hesitations again and went back to being the stoic, grumpy man Sarah relied on.

"I believe you. Though I may find myself needing to repeat that mantra, I believe you. Please, continue," he said curtly. "What does all this have to do with you being here?"

"You remember about my family history project I worked on back home?"

"Yes."

"Okay, hear me out. I think I'm here to help Ramon in some way. If I can find a way for him to not contract typhoid fever, imagine what that'll mean for my family. He wouldn't have died so young, and my grandmother would have had a father. Helen would have had a husband. She wouldn't have had to endure a lifetime alone." Sarah stopped for a moment, the enormity of the situation hitting her like a Mack truck. "Jacob, that's what I have to do. I'm going to keep Ramon from dying in that hospital."

The dots had finally started to connect for Sarah, which was a relief because nothing up until now had made a lick of sense. She still had no idea how she got here, how she would get home, or any of the in-between, but those questions didn't terrify her like they did before.

What truly did terrify her, though, was going back to the life she had. Back home, her mounting inadequacies threatened to consume her. The cycle was exhausting: She wasn't good enough at her job, which hindered her from measuring up against the men she dated who were further along in their careers. She wasn't married because prospective boyfriends didn't want to start out a relationship knowing they'd have to financially carry a so-so medical writer. Lack of a spouse led to lack of kids. And, well, when Aunt Sarah showed up for Christmas with stacks of exciting presents for the nieces and nephews and all she had waiting for her were the same old gift cards each year, it sent a message: She was lackluster, and everyone knew it. She had firmly hoped to eradicate that image with the reunion, though. Show everyone she was worthy of people's esteem despite her crummy job and kidless condo.

Slowly, the puzzle pieces began to align. Why was she here? She couldn't ignore the exact date and time to which she had been whisked back. It was all deliberate. Had to be. Something was steering her in a direction. Heck, she'd just run into her great-grandfather in the freaking hallway! What if she could change things? Like, *really* change things? A big, monumental keep-Ramon-from-dying type of change? Once her mind went down that path of possibilities, she couldn't shake it. If she could save Ramon's life, the implications would be huge. So, with both feet, she leaped in.

Jacob sat there on the edge of the bed like a sponge. He had listened to every cooky detail and hadn't yet run out on her to call the authorities. That was encouraging, Sarah figured. Jacob took a slow, deep inhale once she finished speaking, staring absentmindedly at the carpet. The sight of his chest as it swelled up reminded her of the man's physical presence in the room.

Letting out the breath, Jacob looked at her and officially set her course. "I suppose I'll need to make arrangements to extend my stay in the city for a few more days. Now that I know you have no one here to vouch for you, I can work on arrangements for you as well if you need them. I don't presume you thought through any of those magical little details, Woman of the Future, like where to rest your head in between your jaunts through time."

The widest damn smile Sarah had ever managed suddenly crept across her face.

"You read me like a book, Grumpy."

CHAPTER 9

J acob had just opened the door to his hotel room after completing his errand at the front desk to extend their stay when the sight before him froze him catatonic. Sarah sat in the middle of the bed, *his bed*, cross-legged and barefoot. Her black Mary Janes had been kicked off and lay haphazardly along the far wall underneath the window. In the center of the mattress, on top of the standard-issue white cotton blanket, Sarah's bare feet and legs peeked out below her black skirt, which she had hiked up slightly above her knee to allow for the range of motion, no doubt.

The blue-and-white button-down pinstripe blouse had its first two top buttons undone so her neck was no longer confined and showed more of Sarah's fair skin. The winter sun that shone through the window streaked across her chest and torso, the ribbon of light emblazoned like Zeus' thunderbolt. Between her exposed skin, the sun's illumination, the way she rested her slender hands in her lap, and the innocent yet determined way she looked at him, he was dumbstruck. She was Athena personified: goddess of both wisdom and war strategy. *His spitfire.*

But, no, he shouldn't think of her in that way. She wasn't his anything.

"You okay?" she asked when he didn't move from the doorway. Heck, he hadn't even closed the door yet.

He quickly cleared his throat, closed the door, and threw the key on top of the dresser. "Yes, I'm fine. Comfortable?" he said as he eyed her bare legs.

At that, she tracked his eyes and saw where they landed. "Shit...shoot...sorry," she said as she uncrossed her legs, laid them straight out in front of her, crossed her ankles, and smoothed her skirt back down so only her feet were exposed. "I, uh, I still need to learn some social etiquette for your time. I take it that women here tend to dress more conservatively?"

"Yes, women's fashions are a bit different."

"Yes, of course. I'll need to learn a little more before I head back to the hospital."

Jacob did a double take at that. "You want to go back? Why?"

"I want to see whether I can find Ramon again. Figure out a way to keep him from getting typhoid fever." Once the statement left Sarah's mouth, she blinked up at him a few times. Her declaration was so casual and certain in its deliverance she might as well have said she'd go jump out a ten-story window instead of take the stairs because it was the quickest and most direct way. Naturally.

"I see," Jacob said as he took a seat in the chair across from the bed —the same bed he had been sleeping in not three hours before, and where Sarah had decided was a better place from which to deliver her plan of attack—and turned it around to face her. God, it would be easier to stop thinking about her in his bed if she weren't actually *in* his bed.

"So apprise me. Before you plan to do an about-face and storm the hospital, what will you tell people who notice you? Or, for that matter, how do you plan to provide for yourself should things not go your way? Have you given any thought to your situation beyond your magical motive to restore your family?" He wasn't trying to be a cad, but he still had so many questions. They both needed intel and a plan. "Forgive me, Sarah, but in my previous line of work, I learned that going off half-cocked is a surefire way to end your journey before it begins."

Sarah narrowed her eyes at him, which he deserved. "Well, Grumpy, care to elaborate on your previous line of work, then? I heard the nurse call you corporal."

"Yes, I was an Army corporal with Baltimore's three hundred and thirteenth infantry regiment during the war. That charming fellow you met downstairs, Dick Stevens? Well, we served together. We were both runners for our regiment."

"Runners?"

God, how he hated talking about his time in the conflict.

"Runners were messengers. We carried information back and forth across the front lines, running through trenches, open fire, you name it. Not exactly glamorous work, and by all accounts, I should have been killed ages ago. Stevens and I both should have, actually. When the war ended, we were the only two runners left in our regiment." Jacob's eyes drifted toward a seam between two wooden planks on the floor as his memories slowly resurfaced.

The din of German shell fire and the acrid smell of gunpowder began to invade his memories when he felt her hand close around his own. He hadn't even remembered clenching it into a fist, but when he looked down, Sarah had taken her other hand and began to pry open his fingers one by one, massaging each digit into submission. He looked up at her and was surprised he never heard her move to the edge of the bed across from him. She met his gaze and still didn't let go of his hand.

God, why did she have to be so close? Sarah had leaned forward to grasp his hand, and doing so gave him a direct line of sight to her chest. He wasn't used to seeing women on display in that manner in public.

But he supposed they weren't in public, were they?

The top two undone buttons of her blouse parted the fabric like the Red Sea, and not for the first time, Jacob wondered about this woman's previous life. She had told him she had no husband. How that was possible, he couldn't comprehend. Perhaps an engagement, then? Surely, she must be spoken for.

She was about to say something, but he cut her off with a wave of his hand. No doubt she would pour out her pity for his shell shock and rehabilitation. He had no interest or use for that. Instead, he wanted to know more about her, more about this woman who'd landed in his proverbial lap and decided to dig her heels in.

"Speaking of how we met." Jacob took his hand back from hers and leaned back in the chair. "You had mentioned you didn't have a husband, nor did you live with your father. How are you thirty-one years old with no husband, especially if there is no war in your time? Forgive me for being forward, but you are strong, intelligent..." Beautiful. Beguiling. Though those last two he kept to himself. "Qualities any man would find endearing."

The blush in Sarah's pale cheeks said she wasn't used to hearing those particular accolades. Sarah scooched back a bit on the bed and brought her bare legs up under her again to sit cross-legged. Jacob wouldn't comment this time, as it was clearly a position of comfort for her. And he wanted her to be comfortable.

"Thank you," she whispered as she nervously tucked a few strands of hair behind her ear. "But no, it's just me." At this, her voice returned to its normal volume. "I've had a few boyfriends over the years, but things never stuck, as you can tell. But I have my career, though that seems to have kind of stalled lately. My family, friends, it's all good."

"A career?"

"Oh, yes. I'm a medical writer and editor. I write articles for health websites and cover medical conferences. Mostly, I write about pain management now, but I've dabbled in endocrinology, spine, occasionally I'll do some diabetes work when that department is short-staffed..."

Jacob's mouth hung slack-jawed, his head tilted slightly to the right.

"I'm sorry. I just realized you probably have no idea what any of that is." Sarah balled her hands into fists, brought them up to her forehead, and leaned her head on them, closing her eyes in the process. "Ugh! Shit...shoot...shit. Sorry. I know I stick out like a sore thumb here. I have no idea how I'm going to be able to pass as someone from your time and save Ramon." Sarah still had her eyes closed, her fisted hands seeming to press harder into her sockets.

Jacob snapped out of his stupor long enough to notice her body starting to tremble a bit, as if she were silently sobbing but fighting her hardest to hold back the emotional onslaught. Before he met Sarah, Jacob thought he no longer had a caring bone left in his body, but in that moment, his instincts took over.

When Sarah's subtle wracking didn't let up, Jacob jumped from his chair and landed on his knees at the edge of the bed in front of her. Even sitting up on his knees on the floor, he was still taller than she was as she sat there on the bed. With a swift yet gentle approach, the same tactic he had used on his parents' farm when one of the livestock got spooked, he reached up and grabbed her hands away from her eyes all while making the "shh...shh...shh..." sounds his father had taught him to use on panicked animals.

Once he brought her fists down into her lap, he cradled her upper body against his. Enveloped in his arms, she buried her face in his left shoulder. He suspected she wasn't ready to show her face yet, so he allowed her to hide there for as long as she needed while he used his thumb to rub soothing circles into her biceps.

They sat there like that for as long as Sarah needed to regain her composure. Though Jacob wouldn't have minded if they had stayed like that for longer. As he held her close, he looked down at their hair intermingling on his shoulder: the dark and the light. He liked the contrast and again noticed how he was always being drawn to her spark.

Jacob felt Sarah's eyes give a few blinks against his shoulder, the flutter of her lashes a gentle tickle through his shirt sleeves. She slowly pulled back and looked up at him. There was not a single tear in her eyes, but they were bloodshot, nonetheless. For Christ's sake, this woman would no sooner allow an avalanche to flow down a mountain, let alone a single tear to fall down her cheek.

"Sarah, I haven't known you long, but I am very good at reading people. You, my spitfire, are capable of doing exactly what you intend to." Sarah squinted a bit at that, her head cocked slightly in confusion. "And I will assist you...help you deliver your messages to your great-grandfather."

Sarah's lips slowly grew into a smile.

Jacob lifted his thumb and pointed it at his chest. "I'm a runner, remember? It's what I do."

Sarah launched herself at him in a full bear hug, knocking the breath out of Jacob. "I know I keep saying this," Sarah said softly into his ear. "But thank you."

Jacob could feel much of the tension leaving her body, and he found himself smiling as he returned her hug. He hadn't had a reason to smile in so long, the action felt foreign yet innate. Like riding a bicycle, he supposed.

"You're very welcome," he volleyed back before setting her upright and rising from the floor. "Besides, I think I have an idea of how we can get you back into the hospital without raising too much suspicion." He held his hand out to her. "All right, Miss Writer, let's see how good of an actress you can be."

CHAPTER 10

Sarah's molars clenched as the heel of her shoe slipped in between yet another crack in the brick sidewalk. "Crack" was a kind term. "Crevasse" was probably more apt. In her own time, she always viewed the cobblestone path leading up to her local library as romantic and charming. Likewise, the brick walkway that snaked around the arboretum and botanical garden in the adjacent town made it easy for a gal to become one with her inner Dorothy. Its smooth manicured surface was like that of a runway ready to guide visitors to its inner sanctum. Follow the yellow brick road and all that.

Nope. Not here. Baltimore's sidewalks and plazas in this time were laid with brick so uneven and askew, Sarah felt like playing whack-a-mole with the ball of her foot on every other uneven interlocking paver she came across. Sure, there were things she missed about her own time. Never did she think concrete sealer would be high on that list.

"I swear, woman, you remind me of a newborn giraffe," Jacob said with a snort as he paused, yet again, to wait for Sarah to unstick her heel and right herself before they proceeded down the street. "Do they not walk much in your time?" Jacob muttered under his breath so only she could hear.

Sarah stood to her full height and shook off her boot in Jacob's direction, the dirty road slush and gravel landing on the ankles of his pants. "No, we don't, actually," Sarah bit back while adjusting her hair under the new royal blue bowler hat she wore.

The hat sported a tonal blue ribbon that snaked all the way around its middle, culminating in a modest blue bow on its side right above Sarah's ear. She needed to look the part more, and Jacob insisted wearing a hat would help her cause. He also insisted on helping her out in the new wardrobe department, too, which didn't sit well with her at all, but like she had a choice. Desperate times and all that. Still, she wasn't a hat person, so she couldn't help but constantly fuss and fiddle with the darn thing.

"In the future," Sarah continued, "everyone gets carried around in a litter hoisted by four gorgeous chairmen. Is that not how they do it here?" She turned her head to him, raised her right eyebrow, and stuck out her chin, content to fling the snark back at him as fast as the detritus from her boot.

"You know," Jacob said gruffly as they resumed their walk, nonchalantly shaking off his leg as if her tantrum was of no more importance than a loose thread on his sleeve, "if you want this plan to work, you're going to have to play nice."

"I can play nice."

"Can you now?" he said as he scratched his bearded chin. "When we get to the hospital, I suggest you let me do the talking, at least to start. We wouldn't want you asking for Dr. *Carlson* again, would we?" Jacob bent his head down to remove his olive green wool flat cap. As they walked, he ran his hand through his thick hair a time or two, adjusting the way the tresses fell and scratching at his scalp a bit before he refitted the cap on his head. The routine did not escape Sarah's notice.

"I do have a question for you."

"I'm all ears."

"Why do you wear your hair in such a different style from all the other men I've seen? It seems more common to wear it short."

Jacob shot Sarah the side-eye under the brim of his cap before he righted his gaze on the path ahead. "Preference, Miss Johansson. There was never any time for constant trimmings every three weeks when my brother and I worked to maintain my family's farm. As I am not a neat and tidy man by nature, the length suits me...as does the beard."

Sarah forced herself to stop staring at where his hair fell half-in, half-out of his coat collar near his shoulders and promptly got her eyes back on the sidewalk in front of her. "I'm surprised the Army wouldn't have regulations to the effect of how a soldier should dress. It sure does back in my time," Sarah commented, that last sentence at a lower volume than the rest.

"I will admit, when I was first drafted into service, there were certain decorum rules new recruits had to follow. But as the weeks and months went on, our commanding officers were more consumed with war strategy than hair length or whether one was clean-shaven. After the first month, I started to grow my beard and hair out again and no one really cared. They were all far too concerned with how the government planned to feed and arm us."

"Well, it works on you. I can't imagine you clean-shaven."

Jacob peered down at Sarah for a brief moment. "Likewise, blue is most definitely a favorable color on you."

Sarah let the compliment land and was grateful for the low-slung brim of her bowler hat. She ducked her head down slightly as the flush of heat traveled up her skin to the tips of her ears.

The next ten minutes passed in relative quiet until Sarah heard only the sounds of her own footfalls. A glance back revealed Jacob several feet behind. The wind whipped his hair about his face as he stood stock-still, staring across the street. His tanned complexion had turned sour, his ashen color resembling the gray snow at his feet.

Vibrant blues and reds broke through Sarah's periphery. She turned and took in the solemn draping of the American flag across a casket. The sight stood out against the somber backdrop. A fallen soldier. Two funeral parlor attendants pushed the remains around toward the back of the building. Groups of people in black clothes huddled together as they ascended the stairs to the funeral home.

Once the line of people trickled down to a few stragglers, Sarah glanced back at Jacob.

He was still frozen, and not in the my-tootsies-are-too-cold sense.

She rushed over to him and laid a hand on his forearm. The wool of his coat scratched this time, rather than soothed. "Jacob? What's wrong?"

He didn't answer her, just continued to stare off in the direction of the funeral home. His eyes never even glanced down to her hand on his sleeve. Concerned, she inched up his sleeve and laid two fingers along his wrist. His pulse hammered out a faster-than-normal rhythm for someone doing little more than breathing.

"Jacob," she said firmly, placing her hands on each side of his face. "Grumpy, do you hear me?"

A few flutters of his eyelashes preceded a quick inhale before he snapped his attention toward her. His eyebrows dipped down as his gaze danced across her face.

"I'm...excuse me. I'm sorry," he said, clearing his throat and stepping back a pace, leaving her hands empty.

"What happened back there? It seemed like you snuck inside your mind for a second."

"Yes, apologies. It's just that, from time to time, I have...triggers. Reminders of how I'm still here, but others are not. A casket is just one of many lovely images that can bring to mind my guilt from time to time. It's nothing. As you know, I'm working through it."

"But you have nothing to feel guilty for," she said, knowing she should tread lightly. "War is not fair, especially for those conscripted to serve. None of that is your fault. You have to know that."

Jacob stared down at his boots, looking more interested in a rock on the ground than acknowledging her words. But she knew he needed space, time to process. Sometimes, mental wounds were so much harder to heal than physical ones.

"Look," Sarah said to break the silence, "you don't have to talk to me about it. I know it's a personal, private thing that I probably wouldn't understand. I respect that. Just know that if you ever wanted to talk about it, I'd be happy to listen. I won't say a word, I promise. I'd just listen. A judgment-free zone. But you'd be surprised how much lighter you can feel after talking, even if the conversation is one way. Sometimes, it helps to know your words aren't just bouncing off the walls around you."

Jacob kicked the rock in front of his boot. The stone traveled into the street and plunked into a puddle in the middle of the road. The water's surface rippled briefly before stilling again. No evidence of the rock was visible at all. Was Jacob's pain like that rock? Did he think it was better hidden under a fragile shell where no one was the wiser? Gosh, what were the current treatments for mental trauma in 1919? Maybe he didn't know he was allowed to talk about it.

As Sarah mulled over what she knew of post-World War I treatment for mental trauma (a whole lot of nada), the shuffle of Jacob's boot brought her attention back to him.

"Thank you," he said softly, almost so low she nearly missed it. His chin was down, his eyes still not meeting hers, but the mutual understanding was there. That would have to be enough for now. Rising to his full height, he motioned forward and they resumed their walk.

With the moment behind them, Sarah turned her thoughts back to their plan. When they arrived at the hospital, Jacob would re-introduce her formally as one of his old childhood friends for whom he was caring. The lie would continue with Sarah expressing to the nursing staff that she believed she may be two months pregnant, but didn't have the means for a private physician at the moment. With any luck, that story would sell and Sarah would be the newest pregnant patient at Martinsville in need of gynecological services. From her great-grandfather no less, who happened to be a gynecologist about to graduate with his medical degree in a few months.

That wasn't weird at all, really.

Sarah glanced up when she noticed Jacob had stopped walking. Once again, the Martinsville University of Science and Medicine loomed large before her, its stone steps the precipice their plan would live or die on. Jacob hadn't been kidding when he asked her how good her acting skills were. Acting wasn't that different from lying, right? Just with better lighting and a paying audience, she imagined. But as Jacob had so kindly pointed out from their original meet and greet, she was, in fact, a terrible liar.

This should be interesting.

A surprise warmth looped through her left arm and cupped her left elbow. Jacob had inserted his right arm through hers and now held her elbow in the palm of his glove.

"Time to play your part, Miss Johansson. Now, as we discussed, let me do the talking."

"My, you're bossy. One would think you'd know how to take orders better given your recent service," Sarah fired back with a slight smirk, but her mouth fell real quick when she heard the low growl in his throat.

Bending over, Jacob brought his lips to her left ear. His breath, coupled with the biting cold, caused her goosebumps to get goosebumps. "My temperament is the product of war, Miss Johansson. I am an expert in orders of all kinds, but I will not tolerate one that jeopardizes the mission."

Sarah turned her head slightly to the left toward the bone-deep rumble that was quickly becoming something her heart kept pace with. That slight head turn brought her lips within mere inches of his beard, the dark brown pelt threatening to graze the skin of her cheek. Then her damn body started going rogue.

Her lips parted slightly, exhaling the cold air. Her breath's vapor left on a slow puff that seemed to dance and join with Jacob's own, swirling around their mouths and noses like a heady incense. When she spared a glance at Jacob's face, his lips were tightly closed and his breath came in short bursts from his nose. As she stared at the sight of him, he seemed like a pent-up bull about to charge at its matador.

And Sarah was the one holding the red cape.

Jacob had no explanations for his reactions, but that had started to become par for the course when it came to Sarah. The brim of her blue hat was so near to his face that it tickled his eyebrow. He was too close, yet when he tried to back his head away, he was frozen. By some miracle, Sarah hadn't shied away from him.

This woman distracted and disoriented him. She was a riddle he couldn't solve, a magician whose tricks he couldn't decipher. She was damn frustrating...and captivating. In a move he didn't remember making, his hand floated up toward her upper arm where his fingers dug into the sleeve of her blue dress. Not harshly, not as a brute would. No, he would never behave in that manner. But vitally, as if she were his mooring and he'd be set adrift if he didn't lay hold of her.

With his hand on her upper arm and his other arm still linked through hers down at their waists, he pulled her closer to his body. At the sudden urging, she allowed her torso to brush up against his. It was a good thing she'd folded her right arm up against her chest or there would have been very little keeping their bodies from being flush against one another.

Or wasn't it a good thing?

His eyes settled on her lips, which were parted and panting into the crisp air, her breath leaving her lungs in an intoxicating swirl around his senses. He wanted to capture that breath, that essence, whatever it was that seemed to call him home.

Jacob turned his chin toward her cheek, ghosting his beard across her smooth skin until his lips skated across her mouth...and then stopped. There was no kiss. No ravishing. No, just a gentle caress of open mouths, of new sensations. Jacob shut his eyes and breathed in the entire moment.

God, this was heaven. The ultimate balm to his war-ravished soul. He could bask here forever, on the steps of this infernal hospital, until his feet were frozen to the Earth, and he would have no complaints. The longer he stood there in that almost-kiss limbo, the more he realized that, like this moment, his time with Sarah was fleeting. He hated admitting it to himself, but each helping hand he extended to her slowly cut him off at the knees.

And he would have it no other way. He had come to find meaning in her mission, which empowered him more than any other mission of recent memory. So he would continue on his course to aid Sarah for as long as she needed it.

On the next exhale, he released her arm and resumed his stance at her side. Presenting his elbow to her, Jacob glanced down at Sarah, who was still standing there breathless and stoic.

"Shall we, Miss Johansson?" he said after he cleared his throat slightly.

Sarah took a moment to compose herself before she readjusted her hand in the crook of his elbow, closed her lips, and nodded.

As they ambled up the steps to the hospital, Jacob had a heck of a time walking straight.

CHAPTER 11

Sarah was more than elated to know she wouldn't have to suffer through whatever version of a 1900s gynecological exam may have awaited her on the inside of the tiny patient room. When she had originally heard about Jacob's plan for her to see Ramon under the guise of a pregnant woman needing an OB/GYN, she almost abandoned ship right then and there. Yeah, turns out, there were some *huge* gaps to bridge in that department.

She imagined it was uncommon for a pregnant woman to see an obstetrician in the early term of pregnancy by virtue of the fact that they didn't have the medical tools to diagnostically assess the fetus. Ain't no ultrasound being used around here, after all.

No, instead, based on her conversation with the intake nurse, the emphasis was on ensuring the overall health of the mother to carry the baby to term. Only at the end did mothers call in the heavyweights, and that was fine by her. She didn't need the threat of some 103-year-old speculum getting all up and personal with her, thank you very much. They had just needed to rework their original plan of attack a bit.

Sarah sat on the edge of an examination table, which, again, she was *assured* wouldn't be used in that manner, while Jacob stood brooding in the corner of the room, his massive bulk holding up the wall next to the door. After going through Sarah's basic health information, the nurse assured them the doctor would be in momentarily.

She was grateful for the wait, honestly. She still hadn't recovered from whatever the heck kind of chemistry had just combusted all over her and Jacob outside. They had kissed, right? Or didn't they? Sarah had spent the time at the check-in desk replaying the whole encounter in her head, and the more she tried to recall, the fuzzier the details seemed to be. What wasn't fuzzy? The muscle memory that swirled through her body as she relived the feel of the moment.

She used the brim of her hat to shield her eyes as she flicked a glance at Grumpy in the corner, her feet crossed at the ankles and nervously tap-tap-tapping against the leg of the table. The lush of his beard had been the gentlest hint of a caress along her jaw, and when she felt his lips brush across hers, the touch was so minimal, so non-existent, but it had still made her belly bottom out as if she careened down the back end of a three-hundred-foot roller coaster drop.

Sarah thought back to the occasional times she'd ridden her bicycle as a teenager, when she was just coming into her own. How, eeeeeevery so often, if she positioned herself juuuuust right, the slight friction from the bicycle seat against her core would cause her sex to tingle in a barely-there-but-oh-yeah-I-feel-something-building moment, making her ditch the bike and hoof it a bit to cool the heck off. When his lips lightly skated across hers, she felt that bicycle tingle all over again, except this time her nipples had hardened underneath her royal blue cotton dress and her thighs had begun to squeeze together of their own accord. Thank God it was winter and she could blame any unintended high beams on the cold. Whew!

Jacob did something to her, though, and she was afraid to examine it too closely. Physical attraction? Hell, yes. But where would it lead from there? Heck, she didn't even really know much about him other than he was a former corporal in the Army who had spent time recovering in a hospital after his fighting stint in World War I. And, oh, yeah, he grew up on a farm, apparently.

Sarah continued kicking around her internal analysis, while Jacob continued toeing at a scuff mark along the wall, his arms crossed over his chest in annoyance. Before too long, a soft knock on the door sounded and a dark-haired man in a white doctor's coat walked in.

Ramon Mendez stepped through the doorway, and with his entrance into that small exam room, it seemed all the breathable air decided to turn tail and vanish. The man who entered wasn't much taller than Sarah's five-five frame. His hair was cut short, though he wore it with a closer fade on the sides and an inch or so taller on top, but still slicked over with that harsh side part she'd noticed on many of the men in the city. His black coffee-colored eyes scanned the room briefly and then landed on her as he shut the door behind him.

He was the spitting image of his picture, which Sarah still kept tucked away in her clothes. This man, her great-grandfather, Martinsville University School of Medicine's first gynecologist to hail from Puerto Rico, was the greatest mystery in her family's history. And he was about to have a medical consultation with his great-granddaughter about her unintended (but more importantly *fake*) pregnancy.

"Hello, Miss Johansson," Ramon piped up through an encouraging smile, as though he had done this a million times before with patients. "I'm Dr. Mendez, one of the gynecologists at the hospital." His accent was prominent to her ears, but she could tell he had worked very hard to adapt his vernacular to his new life in Baltimore. "Well, technically," Ramon said with a shy grin, his hand reaching up and around to rub the back of his neck, "I'm due to receive my medical doctorate in a few months when I graduate, but most of us have had our training expedited and called into hospital service early due to the war."

Realizing his misstep in admitting he wasn't, in fact, a licensed doctor, he threw his hands up wildly in front of Sarah as if he were wiping a smudge off a window. "No, no, no. I apologize! I didn't mean to give you the impression I am not qualified to care for you. It's just that, you know, call of duty and all that. My fellow gynecologists and I are even seeing more and more obstetric patients such as yourself. I'm here to help in any way I can."

Whatever ideas she had about Ramon had just flown right out the window. He was a *baby*. At least in the grand scheme of life. She recalled that back in 1919, he would have only been twenty-four years

76

old. Hell, Sarah had barely been off her parents' car insurance policy when she was twenty-four. And here Ramon was, having traveled from Puerto Rico to attend medical school in a different country, learned a new language, built a life from the ground up and, oh, yeah, did it amid a freaking *war*. When she began to connect all the dots, she had to smile at his mettle.

"Think nothing of it, Dr. Mendez. I completely understand." Sarah beamed like a fool as she offered to shake his hand, enclosing it between both of hers. The moment her fingers pressed into his skin, a low hum of electricity prickled inside her ears, and a slight pressure began to build, the kind she always chewed gum or sucked on a hard candy to alleviate on airplanes during takeoff. The force swelled to a buzzing and caused Sarah to squint a bit in distraction until a low grunt from the corner broke up the party and she realized she'd forgotten all about Jacob.

"Oh, goodness!" she cried when she dropped her hands from Ramon's and they flew to the top of her hat. She blinked several times to assess and reset the scene. The sudden spike in her heart rate surprised her, but the sensations subsided as fast as they came on. "I should apologize as well." Sarah exhaled in an attempt to regain composure. What was she about to say? Oh, yes, saved by the Bellamy. "This is my...um...caregiver, Corporal Jacob Bellamy. He's been kind enough to assist in arranging this visit."

Jacob's eyes acknowledged Sarah for a moment before he kicked off from the wall and turned his attention to the doctor. Hand held out, he shook Ramon's and nodded curtly before resuming his stance as building support.

"So, Miss Johansson, I understand you believe you are roughly two months along in your pregnancy. Is that correct?"

"Yes, sir."

"Have you had any new or worsening medical symptoms?"

"No, I haven't."

The two of them went back and forth with the standard Q and A until the good doctor walked over to her to do a basic set of vitals. While he worked to remove his stopwatch from his pocket, Sarah saw her opening and took it.

"Dr. Mendez," Sarah said to the top of the man's head as he sat on the stool before her, nose in her chart. "What are your usual hours at the hospital?"

"Oh, it varies," he remarked as he continued to scribble. "But generally, I'm here every weekday, with occasional weekend and evening rotations." Abruptly, he sat back and looked at Sarah, a soft crease to his brow. "If you'd prefer to see someone else for any future needs, I can certainly arrange…"

"Not at all! Oh, no, I like you just fine. I mean, not *like* you, I just mean…um. I'm comfortable in your care, is what I'm trying to say. I'd like to continue seeing you during the course of my…pregnancy. If possible." When Sarah began to fumble the damn ball, she visibly winced at the blunder and then glanced over to see Jacob silently laughing into his fist. She squinted daggers at the man and promised herself appropriate retribution. Once Jacob caught her glare, his slightly audible laugh died in his throat as he put his fist back behind his back and resumed his stint as Corporal Catatonic.

"Great, I am pleased to hear it. Now, I just need to take a listen to your heart and we'll be finished. Everything looks great."

Ramon slapped his hands on his knees and pushed off before walking around the table where Sarah sat to stand at her back. He removed his stethoscope from around his neck and brought it to rest between Sarah's shoulder blades. A moment later, Ramon adjusted his angle and placed his left hand on her left shoulder to steady the stethoscope.

As soon as the contact was made, Sarah hissed a breath in through her teeth and clenched her jaw so hard she bit the inside of her mouth. The pain that flashed through her frontal lobe behind her closed eyes was so intense she didn't even realize something was wrong until the sensation of warm coppery liquid began to drip down the back of her throat.

Ramon immediately jumped back in shock and ran around to face Sarah. He hesitantly ran his hands over her body where he had touched her in case he did something to cause her pain. But the hand on his shoulder that urged him back a few paces paused his sudden

78

panic. Jacob had leaped from his station and all but threw the young doctor to the side as he barreled toward Sarah.

When the connection between Ramon and Sarah had been severed, she slumped over into her lap. The tension in her head had evaporated as fast as it had come on, but the pain. God, she had never felt pain like that before in her life. She imagined her brain as the cork in a wine bottle, a sharp metal corkscrew slowly impaling her cerebrum, her brain matter being harpooned into shards. Then, all at once, the pain retreated, the pressure jettisoned out like a deflated balloon. Her head was between her knees, lolling back and forth, when her traumatized equilibrium caught up with her and violently emptied her stomach all over the floor.

Jacob stopped his forward momentum and jumped out to Sarah's side, as did Ramon. Coming around to her back, Jacob cradled her shoulders in his large hands and rubbed soothing circles in her back until her heaves had subsided and her mouth was left coated in stomach bile and blood.

She couldn't open her eyes, couldn't even take a deep breath. All Sarah managed to do was fall back into Jacob's hands as he gently laid her down on the examination table. She heard orders being barked, some in Jacob's voice and some in Ramon's. Her mouth, chin, and neck were wiped down with a cold washcloth. Her overcoat was removed, shoes unbuckled. In the hazy aftermath of the worst pain she had ever known, she tried to piece together what she could of the voices.

"...common symptom during the first trimester...bed rest is recommended for the next month..."

"...cabin outside the city on my family's farm...recuperate."

"...another visit next week..."

"Shh... rest, Sarah."

As the agony in Sarah's head finally began to subside, her consciousness drifted off to Jacob's baritone rumblings purring in her ear.

CHAPTER 12

Fear was a funny thing. It was probably the most useful emotion Jacob could immediately name. Sure, guilt may seem to be a strong contender on the surface. After all, guilt could get the pretty girl to finally take you up on spending time together. It could lead a sinner back into the arms of the Lord for a time. Heck, it could even cause you to enlist in the Army and put your life on the line for God and country.

But guilt wasn't lasting. Sooner or later, the pretty girl would remember why she said no to you in the first, second, and third place. The sinner would find his temptation in the same dark corners it always inhabited. And, in all honesty, guilt was wasted on the dead.

But fear, now that's one giant motivator.

Jacob had spent the last year of his life running head-on into enemy fire through the trenches of war. He had always assumed fear lit the fire under his hide to propel him to keep up with the hustle. But looking back on it, no, that wasn't fear. That was more adrenaline and reflexes than anything. True fear, Jacob realized, was seeing Sarah doubled over in agony the second that great-grandfather doctor of hers got in close.

God, he'd felt helpless in that moment and clueless in the next. Who was the enemy he was trying to defend her from? Was it the doctor? Some unseen sickness? He hadn't the foggiest, but when she collapsed into his arms after her body was spent from the vomiting, he gently cradled this woman down to the exam table. This woman who, in such a short time, had become the orbital force in his tiny insignificant world. And seeing her ill like that, covered in her own sick with her teeth clenched shut and blood dribbling out the side of her mouth while she lay unconscious—that was goddamn fear.

The nurses had come in shortly after to clean Sarah up and get her resting in a different room. Dr. Mendez did another patient assessment, repeatedly assured Jacob that she would be fine. The official diagnosis? Hyperemesis gravidarum, or, as it was explained to him, severe vomiting during pregnancy. Natural progression through the trimesters would cure Sarah of the ailment. The only problem? Unbeknownst to the good doctor, Sarah wasn't *actually* pregnant.

Jacob sat in the chair across from Sarah's hospital bed. He couldn't help but acknowledge the irony in their circumstances now. He had the chair propped up against the opposing wall, his left leg bent at an angle and his right leg kicked all the way out. His head mildly thumped against the back of the wall in time with the second hand on the clock above the door. He couldn't take his eyes off her resting form.

The mellow rise and fall of her chest was such a counterbalance to the physical trauma she'd gone through. Her hair had been washed and lay in slightly damp lengths down her shoulders. During her time with the nursing staff, Jacob had made arrangements with the hotel to check out of their rooms and collect their belongings. For Sarah, that wasn't much and only included the three outfits and a toiletry kit Jacob had purchased for her at the five-and-dime. But the clothes were clean, and she would need them.

The dark green blouse she had been changed into reminded him of pine needles and the forest behind his family's cabin. He imagined Sarah in that backdrop, walking by his side down the small trail from the cabin to Lake Roland. The image soothed him. Actually, if he were being honest with himself, it was Sarah who did the trick. He had connected with her in a manner he hadn't done with any woman before her. She was quick-witted, smart, and a career woman in her time, no less! Her familial passion spoke volumes about her character, her selflessness and determination the stuff seasoned commanding officers sorely lacked.

His Athena, goddess of war and wisdom.

And what a goddess she was.

Jacob stopped keeping time with his head banging against the wall and just drank her in. Even under the thin blanket, he could make out the shape of her. He was no saint, and while he would never touch a woman if it displeased her, the scoundrel in him couldn't help but look his fill. Especially if memories of almost kissing that woman would serve as a preamble of other offerings.

He had been assured she was just resting and would recover fully. He had put his faith in that thought, and only because of that did he permit his mind to further wander. God, the woman's breasts were like manna to a starving man. More than ample enough to fill his large hands. He imagined feasting on them for days and never being satisfied.

Jacob drifted his eyes closed and let his mind roam with the possibilities that could never be. The war had left him so triggered and tightly coiled, even the common backfire of an automobile engine spiked his pulse automatically. And then there was his family he had lost. His parents, his baby brother. What kind of companionship could he offer a woman when his everyday thoughts were so morose? Besides, Sarah was only a woman passing through. But it was precisely because of her temporary situation that he allowed himself to daydream, imagine more with her.

A quiet cough snapped him out of his perverted trance.

Sarah groggily opened her eyes and cleared her throat another time or two before she took stock of her surroundings. When she registered that she was in yet another hospital room, though she was the patient in bed this time, her brows furrowed in confusion. Sensing someone else in the room, she looked up in his direction.

God, she captivated him. Even in a disheveled and confused state, he imagined he would bite off his foot if she asked him to just for the opportunity to see her mouth lift in a smile.

"Jacob," she croaked softly through cracked lips. "What the heck happened?"

The more words she got out, the more she winced. She tried to sit up a bit straighter in the bed, but Jacob had already rushed to the chair immediately at her side and settled his hand on her shoulder, urging her to remain settled.

"Here, drink first. Then I'll update you." He handed her a tall glass of water from the table next to the bed and watched as she started to gulp the water, but her lips were so dry she had difficulty forming a seal around the glass. The water dribbled out of the corner of her mouth and trickled slowly into the valley of her breasts beneath the fabric. Cad that he was, he clenched his teeth as he followed the water's path before he righted his gaze to Sarah's eyes, where it should have stayed all along.

Sarah had used the backs of her hands to wipe away the excess water and leaned her head back against the pillow again. She met his gaze and stayed silent, impatient expectation written across her face. Jacob took the glass from her hands, resettled it on the table, and proceeded to recap the events of the last few hours.

As he neared the end of the story, Sarah continued to shake her head back and forth in disbelief. "But I'm not really pregnant!"

Jacob stole a quick glance at the door before he hushed her tone. "Yes, I am aware, but *they* don't know that. And whatever caused your reaction is irrelevant in the doctor's eyes. He saw it as a symptom of pregnancy and ordered you on bed rest for the next week."

"Well, that's not happening, obviously," she said with a snort as she gripped the edge of the sheets and threw them across her legs to get out of bed. Jacob halted her progress by putting his hand on her knee and applying gentle pressure, just enough to stop the forward movement. Sarah huffed out a breath through her nose, her lips set in a thin line. She glanced down to his hand on her leg, then shot her eyes back up to his and arched her eyebrow. A more straightforward warning of move-it-or-lose-it he had never seen. But he had to make her see reason, so he proceeded.

"Listen. Please be calm and listen to me." He began to rub small circles with his thumb on the outside of her knee. Her shoulders released the tension slightly. "If you want to remain close to Ramon, this is the smartest way to do so. I've arranged a follow-up appointment a week from now and told him I'd take you to my family's cabin outside the city near Lake Roland to recover and rest."

At that, she lowered her eyebrow, and Jacob could see the wheels turning behind her eyes. She finally saw where he was going with this.

"If you want any chance of connecting with him again, you have to continue to play the part. If you stay in Baltimore, you run the risk of Ramon or other hospital staff seeing you in the city. It would raise suspicion, especially since they're all under the impression I had to pull some strings to arrange for your care."

Sarah turned her head toward the window and surveyed the overcast gray of another winter's day. He sensed she'd run out of options, and this didn't sit well with her. But there was one more thing he needed to make her understand.

He removed his hand from her knee and grabbed both of her hands together in her lap. His thumbs resumed that circling motion that seemed to calm her. "Sarah, when you had your attack, for I don't know what else to call it, I was scared to death. And I assure you, I have never been known to scare easily."

Sarah's lips slightly parted at that, and her eyes dropped to her lap where their hands were entangled. "Jacob," she said through still-abused vocal cords, "I don't know why that happened. But I'd be lying if I said I wasn't scared, too. I've never experienced that before. When Ramon touched me like that," she glanced back up at him, her eyes taking on a sheen of mist, "I thought I would die. I know it sounds melodramatic, but the pain...God."

The healthy glow that had slowly been returning to her face since she woke up started to fade into that ghostly pallor that overtook her during the attack. The fear returned for each of them, slowly consuming the progress they'd made. Without thinking, Jacob beat it back the only way he could think to do so. He released one of his hands, snaked it around the back of her neck, and lifted her mouth to his own.

She was surprised, as was he. For Christ's sake, she had just almost died! At least, she thought she did. But at that moment, he didn't care.

84

She needed to be grounded, to know she had an ally. And he needed, well, Sarah.

He was careful of her cracked lips and gently tried to massage away the irritation with his own as best he could, but he was concerned the coarseness of his beard would prove too much of a discomfort for her. He started to pull away when he felt her own hand touching the ends of his hair down by his shoulder. When she began to return the kiss in earnest, his heart raced for a different reason.

Out of the frying pan and into the fryer, and all that.

Jacob took his other hand and cupped her cheek as he licked her delicate lips. Cad. Scoundrel. Whatever. The woman, his woman, didn't seem to care. She gave as good as she got, and when she began to arch out of the bed, inviting her tongue to tangle with his own, he had to grit his teeth and come back down to Earth lest they both get intruded upon at any moment.

His hands cupped her shoulders and gently guided her back down to the mattress. Once he was certain she wouldn't rise again, he reluctantly broke apart from her in a panting exhale and sat back in his chair, eyes cast downward. God, the broken connection was painful. He wanted more, wanted his mouth on hers and elsewhere, but it was neither the time nor the place. When his heart rate had begun to settle a bit, he raised his head to hers, his hands still resting on her shoulders.

"Sarah," he forced out in a gravelly whisper, "my family owns a cabin about an hour's train ride outside of the city. You will come with me there for the week and we will parse all of this out. Now that you're awake, I'll arrange for your discharge and we'll leave this afternoon."

Sarah was slightly panting as well, and when Jacob delivered his marching orders, his feisty patient didn't miss a beat.

"Are we now?" Her eyebrow raised again after a slight delay, though this time she also rewarded him with a smile.

"Yes, spitfire. Doctor's orders and all that," he said with a wink.

CHAPTER 13

The giant railyard felt like home, with all its hustle and bustle of people shouting, train whistles blaring, and the loud puffs of steam that never failed to startle Sarah even though she knew to expect it. And boy, did she need something solidly familiar in that moment.

That kiss with Jacob had completely unhinged her. It was unexpected, a bit terrifying, and so absolutely *needed*. She hadn't been lying when she'd told him she thought she would die. That whole exercise in her first near-death experience had rattled her confidence and sanity. Once the heaves had started wracking her body, all the questions and goals she had been focusing on since she learned where she was, all the determination she threw into this ridiculous fact-finding mission, had flown out the window.

She was scared. More than scared. She was done and ready to give in to what may be. But for some reason, being with Jacob gave her the courage to keep fighting. So she would. Without her realizing it, he had quickly scaled to the top of her list of people she refused to let down. He had turned into her summit, her true north, and she wasn't entirely sure how she felt about that. But at least, as she sat there in the busy train station, she sought comfort in the little familiar things.

Sarah sat on a long wooden pew inside the grand open central cavity of the station. The floor was white and black mosaic tile, and depending on how she clicked her heels against it, each tap of her foot gave off a different sort of note. It called to mind images of Fred and Ginger foxtrotting across the floor. When she leaned her head back and peered up at the ceiling, the roof peaked into a marvelous frosted-glass dome lined with wrought iron supports. The architecture was stunning and bathed the entire station with the perfect amount of light. This calmed her immensely.

Having grown up in central New Jersey, and with her hometown being basically a suburb of New York City, the train was a way of life for her. She was more comfortable riding a train than any other mode of transportation. This small comfort, with her head leaning back against the wooden bench and the filtered sun grazing her face while travelers whirled around her, was a balm to her shocked soul.

"Our train should be here in the next five minutes and will be arriving on track five. Come, let's go wait for it." Jacob had just walked back from the ticket booth to collect Sarah and their belongings. Well, she supposed *belongings* was a relative term. Nothing belonged to her here. Not the clothes she wore, nor the man who bought them. It was yet another stark reminder of the circumstances she found herself in. She had to find a way back home, and though she couldn't explain why, she believed down to her core that saving Ramon from contracting typhoid fever and dying was her ticket back to her time, her purpose in this whole crazy mess. But if she were honest with herself, the thought of leaving Jacob behind sat like a heavy stone on her heart. She cared for him, that much she knew, but where could things go? How could this possibly work out in the end?

Sarah continued to run through the facts as they climbed the stairs up to track five. Once at the top, Jacob never strayed too far from her, though he noticeably made sure he didn't touch her. Perhaps he'd come to the same awkward conclusion she'd drawn up? That, despite their chemistry, their waters were muddy at best? She wasn't sure, but she was stuck. Maybe some time in a cabin away from the city would allow her to regroup and strategize.

The smell of the engine oil wafting through the steam tinged the air on the track, and Sarah's heart began to race faster, as it always did once a train approached. The hair around her shoulders started to dance a bit, and when she turned her head to the left, she saw the black engine of a locomotive barreling toward their track. Stepping back from the edge, as was second nature, she covered her ears as the high-pitched squeal of brake lines pierced the air.

Yup, some things never changed.

When the train rolled to a stop, the doors opened, and the conductors exited first. Then, a barrage of passengers stepped out and dispersed throughout the station like ants at a picnic. The thought made her smile, though it was laced with a bit of sadness. She missed her home, missed her life.

Seeing the swarm of people exit the train, the purpose on their faces as they walked with intent toward their destination, stung. It reminded her of her morning coffee shop runs, the long line of customers that always moved quicker than she expected. Everyone ordering their usual to help jumpstart their days. Sarah's eyes began to mist over as she mourned the loss of her former morning routine. It was such a small part of her daily life, but it was something she took for granted. Feeling sorry for herself, though, wouldn't serve her any good.

With the most discreet of sniffles, she stepped closer to Jacob and clutched his gloved hand as he squinted through the din of the passengers and steam. "C'mon, let's go. Show me this cabin of yours."

Jacob looked at her with a puzzled expression and then trailed behind her as she led the way toward the nearest train entrance. Still gripping his hand, she waited for the last passenger to exit before she led them up the three steps and into the train car.

Dick Stevens slammed back the last of his scotch and pocketed his flask inside his coat pocket. Feeling for all the world like the cat who licked the cream, he couldn't imagine his luck being any better. He watched from the end of the platform as Bellamy and Miss Johansson waited to board the train north out of the city.

His poker game the night before had been very kind to him, or, should he say, his own ability to lie through his teeth had been very kind to him. The bum he'd bested couldn't afford all the payout owed to Dick following the game so, after some physical persuasion on Dick's part, there was a mutual agreement to meet at the very public train station the following afternoon to deliver the rest of Dick's money. The payer was wisely reluctant at receiving another dislocated wrist, and Dick could hardly blame him. But when Dick saw a man with shoulder-length dark hair and shoulders as wide as the damn Appalachians toting a delicious little blonde morsel onto the same track, serendipity smiled down upon him.

Fucking Bellamy and the lovely Miss Johansson. And they appeared to be leaving in a hurry. Dick knew Bellamy originally hailed from north of the city, a farm of some sort. He had never cared to find out the town, but he'd be lying if he said his curiosity wasn't piqued. Where would those two be heading? Sure, Dick had stayed an extra few nights at the hotel where Bellamy and the broad were staying, but he wasn't able to garner any more information. In fact, it was only a few days after he saw them eating breakfast initially when he had overheard the front desk receptionist hit on the subject. Apparently, Corporal Bellamy had checked out and required arrangements for his and his female companion's belongings.

Female companion my left nut, Dick thought to himself. He leered on from under the brim of his hat as the train pulled up next to the track. Miss Johansson raised her hands to cover her ears from the onslaught of noise though, ironically, she didn't seem bothered by it. More of a necessary and anticipated precaution.

As her hair whipped around her wrists when the first of the train cars blew past, she looked regal, like a siren being thrown about in a tempest but with not a care in the world. The breath escaped Dick's lungs in a rush in time with the whirring wind left in the train's wake. Miss Johansson's calf-length A-line black skirt whirled higher and higher around her knees in the wind, flashing hints of creamy bare skin and thick, toned thighs. Even from a hundred feet away, Dick could tell she didn't wear any stockings. His nostrils flared at the temptation.

The spark of an idea had begun to form in Dick's mind. What

would happen if he joined them on their little trek north? After all, thanks to his poker game, he had the funds for fun at the moment and more than idle enough hands to toy with Bellamy. He also wouldn't mind if Miss Johansson played a starring role in his endeavor, and Bellamy could stay the fuck away on his little hovel of a farm and out of Dick's ass. Bellamy would learn what it was like to have something precious taken from him, and Dick was in more than a teachable mood.

With his good ear toward the tracks, he listened as the conductor gave the final "All aboard!" before the conductor climbed the steps and began to shut the train doors. As the door to the last car began to slam shut, Dick sprinted across the track and up the three steps to the car of the train, his coattails narrowly escaping the door's closure before it sealed him in. Turning to his right, he prowled through the cars like a panther until he noticed the top of Bellamy's flat cap seated next to Miss Johansson's blond head, both facing forward on the right side of the car. Dick grabbed the furthermost seat in the back of the car, adjusted the brim of his hat down lower, and settled in for the ride.

A piercing screech jarred Jacob awake and clutched at his heart. Blood pounded in his ears as panic constricted his chest. His eyes flew open, arms arced above his head in protection. Eyes down, breaths panting. Images whirled past him to his right. Trees filled his periphery through a small window. The dizziness of the imagery confused his senses, though the steady rumble of the convoy's Army vehicle vibrated beneath him.

The trees were lush and green. Not gray and barren from mustard gas exposure. But how was that possible when his body recognized the howl of enemy fighter aircraft? Confusion caused his sweaty brow to crease. Jacob hurriedly reached for the trench knife at his waist, and his elbow bumped into something.

Sarah lay back in the seat next to him, a soft snore fluttering past her parted lips. Her head had fallen slightly, nudging him in his arm. Relief washed over him as he took in his surroundings, his pulse slowly falling to a normal tempo. He was on a train, not a convoy vehicle, escorting Sarah to his childhood home. Dots were finally connecting as the same noise as earlier pierced through the cabin. Engine brakes. By his side, Sarah rested her head on his shoulder. Her long lashes looked so soft and inviting. Her lips, with the top one being enticingly larger than the bottom, were slightly open. For a woman who had almost died not even eight hours before, she looked utterly at peace.

God, how he envied her that peace. Not fearing the dark shroud of sleep each night, but instead welcoming it as a harbinger of rejuvenation. Leaning into it, instead of worrying about the haunting nightmares it would bring.

A quick glance out the train window told Jacob they would be arriving at their destination momentarily. He turned his head back to Sarah and gently skated his mouth over her forehead. In this one stolen moment, he pressed his lips to her smooth skin and inhaled the sweet scent of her hair. His heart rate continued to normalize, his nerves calming just from his proximity to her. This woman could chase away his darkest terrors even in her sleep. How she grounded him.

As if she knew he was thinking about her, Sarah's nose started to scrunch up. While he had selfishly been pilfering a kiss, he'd been unaware that his beard had scraped right across her delicate nose. Rather than the soothing arousal he'd hoped to give her, Sarah shirked back from his arm, eyes still closed, and released the loudest, wettest sneeze right between his eyes. The force of the spray took him by surprise as he quickly slammed his eyes shut and reached into his back pocket for his handkerchief.

Serves you right, bastard.

Sarah opened her eyes wide and sat up straight in her seat, completely oblivious to the shoulder-sleep-kiss-nose-spray-in-face incident, which was just fine by Jacob. She craned her head around the car briefly and then put her hands behind her lower back.

"How much longer, do you think?" she asked as she pushed her hands forward and arched her lower back out, working out the stiffness.

As if right on cue, the conductor announced to their car that those getting off for Lake Roland should exit the train at the next stop.

"This is us, Miss Johansson," Jacob said with a wink. "My family's land is not that far from town, maybe a fifteen- to twenty-minute walk from the station. It's the best of both worlds: seclusion as well as close proximity to commerce." He beamed at her, pride shining through in his voice. He couldn't help but puff out his chest a bit when he thought of his family's estate.

When Jacob was a boy, the sprawling acres had been a young lad's dream. They grew every kind of crop one could think of, sold most of it in town, and only housed what livestock they needed. He and his brother, Isaac, worked hard and played harder in some cases, Jacob recalled with a smirk. Times had changed, though, and life wasn't what it once was.

The train rolled to a stop in front of a red-brick train station. Behind it was a town plaza with much foot traffic, but nowhere near as much as the city. It was a weekday afternoon, which was busy for a small town, but even that type of busy was relatively quiet compared to the metropolises of the world.

Sarah and Jacob retrieved their bags and made their way down the steps of the train. The late-day sun's tangerine rays bubbled up behind the clouds. Bright fissures burst through the gray masses. As if calling to her, Sarah dropped her head back and let the rays soak in. It was still cold, but nothing a brisk walk couldn't remedy.

Shirking off the chill, Jacob led them down the track. The swarms of people mulling about unnerved him, but it wasn't just the crowd that perked up his senses. Goosebumps settled on his upper arms. He was no stranger to cold weather, but this was different. Jacob halted his stride and peered over his shoulder toward the end of the track. A family with a young boy hurried down the sidewalk while another man nearby stopped to light a cigarette. Jacob found nothing to explain his unease. Dismissing the feeling as a cold draft, he turned back to his traveling companion.

"Welcome to Lake Roland," Jacob said through a wide smile, his composure regained. It was true, being home was a comfort to him.

"Is that a smile I see?"

Jacob looked down at Sarah and saw her standing there with her hand on her hip, her lips upturned on one side. She teased him, and he ate up every drop. "Yes, Miss Johansson, you have just witnessed a rare event. I hope you recorded the image to memory."

When he fired the barb back, he waited to hear what she'd throw his way. Instead, she just stood there staring at him. A few more seconds went by, and when she opened her mouth to speak, her lips quickly closed again.

He had silenced his warrior goddess, it seemed. And God, that satisfaction was delicious.

"This way, Miss Johansson," he called out to her as he turned and proceeded down the sidewalk. "And be sure to watch where you step. I'm afraid we don't have any litters and chairmen to carry you around this far out in the country should you stumble."

CHAPTER 14

The sun had just started to crest over the tops of the trees that were coming into view off the western side of Lake Roland as Sarah and Jacob trudged up to the property line. The crunch of the dried leaves under her boots reminded Sarah of wrapping paper, how she'd crumple up the wadded balls and shoot them into the wastepaper baskets as a game her family played during the holidays. When she glanced out at the lake, the sun's orange hues reflected off the water's edge and caused the ripples to dance like the Christmas twinkle lights she was so fond of back home.

God, home. Her family.

As she trudged along the dirt path, she started to think about all the things she missed from her time, like her memory foam mattress or standing under the rainfall showerhead for so long the hot water ran out. And she couldn't overlook how vital personal transportation and her own job were. Speaking of work, she had missed so much work already she was sure she wouldn't have a job to go back to. What only felt like the better part of a week here included three missed deadlines. One of those deadlines was for next month's print journal. She had been banking on her latest interview with this rising star in the pain management field to finally catch the eye of upper management.

So much for that.

But work aside, she had spent so much time thinking about her family *here*, had her family back home even noticed she was gone? This whole family reunion was her idea, after all, and the subject, if she were a little honest with herself, may have been more forced on her part than she'd like to admit. If she hadn't laid on the guilt good and thick about the lack of family time, would anyone have cared? That was a depressing thought.

Speaking of thought, her brain had been running nonstop this whole time with questions, and she couldn't escape the impending sense of urgency that bared down on her. When it came to sussing out the answers to her questions, time was not on her side.

Why her? How did she get back? What would become of Jacob?

Jacob.

That last one stopped her mental hamster wheel short. She would miss Jacob. And she would *not* be okay with that.

Her Mack truck of a realization caused her to lose track of her surroundings a bit. She narrowly escaped face-planting over the tree root in front of her. Unfortunately, her almost-tumble didn't escape the notice of her burly trail guide.

"Everything all right, Miss Johansson?" Jacob looked back at her with a raised eyebrow and a smirk. The clod.

"Perfectly fine, Corporal Bellamy," she said through gritted teeth as she hiked up her skirt a little higher in an overt show that she was, in fact, capable of watching her damn step. The low chuckle that escaped his throat rumbled over her skin and slowly lit her up from the inside. The bastard was a walking stick of sexy dynamite just waiting for her to throw a spark.

And he friggin' knew it.

Before she took drastic recourse and dove into the lake to cool off, she quickly changed the subject. "Is that your cabin?"

Up ahead, nestled within the shade of the large maple trees, sat a classic log cabin ripped straight from a Thomas Kinkade Hallmark card, right down to the red-brick chimney and the steep-sloped roof overhanging the front porch. It was so quaint and absolutely charmed the pants off her. But unlike the greeting card images of her time, this cabin lacked the glowing light shining through the windowpanes. There was no wood-burning stove sending up plumes of nose-stickling smoke out into the forest. There was no rocking chair on the porch or straw-bound broom slouching under the eaves of the front door. It had been quite some time since anyone had lived here.

Jacob's footsteps slowed as the cabin came into view. "Yes, it is," he said in a hushed voice, almost to himself, after standing there a few seconds. Like a dog reuniting with its owner, he half jogged, half speed-walked toward the front door as if the luggage in his hand weighed nothing. Sarah recalled that his parents and brother had passed away, though she didn't know the circumstances. Come to think of it, she didn't even know Jacob's age.

More damn questions.

Nonetheless, he was obviously eager to return home. She could relate.

After Jacob sped up to the cabin, Sarah decided to slow her pace a bit and give him the time he needed in his family's home. Two minutes later, she crept up to the two small steps of the front porch, wiped her feet on the worn foot mat, and crossed the threshold, the creaking floorboards announcing her entry.

The cabin's front door opened into a main living/common room with a mahogany rocking chair in the corner, a quilted blanket draped over its back. A rectangular wooden table sat centrally in the room, with four chairs all around it, its edges showing the scratches and nicks of many meals eaten there together. Along the wall rested a high-backed wicker bench large enough for two.

Next to the bench, Sarah got an eyeful of Jacob stooped over the stone hearth as he blew on a few glowing embers and worked to get the fire started. Above the hearth hung a small assortment of cast iron pots and pans, spoons and ladles. The lighting inside was dim, but the late afternoon rays slanting through the paned windows painted everything in amber hues. It added visual warmth to the place and gave the actual fire in the hearth time to work its way up to full speed.

The *pop-sizzle* of the awakening fire drew Sarah's attention back to Jacob as he rose to his full height and started rubbing his hands together, blowing into them. Standing in the small living space, just the two of them, she suddenly felt hyperaware of the situation. Jacob was the master of his castle here, the giant at the top of the beanstalk. He was all-consuming. In that moment, he was the open airplane cabin window sucking out all of Sarah's spare oxygen.

"Sarah, come in," he said through a boyish grin. He was clearly happy to be her host. "Welcome to Blossom House, my family's cabin."

At hearing the name of the cabin, her ears perked up. Naming buildings in such a fashion wasn't something she was used to.

Jacob noticed her intrigued expression and humored her. "My mother named it," he said with an eye roll as he rubbed the back of his neck. "She had a knack for gardening, and my father had a knack for giving her what she wanted. She wanted to give the cabin a name, so there you go."

"It's lovely," Sarah said with a smile.

"The fire will get going in another minute or two." He relocated their bag to the top of the table and slammed his hands together in a loud clap. "Now, the cabin has two bedrooms, one on each side of the living room," he said, gesturing to the opposing doorways, "and the kitchen's right over there. The hearth is in the center of the house, so the heat spreads outward into the bedrooms from here. There are also two other outbuildings on the property, which were previously used for storing hay and grain, or housing the livestock when we had them."

He unraveled the gray wool scarf around his neck and walked past her to shut the front door, sealing in the burgeoning heat.

Crap. Had she left the door open that whole time? She was so enthralled with how animated and giddy he was, she hadn't even noticed.

After hooking his scarf and hat on the wrought iron coat rack in the corner, he shrugged out of his coat and hung it with its friends. "I'll give you the grand tour tomorrow. Here, let me help you with your coat."

Jacob was in complete host-with-the-most mode and eagerly closed the two-foot gap between them. Stepping up behind her, his gentle side reemerged as he softly placed his hands along the collar of her coat. The touch of his bare skin surprised her. A glance at the fireplace mantle answered her question when she noticed his gloves resting there above the hearth.

Wow. She was so overwhelmed by him in his element, she hadn't even noticed when he removed his gloves.

The tips of his fingers tickled the back of her neck as he gripped the inside of her coat, sending a tremble down her spine.

"Cold?" His breath coasted down her skin, leaving goosebumps in its wake.

"No, I'm warming up."

He slowly slid the coat off her shoulders, and the relief of its weight almost made her knees give out. Turning around on her heel to face him put her mouth just under his bearded jaw. When she glanced up, the now-roaring fire was reflected in his dark brown eyes. The orange glow of dusk pierced through the door slats behind him, his dark features standing out in stark relief. His brows were knit together in concern, the crease lines visible above his eyes. They were sharing the same air, in each other's orbit, yet she was still acutely aware of her perilous circumstances. It was all becoming too much for her. Her confusion and fear were coming to a head, and she needed to grasp on to the only solid thing within reach.

"Jacob," Sarah breathed. "I...uh...I don't..." His eyes locked onto hers, and when his nostrils flared, words left her.

"Yes," Jacob growled out as he threw her coat on the nearby table, his eyes never leaving hers.

"I don't..."

"You don't...what?"

"I...uh...don't...know your age." There! A question he could answer!

His mouth widened into a large Cheshire cat grin. "You'd like to know my age?"

"Yes, I would. I've told you mine."

"Yes, you have. Very well. I'm twenty-nine."

Sarah blinked up at that for a second. Then, with a hint of playfulness about her, though she had no idea where this courage came from, she said, "So, I'm the older woman then."

Jacob nodded at her assessment, his grin never leaving his face. Sarah's newfound confidence eased some of her nerves, her uncertainty. Before the bravado left her, she extended her hand to his shoulder and let the wisps of his dark hair dance through her fingertips.

"What's happening here between us? I'm so confused."

Her heart hammered out a faint drumroll in her chest, and she became emboldened by the rhythm. Her fingers climbed higher through his mane. The backs of her knuckles brushed against the coarse hair of his beard. God, she loved his hair and beard. They had quickly become one of her calming sensory comforts, much in the way a baby has a favorite blanket that soothes them to sleep.

"What I believe is happening here is that you're...petting me."

A very unladylike snort escaped through Sarah's nose, and her hand flew over her mouth to hide her laugh. That hand was quickly captured in Jacob's own.

"I never said to stop. If I may be frank, there is nothing on this Earth that has yet to calm me more completely than your touch." He still held her hand, though his eyes lost focus on a far-away corner of the room. His lips pinched into a tight line before his gaze settled back to hers. "Before you barged in on my respite at the hospital...and don't give me that look, you were very much a bother I wanted to toss out at first...I was in a bad place. A bad mental place, as it were. Depression. Call it whatever you want. But from the moment you crash-landed into my life, I've had a light to turn to when the dark threatened to creep in."

Sarah went stiff at his confession. That must be why he was hospitalized. She didn't have long to dwell on the subject, though.

"My every breath of late has been consumed with you. Where you're from, *when* you're from, clothing you, feeding you, helping you. This list goes on, and I say this not to imply you're a weight to carry. I say this because, in my world, focusing on you is saving me from myself. You have become this great precious thing to me." Jacob slowly guided Sarah's hands northward and clasped them around the back of his neck. "You are healing me. Let me heal you."

The distance between them had rapidly shrunk with Sarah's arms draped over his broad shoulders, yet he didn't move to close the space. Inching up on the balls of her feet, she raised her nose to his and silently rubbed it back and forth before she rested her forehead against his own, her eyes fluttering closed. Sarah's chin moved up and down on the briefest of nods. The word "Yes" drifted over Sarah's lips on the slightest of whispers.

It all happened so fast after that. Jacob lowered his head and captured her lips, stealing her breath in a searing open-mouthed kiss. There was no hesitation this time, no gentle strokes to learn the other person's tastes and preferences. No, this was pure instinct. Every question rocking around in her head, every concern vanished as Jacob cradled her face in his hands and quickly backed her up against the wall next to the door.

Sarah flew so high, she didn't even remember her own name. Her focus, her lifeblood in that moment was Jacob...and the massive erection she could feel digging into her belly button.

Well, didn't that just that spur her on?

Jacob plundered her mouth, entangled his tongue with hers, and drew out every essence of herself. On her next retreat, she scraped her teeth along his bottom lip and held his mouth captive in a seductive nibble. She was rewarded with that magnificent tongue of his snaking down the left column of her neck. When it reached the juncture at her collarbone, he had to pause because her damn blouse collar got in the way.

Before she could think of the fastest way to get out of her blouse, the sound of seams renting pierced the cabin's silence and the chilly winter air assaulted her left shoulder and breast. Jacob's beard danced across her bare skin, down her collarbone, shoulder, and lower. His beard, she realized, was the appetizer for the meal. The soft-yet-rough combination woke every nerve ending in her body. Where his beard had rasped over her skin, his warm tongue followed next. He lapped at her like one savored an Italian sorbet.

Jacob paused in his handiwork to lift his head up and admire her swollen breast. The dark rose of her skin glistened from his kisses. Each roll and pinch of her nipple elicited new moans and mewls from her throat. When his gaze traveled up to her bare shoulder, his skin, which, a second ago had been tan and misted with a slight sheen from his exertion, turned gray and ashen, and his jaw dropped low in an expression of shock. Sarah tried to see what had distressed him and noticed he hadn't taken his eyes away from her shoulder. When she started to turn her head to look at herself, Jacob held her face firmly between his warm hands and forced her to look him in the eyes.

"What is it? You're scaring me."

"Sarah," he exhaled out on a burst. "Your shoulder..."

"What about my shoulder?" She was really starting to panic now as she grabbed onto his wrists and tried to pry his hands off her head. "What's going on?"

He took one more glance at her shoulder before turning back to her. "Your skin...it's green."

"What?"

At that, he dropped his hands, and Sarah immediately grabbed her shoulder and began assessing it. When she looked down, her entire left shoulder, from back to front, was a solid pale green color.

Like the Statue of Liberty.

With trembling fingers, she ran her right hand over her skin where the green ended and her normal skin tone began. There was no discernible difference in touch. She rolled her shoulder around a few times. No difference in movement. She was utterly puzzled and confused...until she saw the edge of the green mass creep lower down her arm by about a quarter of an inch.

Her skin just *moved*.

Sarah screamed. She swiped and clawed at her skin. Panic and terror took root. Her nails dug in and scraped down her arm. She felt as if she were being eaten alive by scarab beetles. She kept scraping, clawing, crying until Jacob wrapped his arms around her in a bear hug and settled her on the floor in front of the fire. His long legs wrapped around her to hold her in place and prevent her from hurting herself. He held her there until the violent terror and wracking sobs subsided, cooing and shushing in her ear as he rocked her back and forth.

Sarah had no doubts about it now.

She was going to die.

CHAPTER 15

The patchwork quilt his mother had made for him when he was a young lad lay buried at the bottom of his old trunk. It was a very simple pattern, she always said, though it looked so ornate to him: royal blue-and-white checkered boxes maneuvered into the shape of a six-pointed star in the center. Simple or not, it was another piece of home and had always brought him comfort. Jacob excavated the folded quilt, closed the trunk, and walked out to the living room to join Sarah, who was still seated cross-legged in front of the fire.

After a brief moment's hesitation, he joined her on the floor and draped the quilt around her shoulders, careful not to touch her left one. Earlier, after she had calmed down, she was able to assess her skin's sensations further and assured him that it didn't hurt, but he didn't want to take any chances.

Sarah's red-rimmed eyes just stared off into the flames, watching the tiny embers break free and flutter around the fireplace like snowflakes. He couldn't blame her for her lack of words. He had never seen anything like that before, either. He had been raised a Christian, though more so the say-grace-at-meals type and not necessarily the go-to-church-every-Sunday type. His knowledge of the Bible and Satan was by no means extensive, but those were the only things his small mind registered as possible reasons for Sarah's skin to change color like that. In other words, he had no clue.

A loud pop rang out from one of the logs on the fire. He expected Sarah to jump or at least startle slightly at the noise, but no. She didn't move a muscle, hadn't done much of anything the last fifteen minutes except stare at the fire. He considered it a small miracle when she'd accepted his offer of tea. The thoughts traipsing through his mind nagged at him, but he could only imagine what she must be thinking. If only she would speak!

Sarah laid her mug of tea down on the floor and extended her long legs out in front of her, leaning back on her arms. After the event, she'd insisted she wanted to change into her "comfy" clothes from her own time. In this small thing, Jacob could help her. So, there she sat in her skin-tight opaque trousers and that oversized cardigan. Her bare feet were outstretched toward the fire, the flames almost licking her toes they seemed so close but she didn't appear to mind.

"Do you think a doctor would be able to help? I mean, I know it's not a...conventional ailment, but..." Jacob was grasping at straws, but the silence and sitting were killing him.

Sarah had already begun shaking her head back and forth until something seemed to click. "Wait, did you say 'doctor'? Oh!" She suddenly sat forward and began rummaging through the pockets of her sweater. Jacob knew what she searched for: the photo of Ramon from her time. She always kept it close, and he wasn't surprised to see it on her now. After her first foray into the right pocket came up empty, she smacked her long hair out of her face and rummaged through the left pocket. From there, she pulled out Ramon's photo and examined it more closely. A moment longer and her hand flew to her forehead, a realization hitting her.

"The green dust!"

"Green...dust?"

"Yes! That's got to have something to do with it. Do you remember when I told you about how I first came here? When I found Ramon's photo and fell off the couch, hitting my head?"

"Yes..."

"There was a green residue on the photo, like a fine powder dusted along the edges. I didn't know what it was at the time, but it got on my skin. When I brought my fingers to my nose to smell it, that's when I fell down the rabbit hole."

He frowned, not following. "Rabbit hole?"

"Yes, it's an expression...from *Alice and Wonderland*...oh, wait. Never mind." She waved her hand. "The point is that this whole thing started with that green dust. The color of the dust was the exact same color as my skin. They've got to be related!"

Now it was Jacob's turn to shake his head back and forth. "I'm sorry, but I'm afraid I don't follow." His eyes traveled up her slender form as she quickly rose from her place on the floor, a new energy invigorating her and breathing life into her once again. "Even if the two things are related, what does that mean?" he asked as he rested his right elbow on his bent knee, his left leg still stretched out in front of him, and watched her pace the length of the small living room floor.

"It means this is a sign. I need to get back," she said as she quickly ran to one of the adjacent bedrooms. Half a minute later, she emerged with the clothes she had worn to travel here. "I feel like I'm losing my way, my focus."

Sarah grabbed the skirt and instead of removing her trousers, she simply stepped into the skirt and shimmied it up over her black-clad legs. It didn't look entirely out of place, as at first glance the "leggings," as she called them, would seem like thick stockings. Regrettably, as a result of Jacob's...enthusiasm...with Sarah's blouse from earlier, the garment could no longer be fastened securely. She decided to simply wear her cotton shirt underneath it tucked into her skirt, and the blouse she wore open over the shirt but its ends she tied in a knot at her waist instead.

At the words "get back," Jacob scrambled to his feet. "No. You just got here! Dr. Mendez said to rest, remember? Yes, I know you're not actually pregnant, but if you were to go back to the city now, you'd be recognized." He rushed toward her as she attempted to pin her hair up with some band from her wrist. With both of her hands engaged, Jacob took the opportunity to wrap his arms around her slight waist and cocoon her body in his own.

At his onslaught, she lowered her arms and settled her hands onto his shoulders, nestling her elbows at ninety degrees into the crooks of his arms. God, she fit perfectly against him, as if they had been both molded from the same piece of clay. He wasn't prepared for her to leave, and he wasn't so proud to tell her so.

He dropped his head to her forehead and breathed in deeply. Even though she had only been in Blossom House a short while, the earthy scent of the woods had permeated her skin, imprinting on him the mingled fragrance of his two poles: Sarah and home. While Jacob warred with himself over her decision and selfishly hoped to keep her, he knew deep down she was never meant to stay here. But that didn't mean he wouldn't help her for as long as God gave him days on this Earth.

"I have to go back," she whispered to him, her slight fingers fisting the fabric of his shirt at his shoulders. "I'm scared, all right? Terrified, if I'm being honest. But I *need* to talk to Ramon. Get back on my original course: saving him from dying. If I can do that, maybe that's my ticket back. It's the only straw I've got left to grasp at." She said all of this without ever lifting her head and meeting his eyes.

She truly was afraid.

Before she could give him a reason to change his mind, he decided to jump headlong down the "rabbit hole" with her, as she called it. Releasing the heaviest of sighs that unburdened not only his lungs but his soul, he relented. "If we head back to the station before it shuts down for the night, we can book tickets on the first train out tomorrow morning."

And just like that, Sarah's smile gave him all the encouragement he needed.

One foot in front of the other, then.

The swift walk back to town didn't feel nearly as cold or long. In truth, it was only about fifteen minutes, but Sarah was so anxious she felt like the Usain Bolt of speedwalkers. Thankfully, Jacob hadn't been peppering her with too many questions. That was good because she wasn't lying to him about being terrified. Every so often, when he wasn't looking, she'd pull the layers of clothing away from her shoulder and peek at the green rash's progress. It hadn't crept down much farther than the quarter inch or so from when she was at the cabin, but her gut told her if she didn't get back to her own time soon, things would go from bad to worse.

Luckily for them, she and Jacob were able to secure tickets on the first train back to Baltimore the following morning. Plan of attack settled, they turned their attention to finding a meal in town at a nearby tavern.

Though the thought of eating anything twisted her gut into a knot of barbed wire, she knew Jacob was exhausted and severely depleted. The man wouldn't say anything but she noticed he had slowed down a bit when they approached the town's plaza, his eyes lined with weariness. Even so, he still refused to let her carry their small, shared satchel.

Stubborn man.

He needed to recharge, even if he wouldn't admit it, and she wouldn't be selfish.

"There's a tavern another block down from the station. It's prime supper time at the moment, so they may be very busy with the evening rush," Jacob said matter-of-factly as they meandered side by side down the red-brick sidewalk next to the plaza. "If we need to, we can purchase some items to take with us instead of waiting."

Sarah's eyes were laser-pinned to her footing, not wanting to misstep and break an ankle. Jacob would never let her hear the end of it.

"Sure, that's fine." She nodded into her chin. Sarah had yet to be out and about in the evening, she realized. Another thing she took for granted: sufficient outside lighting. Sure, there were a few streetlights around, but there weren't as many of them as she was used to seeing, and they weren't as bright. LEDs they were not. The darkness was a problem, and she wasn't sure any amount of squinting on her part would help her cause. Hence the baby steps.

A crowd of voices had Sarah raising her head, and Jacob nodded over to the tavern up on the left, across from the plaza proper. "Big crowd outside. Why don't you rest near one of those boulders along the perimeter of the square and I'll run in and see what I can manage for us?"

With that, he handed her their satchel and trotted off toward the building. Sarah walked toward the sizable stone embankment across the square from the tavern and leaned back against the granite giants, grateful to stand still for a moment. Even though she stopped moving, her brain was still going a mile a minute with worry, trying to figure out what she would do once she returned to Baltimore. How would she get back to Ramon, and what would she say when she did?

"Miss Johansson? Is that you?"

Jarred from her thoughts, she looked up to see the shadow of a male figure ten feet in front of her, but the terrible lighting wasn't doing her eyesight any favors.

"I'm sorry, do I know you?" She tried to wrack her brain and think of who else knew her in this time. The hospital staff, a few hotel workers...

The man walked closer toward her, and though there wasn't a streetlight immediately near her, the moon's glow gave off enough light that she made out the edge of a wide-brimmed hat, khaki in color maybe. As the distance between them closed, her stomach started to somersault and her palms, despite the chilly night air, began to sweat. She didn't know why, but she instinctively backed up a bit until her shoulders were flush with the boulder behind her.

"Oh, I'm so sorry! It's Dick Stevens, miss. A close friend of Jacob Bellamy's, remember?" He closed into her space, and she was able to make out enough of his face to at least identify his features. Yes, there were the pockmarks on the left side of his visage, the scarring reminding her of Two-Face from *Batman*. She immediately recalled the kiss he had given her hand in greeting back at the hotel. That kiss still creeped her out when she thought about how long his lips had been on her skin, how he had simultaneously scraped his fingernail under her palm in a sickeningly encouraging motion.

Sarah laid her palms flat against the rock, the chill of the stone slinking into her skin and crawling up her spine. "Yes, I remember. Nice to see you again. I'm just waiting for Jacob. He went to get us something to eat. He should be back soon," she stammered as her eyes flashed across the plaza, toward the tavern with the swarm of people outside the front.

Please be back soon.

Dick followed her line of sight and glanced back at the tavern entrance. "Excellent. I'd hate to miss an opportunity to see my old friend again." Swinging his head back to hers, he took another step closer, his hulking shoulders beginning to block out the little light coming from the businesses behind him.

Sarah felt the urge to stall for time. This guy made her skin shudder, and she felt ill-equipped to manage the situation. She didn't have her keys with her handheld can of mace on them or a phone to call for help with.

And what good would the phone do in 1919 anyway?

When she finally sized up her situation, warning bells began to fire in her head.

"Miss Johansson, tell me something. How did you and Jacob meet? He's never mentioned you before."

"Old childhood friends," she blurted out.

"Childhood friends. Wonderful! You must be from Lake Roland, then?"

"Yup." Where was Jacob?

"I have to say, and forgive me if I'm being too forward in this," he said with a hand over his chest, his other tucked away in his coat pocket, "but you are absolutely stunning. I can see why Jacob enjoys having you on his arm."

Her eyes kept darting back and forth between the tavern and Dick. If she could pretend to see Jacob and wave over to him, she could exit the conversation and run over to the tavern. Yes, that could work.

"Actually, Dick, I believe I see him right now. Jacob! I'll be right over!" she said, waving her hand. "Excuse me…"

"No, you don't see him, Miss Johansson." He spoke in a slightly bored tone, despite the smirk lifting the right side of his mouth. "Because our Jacob has been apprehended by those wonderful tavern establishment owners who, sad to say, owe me quite a bit of money from a poor poker showing on their part. Bellamy is no doubt swallowing back his own blood from the pummeling I've been promised as barter for their debt."

All her breath rushed out in a torrent. Dick slammed into her, his grimy hand clamping around her throat. Her screams were stifled. Air wouldn't come. His great weight planted her against the boulder.

Dick removed his hat with one hand and set it on top of the boulder as casually as if he were leaving it with a bellman. He brought his mouth to Sarah's right ear, his liquored breath causing her eyes to water. "Now, Miss Johansson, it's time to play your part." He pulled back and captured her eyes, his grip on her throat ensuring she wouldn't be able to move from his gaze.

A smile crept across his face. His hand snaked down her body. With a hard yank, her skirt's waistband ripped. He pulled her behind the large boulder, the rough stone scraping her lower back.

CHAPTER 16

The crowd outside the tavern made him more nervous than he wanted to admit to Sarah, but he did promise her food and would take care of her in that regard.

In every regard, he amended to himself.

Ever since his time in service, crowds in general made him nervous. Yet one of many things he could look forward to "working through," as the doctors called it, in his recovery. Nevertheless, a simple meal should be easy enough for Jacob to procure for the two of them.

Jacob ducked his head slightly as he stepped through the entryway. The density of patrons clogged his path. His pulse ticked up slightly as his unease began to register. On instinct, the tips of his fingers dusted along the leather sheath of his trench knife secured at his back. He scanned the crowd, hoping to see a host of some kind. The undulating cigarette smoke at the bar obscured his vision. He had difficulty seeing men's hands. Reflexively, he kept his back to the wall. He didn't need any surprises. He was just there for a meal. A simple task all around. Another minute went by before a heavyset man greeted Jacob at the front of the bar.

"Hey, my man," Jacob said with all the bravado he could muster.

"Might there be a space for two available? If not, a meal to go shall be fine."

The host seemed to be about Jacob's height, but where Jacob's own waist was fairly narrow, this man's gut protruded beyond the boundaries of his suspenders. The man had his greasy hair slicked to the side in a combover and the sleeves of his dingy white shirt rolled up, though each arm was rolled up to a different length to complete the slovenly look. His eyes traveled up and down Jacob's form, taking in his size, while the man balanced a toothpick on his tongue and volleyed it from side to side in his mouth.

"Sure, we can accommodate," the host said through his clenched teeth around the toothpick. "Name, sir?"

"Corporal Jacob Bellamy." He was normally loath to use his rank, not that it got him much, but if it helped in their service at all, given the size of the crowd, he'd be grateful.

At that, the dingy man smiled, grabbed the toothpick out of his mouth, and replaced the whittled piece of wood with his two club fingers. His fat lips wrapped around the digits on an exhale. The loud whistle rang out through the tavern and got the attention of two large men in the back of the room. Raising their eyes from their conversation, they eyed Jacob and strolled over, each breaking off to flank Jacob on both sides.

A calm steeled over Jacob as the men approached. Their orchestrated movements made no sense, nor why they should be concerned with him. Warning bells flared in his head as he analyzed the situation.

Both men towered half a head above most of the other patrons they passed. Their gaits were lumbering, however. One barely missed a chair leg as he stood. The misstep was slight but visible. The blond fellow who approached from the left had a boxer's fit about him—all arms and torso. But even from where Jacob stood, the man's bloodshot eyes hinted at the prior activities of his evening. His stature intimidated, but his reflexes were off. The other man, bald but still brutish, walked toward Jacob on more solid footing. He had years on his blond friend, though, the creases around his eyes and forehead well sunken in. The knuckles on the man's fingers were gnarled and stiff with age, giving off the permanent appearance of a fist balled at the ready. Yet, he moved slowly—an asset for a more limber opponent.

"I'm sorry, is there something wrong?" Jacob asked when he saw the two brutes come over to him. The situation no longer felt comfortable, and he itched to get back to Sarah. "On second thought, never mind about the meal. Thank you for your time."

He turned to go, but the host put his hand on Jacob's shoulder, halting his progress. "No trouble at all. We just have a job to do. No hard feelings, corporal, but I can't afford to lose my business. Mickey, Alton, please..."

Jacob rolled his shoulder away from the host. He sidestepped and turned toward the blond man. In an instant, Jacob whipped his hand around his back and pulled free his knife. Crouched low, he pawed the blade back and forth, backing up toward the nearest wall. Around him, patrons took note of the commotion. Some stopped their conversations to watch, others scurried out the door. The man before him eyed the knife, though tracking it proved difficult with Jacob's volleys.

Dammit, he didn't need this. He briefly eyed the door. Could he make a run for it? The bottleneck of departing patrons gave him his answer. He spat a curse and prepared to lunge, his knuckles turning white around the knife's hilt. As his back foot left the ground, a large meaty fist connected with his jaw. He doubled over with a grunt, his eyes and body seizing up at the onslaught. The force of the blow launched him into the windows. Had it not been for the wrought iron frame of the windowpane, he would have smashed right through them.

Huddled on the floor, panting and dazed but not done, Jacob whirled around, knife out, and connected with the blond man's beer belly. A loud cry and string of curses rang out. His blade's edge was painted crimson. Dammit all, but he had lost track of the bald fellow. He turned his attention to the second attacker, but his vision blurred at the sight before him.

The swarm of people in the tavern had grown. A bar brawl was just the thing to pique their curiosity. Nausea rose in his gut, from both the head blow and his rising anxiety at the mob. As he struggled to his feet, blood coating his lips, a heavy glass object struck him at the base of his skull. Shards of glass pelted his hair and skin as Jacob dropped to the floor. The scratchy wood of the floorboards cradled his cheek as a warm, coppery liquid seeped into his ear.

A harsh cough protruded up from his lungs. He fought to breathe deeply. On his next inhale, a filthy bar rag was stuffed into his bleeding mouth. His tongue was shoved farther back into his throat, causing him to gag around the cloth. While he struggled to clear his airway, two sets of beefy arms lifted him off the floor and dragged him through the tavern. His last thought as he stared with blurry vision at the heels of his boots scraping the floor in front of him was how he had left Sarah as an easy mark.

Holy shit, this couldn't be happening! No no no...

Her pulse pounded in her ears from the force of the blood that rushed to her head as Dick's grip tightened around her throat. Every other second, he would ease up his grasp slightly to readjust or maneuver the two of them in some manner, but then the vice would clamp down once more. She hadn't taken a full breath in almost a minute, and her vision was starting to haze over.

No, hang on, dammit.

The sound of her skirt tearing was loud to her ringing ears. Pins and needles spasmed across her whole body. She couldn't breathe, couldn't move. Terror began seeping into her oxygen-deprived brain, any remaining hope she had trickling out of her in each tear that cascaded down her cheeks.

C'mon...think!

"Oh, no crying, now, Miss Johansson. By the time you get yourself all worked up, it'll be over." Dick held her flat against the back of the boulder, using the huge bulk of his chest to crush her against the stone, compressing her rib cage. His left hand never left her throat, and even though her hands trembled around his wrist, her jagged, torn fingernails digging into his skin, it was clearly a weak attempt to free herself. While she swallowed another slight gulp of air, Dick's other hand had ripped apart her skirt's waistband entirely. Another sound of split seams and the frigid winter's air assaulted her bare legs, the boulder's icy facade coming into contact with her partially naked backside.

Sarah clenched her eyes shut tight and let the tears fall over Dick's knuckles. No, she would not go out like this. She hadn't traveled back in time more than a hundred years to get raped and murdered in a town plaza by a pissed-off bully with a score to settle. Ramon needed her. Jacob needed her.

And she needed Jacob.

That conviction slammed into her. She was from the future, dammit! There must be something she could use as the upper hand.

"Now, I've seen a lot of women's underthings in my day, especially the fancier stuff you whores like to show off, but these are different, I have to say. Put up a good fight, too, those thick stockings of yours did," Dick remarked casually, as though they each were sharing a cup of coffee and talking about the new paint on a car.

What the heck was he talking about? Oh, her underwear and leggings!

When Jacob had offered to purchase new clothes for Sarah, she'd declined his offer regarding the undergarments and always kept on her own bra and underwear beneath the period trimmings. Corsets and petticoats weren't something she wanted to figure out if she didn't need to. It wasn't like she ever envisioned a circumstance where those would become a topic of conversation. But apparently, Sarah's cotton bikini briefs piqued her attacker's interest.

Yes, a distraction!

Dick pulled away from Sarah slightly. Leaning down, he raised an eyebrow in curiosity at her torn underwear. His movement relieved the pressure on Sarah's throat. She quickly pulled in several large, silent gulps of air. She stayed frozen, however, her hands clenched on Dick's wrist. The humiliation was palpable as he further scrutinized her exposed lower body. But she'd rather be alive and embarrassed than dead and unashamed.

"What is this?" Dick said as he picked up the hanging magenta cotton fabric with two fingers. Reflexively, she tried to knee him in the face when he got too close again, but that just made him retighten his grip on her throat. This time, though, she was ready for it.

"Now, now, Sarah...Do you mind if I call you Sarah? After all, we are now on a much more familiar footing." He stood up to his full height again and peered into Sarah's eyes. "My, you are intriguing. I wonder what else you're hiding under there. It's very unlike Jacob not to share, perfect fucking pissant that he is." Dick's free hand grasped her breast through her blouse and cotton shirt and squeezed. His nails dug into Sarah's flesh like he was wringing out a sponge. Sarah pinched her eyes shut briefly, the intense sting and deep muscle bruising distracting her from her plan.

To Sarah's surprise, the pressure on her breast let up almost as soon as it began. Confused, she cracked her eyes open. Dick still had his hands on her, but his gaze had settled on the ground. Seemingly distracted, he halted his assault. His lips had set in a grim line, his brow furrowed. Why was he hesitating? He raised his head slowly and captured her gaze, a far-away expression replacing the menacing intent from a moment ago. His blue eyes bore into hers as if he were pleading. Was that regret? A shake of his head ended the trance almost as fast as it began. Like hell Sarah would miss her cue.

Sarah dropped her hands from his wrist and stabbed her thumbs into his eye sockets. Her remaining fingers clamped around his face. Tension threatened to crack his skull as she clenched her hands tight. Determination to survive invigorated her. She rammed her thumbs in harder, cringing against the feel of the orbs beneath her skin. Crescents of blood began to bloom beneath her fingernails along his eyelids. Still, she kept pushing.

It was Dick's turn to scream, his hands grabbing at Sarah's wrists as he flailed and twisted to break free. She wasn't in the market to hang on longer than needed. Once she saw blood dripping from underneath his left eye socket, she dropped her hands and ran, offering up a silent prayer to every single blockbuster action movie she'd ever seen.

The sting of astringent invaded Jacob's nostrils and immediately triggered his gag reflex. His stomach rolled at the onslaught, forcing him to quickly turn his head and dry heave onto the dank wooden floor. As the fog began to clear, he recalled the rag being removed from his throat sometime earlier, but the damn thing had been soaked in moonshine or some such other spirit. His throat felt like it was coated in battery acid.

"Wakey, wakey, Army boy."

All at once, Jacob's circumstances flooded back to him. The barman at the front, his two lackeys, something about not losing a business.

Sarah.

Christ, he had left her in the plaza! And given that these men knew Jacob by name and had appeared to be waiting for him, he feared what may be waiting for her if her connection to him was discovered.

Easy, Bellamy. Walk before you run.

A harsh voice Jacob recognized echoed through his ringing ears—the corpulent tavern host with the greasy fingers. Eyes still closed, he extended his senses further. The throbbing in his head tapped out a distracting drumbeat, but one that progressed to more of a moderate nuisance as the minutes passed. His jaw was another matter, however. A side-to-side wiggle confirmed nothing was dislocated, but the tenderness and swelling were severe. A swipe of his tongue across his teeth vouched for everyone still being in attendance, but his bite felt off now, as if his teeth no longer fit together properly.

The air around him was only mildly warmer than the outside. He figured he must be in the basement of the tavern judging by the strong smell of yeast and hops. He sat on a dank floor, legs outstretched in front of him, with his arms curled behind him and wrapped around a wooden support beam. His wrists were bound with another bar rag, judging by the gauge of the fibers. Jacob gave a slight tug on his bindings to test its holding.

Solid, but not impossible. Thank God for small blessings. If they had used any sort of leather strapping, he would have had a real challenge on his hands.

Jacob raised his head when the footsteps got closer and slowly cracked his eyes open. Sure enough, the barman with the belly had shuffled across the floor, scraping a four-legged stool behind him. When he was a few feet away from Jacob, he planted the stool and rested his booted feet on a canvas bag of malt nearby.

"I've got to tell you," the barman said as he reached into the back of his pocket to grab another toothpick, "I thought this would be much harder. Your buddy is one crafty fuck, but I do appreciate a good businessman. Glad he was open to this compromise."

Jacob said nothing as the fog in his head began to clear, his vision sharpening. Canvas sacks of malt and hops stacked four high lined the perimeter. The support beam he was tied to was one of many. Yes, he was definitely in the tavern's cellar. The light was low—only a few bare bulbs hung about the space. The dim glow was enough to cast a sheen on the iron banister toward the back, however. A banister that would accompany the stairs out.

As Jacob's circumstances continued to settle, he began forming his exit strategy. Damn, his face hurt. Working his jaw back and forth, he finally processed what the barman said. What buddy? Though he was grateful his suspicions regarding premeditation were accurate, his stomach soured at the implication.

The barman removed the toothpick, snorted back an obscene amount of phlegm, and hocked a monstrous loogie at Jacob's feet. Resettling himself on the stool, he eyed up Jacob again. "Not much to say, then?"

Jacob subtly tried to shake out his neck to remove the speckles of glass fragments in his hair from earlier, but otherwise, he just held his captor's gaze and let the man talk. Jacob needed that time to think and plan.

None of this made any sense. He didn't know this man from Adam and, for the life of him, couldn't comprehend why he'd been targeted and attacked. No matter, he needed out and to make his way back to Sarah.

"Very well. Let me enlighten you. I'm Mack, the owner of this fine establishment. And let's just say I made a deal with a bit of a devil. I believe you know him by the name of Dick Stevens."

At the mention of Steven's name, Jacob was all ears. He tried to hide his intrigue by looking elsewhere, but Mack caught the way Jacob tilted his head to the side briefly.

"Yeah, that's right. Turns out we all have our weaknesses. Mine's pride...no, wait, what does the Good Book call it? Hubris, right? Yeah, that's it. Well, when you're so cocksure with the cards in your hand and the whiskey that puts the money in your pocket, one can get boastful."

Jacob half listened to Mack as he discreetly moved his wrists around behind his back, trying to get a lay of the land. When the backs of his knuckles suddenly recoiled from a pinprick, Jacob circled back to reassess. His fingers grazed the tiniest tip of a thin rusty nail protruding out of the base of the beam. Jacob felt it again. The nail's edge couldn't be poking out more than an eighth of an inch from the wood, virtually hidden if you weren't looking for it.

"...as it happened, my straight flush should have won me that pot, but then Stevens pulled the fucking king of hearts from the deck and..."

Jacob began rubbing the bar rag that secured his wrists back and forth over the nail's tip, hoping it would catch and the fibers would separate. He couldn't move his arms too much, though. Any outward movement would be easily seen if you were staring at Jacob head-on. Thankfully, Mack was distracted by his own tale.

Hubris was right. The man loved a captive audience. Literally.

"...shouldn't have bet on the tavern, but I was so sure! So goddamn sure..."

As Jacob kept up with his whittling, the picture became clearer. This man, Mack, was no bright bulb, to be sure.

"When I couldn't pay out, Dick issued the deal: I find you out and rough you up enough to land you back in Martinsville, and he'd leave me the tavern. Dick mentioned you were from here, on the outskirts a bit. I had planned to ask around, but it would seem serendipity was my temptress today."

A tear in the fiber of the rag finally allowed Jacob to release the tension in his shoulders a bit. Folding his fingers in, he palpated the tear. Dammit. It wasn't large, but it would have to be enough.

"Which leaves me to this next part." Mack rose from his stool. A set of shiny brass knuckles glistened on his right hand. Jacob had been so focused on the rag, he'd neglected the immediate threat in front of him. Mack took a few more steps closer to Jacob and leaned down to look at his face, squinting at the swelling that had begun to bloom.

Mack shook his head a bit, tsked a few times, then said, "That jaw's nowhere near as broken as it needs to be. Whelp, let's get to work. Don't got all night." He pumped his meaty fist a few times for effect before he pulled it back. Like a battering ram, he released his arm toward Jacob's already throbbing jaw.

At the last second before contact, Jacob ducked his head to the right and caught Mack's pudgy wrist with his left hand. The confusion on Mack's face registered as he glanced down at the partially shredded fabric hanging from Jacob's wrist. Before Mack could act, Jacob sprung up, legs bent under him, and tackled Mack to the ground.

Mack landed in a thud on the filthy planks, his head absorbing the impact. He rose shakily to his feet. As the barman steadied himself, Jacob towered above him. His biceps supported a fifty-pound burlap sack of malt held high above his head. Jacob's thighs strained in a deadlift stance under the weight. He shunted his remaining strength to his core. Half a second later, Jacob slammed the malt down on Mack's face. The barman's brief scream was quickly silenced, his legs and arms stilled.

Wasting no time, Jacob sprinted up the cellar steps. When he burst through, he emptied out into a hallway. To his left, he heard the voices of patrons. Avoiding notice, he went right and stumbled out the second door. The night's glacial air accosted his senses.

Ignoring the cold shock, he turned quickly and pumped his legs around the side of the tavern, back toward the plaza. Back to Sarah. Rounding the blind corner, his chin collided with someone's head. A smaller someone. Head thrown back, jaw throbbing, he gripped his chin. His other hand went for the sheath at his back. Empty. Dammit. As his hand fell, a soft curse rose up in front of him. From a woman.

Shit.

"Miss, I'm so sorry! Are you hurt?" He tried to feel around in the dark for the woman, but before he could go any farther, the trembling name that fell from her lips froze him cold.

"Jacob? Is that you?"

"Sarah!" The moon provided pitiful light, but he could just barely make out her form. She stood there with her arms wrapped around herself. Though faint to see, tear tracks glistened through her dirt-streaked skin. Her legs were bare, and that caused him to see red.

CHAPTER 17

"Sarah! Dear God, what happened?" He pulled back briefly, bringing his hands to the sides of her face. His thumbs gently wiped at the dried tear tracks. His eyes quickly scanned over her and landed on her neck where red marks were beginning to appear from Dick's chokehold.

Not wanting to worry him, but also terrified by what she saw staring back at her, she grabbed his wrists and leaned into them, rubbing her cheek against his calloused skin.

"I'm fine now. I just...Jacob, your face..." Beneath his dark beard, his jaw had begun to flesh out from the swelling, his previously chiseled cheeks and chin losing their sharp edges. Along the tips of his ears, hairline, and neck were little bleeding nicks and scrapes, which looked worrisome as a whole but she knew were minor injuries. What was worrisome, however? The crown of Jacob's head was matted with deep red blood that painted rivers of crimson all down his neck and continued into the cavern of his open-necked shirt. His coat was gone.

"Come, we need to get out of here. Follow me. Quickly!"

He grabbed her hand, and the contact anchored her once again before she took off after him down the street behind the tavern and the other buildings. They ran for another four blocks as she struggled to keep pace, but her heels still managed to keep time with his own before Jacob slowed their charge and halted them in front of a red-brick house with four matching steps that led up to the front door. Jacob, never having once let go of her, turned around and took both of her hands in his. Despite the cold, the exertion made his hands fire-poker-hot. The heat was more than a welcome comfort.

"A friend of mine lives here and he's been hanging onto something for me. I had meant to pick it up once I was back and settled for a few days, but I need it now. Stay close. This should be quick."

Sarah nodded her agreement. After all, what else was she going to do?

Jacob climbed the steps and tapped the black cast iron door knocker three times against the front door, then impatiently shot his gaze down to his boots and waited. Another few seconds ticked by, and it was clear Jacob began to get impatient from his aggressive pacing on the four-foot stoop. Every ten seconds or so, he shunted his hand through his hair in frustration.

"C'mon...c'mon. Open up, Michael! It's Jacob." He slammed the door knocker down again and cast his eye across the vacant block while he waited. A loud thud snapped Jacob's head back to the door. The metal of the deadbolt resisted slightly as it was sent home and the door was cracked four inches, the shocked blue eyes and blond bearded chin of a man in his seventies jutting out of the opening in apprehension.

"Jacob? Well, Malorie and I weren't expecting you to be back in town for another few days. Is everything all right? Son, you look like hell!"

"I'm fine, Michael, but I need my car. It's urgent. Is it still around back?"

The old man nodded frantically and opened the door wider to converse. "Oh, yes, of course. Same spot. All fueled up and everything. Just let me go grab the keys for you. Oh! Hello, miss."

Sarah didn't know who this person was beyond being Jacob's friend, but if Jacob trusted him, that was good enough for her. "Hello, sir. My name's Sarah."

"Sarah's a close friend of mine, but there's no time now for introductions. We've run into a bit of trouble and need to quickly get out of here. I apologize for the brevity, but we're in a bind."

"Oh, yes, right. Of course. One moment." The man shuffled back inside, letting the door mostly close behind him. When he returned, he opened the door again and held out a set of keys to Jacob.

"There you are, boy. Now, off with you and Miss Sarah. Go on! I never saw either of you." The old man brushed the two of them off with the backs of his hands the way Sarah imagined mothers shooing children out of the kitchen while they were trying to get dinner ready.

"Thank you." Keys in hand, Jacob leaped off the four steps and jogged around the back of Michael's property, Sarah in tow. In front of them was a row of carports, all housing various colored Model Ts. Sarah couldn't believe what she saw. Up until now, aside from the clothes and commerce, she hadn't largely experienced any excruciatingly jarring time warp moments. Things had been different, sure, but manageable, relatable, and exactly what she envisioned for the time period. Staring down the row of brand-new cars, as in brand new to humanity's existence, she was reminded starkly of how she didn't belong here.

Jacob examined the row of vehicles until he came to a carport housing a black vintage automobile with tires so thin for a car they looked like they belonged on dirt bikes instead of cars.

Remember, Sarah, these aren't vintage here.

The front body of the car reminded her of the long black nose of a Doberman Pinscher, accented in the front with two symmetrically circular headlights. They were so close together they looked like eyes. The car was a convertible, with leather seats large enough for two passengers. The oversized steering wheel stood out from the interior and peeked through the front windshield. Was she actually going to get an opportunity to ride in this thing?

Without bothering to open the door, Jacob climbed up and extended his giant leg over the compartment entrance. Settling in, he used the key to unlock the ignition, and a moment later, the engine roared to life. Leaving the car to idle in its place, he hopped back out again and jogged over to her.

"This is my family's car. Before I shipped out, I gave it to Michael and Malorie to watch over while I was gone. They've known my family since my brother and I were but a thought. It's not ideal for winter, but it'll get us back to the cabin in a flash."

As if he could tell her head was still spinning, he cradled the sides of her face in his warm hands and just held her there. "God, Sarah," he whispered into the night air. "I'm so sorry. So *fucking* sorry."

Even in the dim light, Sarah could clearly see the anguish on Jacob's face. He bit his bottom lip so hard, she thought he'd puncture his canine through the skin. The creases at the corners of his eyes were so sharp, she could tell he held back the floodgates on a tsunami of emotion. He tried immensely to be strong for her, even though this man was clearly a hand grenade whose pin had just been pulled. Despite his own ordeal, his own trauma, he fought to be her champion.

God, how would she ever be able to leave him?

The vibration under his flanks from the engine was a welcome sensation as he coasted his Chevrolet 490 to a stop in front of the cabin. His jaw ached from the punches, and his neck itched like crazy from what he suspected were still tiny glass shards hitching a ride in his hair. Christ, he needed a bath and a drink. But first, he needed to tend to Sarah.

She'd sat still the whole drive back, not that it was a terribly long one. Five minutes driving at forty miles per hour compared to the fifteen to twenty minutes it took to walk. But still, the car had no roof and she'd been outside in the elements ever since they left the cabin originally. God, she must be freezing.

On instinct, he reached across the gear shift and grabbed her fingers, squeezing and kneading her skin to get the blood flow going in her extremities again. The very tips of her fingers were a dark red compared to the alabaster of her palms and wrists, but she still sat silently staring out ahead through the windshield.

"Let's get inside. I'll get the fire going and you can warm up." When she nodded silently, as if she heard him but not really, he got out of the car, closed his door, and walked around to her side. When he got to her door, she looked down at the handle, her brows creased in confusion. "What?"

"I...uh..." She shook her head and looked to be fighting back tears a bit. "This is going to sound crazy, but I don't know how to open this door. The handle...it's not intuitive to me. Do I pull it toward me? Or up?"

Jacob looked down at the silver, flat door latch with the rounded edge. A simple push down would release it, but he sensed something greater at play. Concern pierced his heart. Before he could answer, a deluge came pouring out of Sarah.

"I know very well how to drive a friggin' car, Jacob," she began to sob, "and I thought being in one again, no matter how old...sorry...*different*...would offer me some small sense of feeling like I was back home, but it doesn't." Sarah started to raise her volume just then, the high-pitched trill going in and out and making her voice crack at times. She waved her hands frantically around and finally unburdened onto him, which he gladly bore with everything he had.

"I can't manage a simple car door, Jacob! I can't manage being attacked! I can't manage a fake pregnancy, and I sure as shit can't manage what's happening to my body!" She sought out his eyes in the dim moonlight. "I'm all out of strong, independent woman!" she half yelled, half cried into his face. "I just want to go home!"

Whatever dam she had built up burst free. That last plea, though, broke through Jacob's armor. On a shot, he climbed the single step leading up to her car door, scooped her out of the vehicle, and marched into the cabin, her hunched body high on his chest. His body absorbed every sob and hiccup that escaped Sarah's exasperated cries. He cradled her to his chest as if she were his sole charge on this Earth.

Jacob bypassed the fireplace and made a left turn down the hall, taking her straight to his room. She was still so incoherent, he doubted she even knew where she was in the cabin. He nestled her onto the mattress before briefly leaving to kindle the hearth. When he returned, Sarah lay on her side, curled in on herself. She clenched her arms around her legs and her bloodshot eyes tracked him as he entered from the doorway.

The fight had gone out of his spitfire, and Jacob respected how monumental it was that she would let him witness her in such a state.

He respected her all the more for it.

On a rush, he took three quick strides to the bed. Walking around to the other side, he crawled into the center of the bed, the mattress dipping under the targeted weight from his knees. Once he was situated with his back to the headboard, he gently lifted her onto his lap. Sarah was settled in the crook of his arm. Jacob stroked her hair and fanned it out over her back. The strands wrapped and weaved themselves around his fingers like an octopus claiming its prey in the webbing of its tentacles.

Yes, she has claimed me a thousand times over and doesn't even know it.

Jacob mulled that thought over as he continued to whisper shushing sounds of comfort to his injured warrior. He would stay here like this until the tremors passed or until she sent him away. Whatever she needed.

"Jacob?" Sarah asked in a voice so slight he almost missed it.

"Yes?"

She turned her head to his, the moonlight from the window making her look paler than she was. The silence ticked on for another minute, but he had no intention of rushing her. She needed space to heal and be heard in her own time.

When she finally released her soft shuddering exhale, Jacob sat back and prepared to listen.

"When Dick attacked me and told me what he had arranged to have happen to you at the tavern"—Jacob's upper lip snarled and a predatory growl sat waiting in the back of his throat—"you were the first thought in my mind."

His mind stalled out flat.

In a shaky voice, Sarah went on. "In spite of everything that's happened to me, of all the things I can't manage, losing you was at the top of my list...and I don't know how to handle that."

His breath left him in a rush, as if a battering ram had done its worst to his midsection, heart, and head all in one shot. All logic escaped him. His heart, what once was so dead and war-ravaged, had finally begun to feel the first soft beats of life again.

This woman, this amazing woman who had just been through hell and come to her own rescue, doubted herself? Not only that, but he had somehow managed to carve out a precious place in her heart? A place so prized as to cause her duress with his absence?

Jacob tried to form words back to her, but nothing fit. Nothing was right. Nothing was worthy of these revitalized sensations.

Instead, ever the man of action, he did what he had been longing to do every time that woman drifted too close to his orbit. He would show her, let her feel what he felt. Perhaps logic and reasoning weren't the most useful tools to help her see what was before her.

Jacob slowly lifted Sarah's lithe body closer to his face, noticed how her eyelashes glistened with unshed tears, and captured her quivering lips in a kiss.

He would show her exactly how capable of managing things she was.

CHAPTER 18

W hen the warmth of Jacob's mouth hit her lips, Sarah was done thinking.

Finally.

Since she first emerged in that alley bloody and confused, her mind had had to stay ten steps ahead of her circumstances. No more. She was done. All she cared about was Jacob.

Her fingertips tingled painfully as she lifted them to Jacob's face, combing them through his hair. The intense thaw got the blood flowing to her previously frozen hands. On instinct, she made fists to aid in the heat transfer, trapping Jacob's hair in the center of her hands. Jacob grunted at the surprise tug on his locks and mistook her hair pulling for something more. Not that she would complain. She needed rough. She needed him.

The brush of his beard sent a chill up her spine and made her fidget in his arms. An uncomfortable heaviness grew between her legs the more Jacob's chin caressed her with his beard. She tried her best to squeeze her thighs together to alleviate the pressure, but her position in his arms made that challenging. She still sat draped over his lap, her backside directly over his groin, and she could feel his length growing and hardening with every pseudo-squeeze of her thighs she was able to manage.

Jacob's tongue plundered every inch of her mouth. He was the painter, his vibrant colors emblazoned on her drab canvas. Every ray of color, light, and energy fused inside her. She inhaled every bit of it.

"I need you. More of you," Jacob breathed into her mouth between pants. He broke the kiss for the briefest of moments before he lifted her from the bed and whisked them out to the living room, nipping and licking every spare inch of visible skin.

"Jacob," Sarah said on a breathy half-giggle, "you do realize you already had me in a bed, right?" She raised one eyebrow at him, utterly confused but not wanting to delay things too long with idle chitchat.

Jacob had carted her over to the fireplace. The flames roared with heat, dancing and popping in its open stone cage. "That mouth, Miss Johansson, is going to get you into trouble." On the last word, he dropped her legs like a sack of grain and she let out a brief yelp before she righted herself.

He walked over to a chest in the corner of the room, tucked behind the rocking chair, and pulled out a dark brown fur rug large enough to cover the entire floor of the living room. It was massive. Jacob spread the rug out on the floor, getting one of the short edges as close to the fire as safely possible. Pride beamed through his eyes as he smoothed out the wrinkles and tried to remain stoic, but the dimple that indented his cheek clearly gave away the emotion.

"Why, Corporal Bellamy, you wouldn't have had anything to do with this prize, would you?"

A quick chuckle from Jacob's chest and the wide smile returned to his grumpy demeanor. "You could say that, Miss Johansson."

Jacob was still bent down over the pelt, running his fingers through the bristly fur. Sarah knelt down to join him, running the backs of her knuckles along the fibers.

"Several years back, my younger brother, Isaac, and I had heard some of our farming neighbors talk about a pack of brown bears who weren't keeping to themselves, getting too close to the crops and creating a real headache for the farms out here. My family and I hadn't experienced any problems directly, but this happened around the time that the suburban development offers were rolling in. With the train line extending farther and farther out from Baltimore, Lake Roland became a nice little slice of home away from home for city dwellers. As you can imagine, when more people moved in, the wildlife had to move out. In the case of this particular pack of brown bears, Isaac and I suspected their habitat was demolished as a result of all that building development, so they were showing up more where people didn't want them."

Sarah loved listening to Jacob talk about his family, his smooth soft baritone voice taking on a more pleasant cadence. If they were back home—and by home, she meant her own time—he'd make a wonderful narrator for movies or audiobooks. She couldn't imagine ever getting tired of his voice.

"One early January morning, Isaac and I went out to, well, do our part, I guess you could say. Our mother urged us along, saying it was for the good of the town and all. God, when we stumbled onto the den, just the entry hole was twice the size of any we'd ever seen. I remember walking up to it with all the bravado of a young-and-dumb kid."

"How old were you?"

"I was twenty-one, Isaac was nineteen. In spite of me being older, he was the one who saved my hide in the end. Even though it was in the middle of winter and I was so sure the bear would already have been in the den for its hibernation, the damn thing attacked from a forest ledge behind and caught us off guard. Well, it caught *me* off guard. Isaac was so quick to react, his hunting rifle at the ready."

Jacob's expression froze in thought as he stared into the flames, his face becoming taught and pained. "Isaac took him down in two shots. He was so damn proud, and I couldn't have been more thrilled for him." Jacob cleared his throat a few times before resuming. "He and I made the pelt together...his well-deserved trophy for being the savior of Lake Roland."

"What happened to Isaac?" she asked, though her gut told her she knew the answer.

"Killed in action six months ago." Jacob was hardly able to get the words out, his voice growing so quiet Sarah had to lean forward to hear him at all. "And then, shortly before the armistice, I got word that my parents had grown ill, a new strain of flu or something. I'm not entirely sure. Several people in town had gotten sick, as well as throughout the city. They died four months ago."

The familiar prickle of tears formed in her eyes, but she willed them back. No, she wouldn't cry for this man. He needed strength, support.

Love.

Sarah rose to her feet on shaky legs, her ankles barely supporting her weight. Jacob looked up at her from the floor, the fire's flames reflected back at her in his slightly glossy eyes. When she approached, he rose to greet her, his chest puffing out with a great inhale that no doubt helped steady himself. He was this massive Titan on the outside, capable of running into hellfire and strong enough to withstand the worst artillery humanity could throw at him. Yet, on the inside, he was as brittle as the rest of them. In that moment, Sarah knew she loved Jacob, and the realization hit her like a blow to the head.

Her hands, now warmer from being near the fire, cupped the sides of his anguished face, careful to avoid his injuries, the fibers of his beard cushioning her grasp. Her heels rose of their own accord and carried her up to meet his soft lips, but before she could claim his mouth, he halted her progress by placing the rough pad of his thumb over her bottom lip.

"When you first met me at Martinsville, I told you I was recovering from the war."

She nodded with trepidation at his statement. "Yes."

"That is true in the broader sense. But I need you to know. And if you want nothing to do with me from this moment on, I will still support you as I always have."

A great weight settled in the pit of Sarah's stomach. She didn't think she liked where this would go.

"God, my fierce, strong spitfire." It was Jacob's opportunity to turn pleading eyes her way. "I was in Martinsville because I tried to kill myself."

The shame was so great, he could hardly get the words out. He had never spoken it aloud to anyone outside of the doctors assigned to his chart. And now, as he held Sarah in his arms and watched her expression change, it absolutely gutted him. But he needed to continue. He had come this far, after all.

"I have bad days, days where I wake in cold sweats and want to shut out the world. Oftentimes, I've dreaded going to sleep because I knew I'd have to wake up and start my life all over again the next day. But I'm learning to manage..." The words left him in a rush for fear she'd turn and run. "And honestly," he gritted out, his hand running through his hair, "I've only known you a short while but just being around you, it's...Christ. I'm fumbling here. I don't know, but you've been this great therapy to me. When I can't even contemplate the prospect of another moment in the sun, I think of you and recall that you may be just a little bit as lost as I am at times. You've been my beacon ever since I left Martinsville holding your hand. I imagine you thought it was me escorting you through this new circumstance you'd found yourself in, but in actuality, you've been holding me up every step of the way."

There was no going back now. He just stood there and waited to see what she said. And whatever the outcome, he would take it. If she ran, it would kill him, but he would take it.

A sharp creak of the floorboard beneath their feet pierced the deafening silence of the living room, shaking him from his thoughts. Sarah had taken another step toward him, instead of retreating.

This is good. Please don't run from me.

She reached out for his hands, slowly prying open his calloused fingers until they lay flat. His left hand she interlaced with her own fingers, forming a solid fist of unity. His right hand, however, she held up flat and out, facing her chest. With purpose, she guided his hand toward her until she rested it on her breast, enclosing the soft mound with both of their hands locked together. Jacob's eyes couldn't move from their hands and what she was hopefully inviting him to do.

Could this mean she accepted him?

His head still spinning from her gentle advance, he watched her hand that encased his. She gave a gentle knead, and Jacob's unspoken instruction was clear.

"Sarah…"

Before he could finish, her hot mouth was on his own, and the message rang loud and clear in his addled brain: The time for talking was over. And he was more than fine with that.

Their tongues collided in a rush of heat and need, and Jacob took over with focused determination. His one hand remained glued to her, pawing that perfect teardrop of temptation through way too many damn layers of clothing. To rectify the situation, Jacob took his other hand and slid the open blouse over her left shoulder, always careful of her skin, hoping she would aid him in the rest. As if right on cue, she shrugged the remainder of the way out of her top, her mouth never leaving his own and his hand blissfully never leaving her chest.

Jacob snaked his arm around her waist and lifted her off the ground. He needed closer contact, was being driven mad without it. To his delight, Sarah granted him his wish and wrapped both of her legs around his waist. He had never been so happy ensnared in such a vice grip. The tension in her thighs increased and so did the pressure in his cock. He felt like a grenade a hairbreadth away from exploding. One gentle knock and his shaking pin would dislodge. No way in hell this would be over before it began.

Jacob lowered Sarah to the ground, so excited he nearly dropped her, but the bristly fibers of the bearskin rug were there to cradle her body. He would have been content to spend the next year of his life savoring the taste of her lips, but he had other things in mind and wouldn't let this little rogue deter his mission.

He slowed down his oral advances, dragging one final lick across her kiss-swollen lips before sealing them with a peck.

"Why are you stopping?" Sarah looked up at him in confusion.

"That is need-to-know information, I'm afraid. But we are by no means finished. There's more to this training exercise, Miss Johansson. Now, lie still. That's an order from your commanding officer." The wink he gave her silenced her questions. God, he couldn't remember the last time he had the urge to be playful, and it felt remarkable.

But playtime was over.

Jacob scooted down her lithe body and peeled back her cotton shirt, exposing the creamy skin of her abdomen. Of its own accord, his tongue painted a path along the edge of the remaining waistband of her skirt. The chill of the night air left a breadcrumbs trail of goosebumps where his tongue had been, and the imagery of marking her emboldened his cock even more.

Patience, soldier.

Higher up he tasted her, dipping into the valley of her belly button and traveling across the grooves of her rib cage. A quick glance showed Sarah's head fallen back, eyes squinted shut, and short pants huffing out of her swollen lips. The sight was exquisite. He needed more.

In one rapid swoop, he pushed her shirt up and over her head, freeing it from her arms and tossing it to the side. The firelight bathed her skin in orange and yellow, her body lit up like a bonfire. A moment later, his mouth was on her, feasting on one nipple while pinching the other. Sarah pulled in a short hiss through her teeth, and the satisfaction made Jacob preen like a peacock.

The living room was dark except for the fire, shadows and light being thrown all across the room. But he didn't need his vision right then. Hell, he could have been blind in that moment and he was convinced he would have muddled through things just damn fine. But her little pants and breaths were egging him on, and his cock was so full to bursting he didn't know how much more disciplined he could be.

"Jacob, I need you inside me. Please. Just, please..." Sarah's eyes were still closed, but her brows were knitted together and her tempting tongue kept darting out to remoisten her bottom lip. The sheen from the wetness was what did him in. On a lunge, he curled his fingers into the waistband of her skirt and opaque stockings he'd heard her call "leggings" and yanked every single piece of fabric that had the audacity to get in his way down to her ankles. He was tempted to toss every last stitch into the fire, but quickly considered she may not appreciate that.

To be an officer and a gentleman and all that.

Before him, Sarah was laid bare on *his* rug in *his* cabin. As he sat back on his heels, hands on his knees, he swore a luckier man did not exist, surely. And, God, she was a sight. If he thought her his Athena before, the real thing held no contest. There she lay on her back, her breasts overflowing and her nipples red from his attention. The dips of her waist invited him to explore every inch of her, like a pioneer blazing a trail through uncharted lands. The swell of her hips framed her powerful thighs, calling him home. One of those long legs was coyly draped over her sex, barely hiding the neatly trimmed curls that called to him like manna from heaven.

"You're overdressed, corporal." Sarah eyed Jacob, issuing the dare. His little hellion slowly grazed her right hand down over her breasts, through the V of her thighs, and into her sex until her fingers landed deftly on that little nub of pleasure. And then she began moving her fingers back and forth.

Challenge accepted.

Standing to his full height, one by one, he removed every article of clothing. Could he have done it sitting down? Of course, but he needed her to see all of him. He was a big fellow, and he often hated using his size to fit preconceived notions. But in this, oh, he had no problem. On the contrary, he wanted her to see how big he was, he wanted her to see how heavy and engorged his cock was for her. He needed her to know the effect she had on him, and what she asked for in return.

With his back to the fire, Jacob stood before Sarah, naked and proud. Effecting her game, he brought his muscled arm down to his erection and lifted its heavy weight in his hand. His biceps bunched as he gave it a few solid tugs before he dropped down to the rug one knee at a time to worship at his goddess's altar. He noticed her fingers had been entangled in the fur of the rug, and he planned on giving her more reasons to hang on as well.

Crawling up her body at a snail's pace, Jacob intentionally caressed every inch of her skin with his beard on his trek northward. He loved seeing how her nipples tightened and grew in response to him, how goosebumps peppered her landscape from his touch. His mouth hovered over hers a brief moment before Sarah's hands came up to gently cage in his head.

"I need you to know that I'm on the...well. Just know that I take medication to ensure I don't get pregnant."

Jacob quirked his head to the side at that. "What do you mean?"

"I mean, in my time, women and men have protection available to prevent unwanted pregnancies." His jaw dropped a bit at that, myriad questions coming to mind. Before he could get the first one out, she paused his effort by placing her index finger over his lips. "I have every intention of making love to you right now. I just wanted you to know that we don't have to worry about a *real* pregnancy, all right? Do you trust me?"

"Oh, Sarah. I have a lot to learn, but I will trust you in all things."

The brightness of her smile could have rivaled the sun, which made perfect sense. She was undoubtedly his eternal sun.

He brought his lips down to hers in an urgent kiss, their tongues dancing in time to their heartbeats. Farther down, Jacob took his length in his hand and gently prodded it at her soaking wet entrance, rubbing his swollen head up and down a few times in her slickness. When Sarah let out a moan, he notched his cock at her sex and thrust.

The warmth and tightness felt so good. Yet, as he entered and retreated, he quickly realized it had been too long. He doubted he could keep this going. But, dammit, he would try. Jacob snapped his hips forward, and Sarah released a guttural grunt from deep in her throat.

"Harder, Jacob."

He took her cue and slowly slid out, only to ram back in as he gripped the back of her thighs in his palms, pushing her legs forward toward her chest. Leaning back on his knees, he held her legs and watched her breasts bounce as he pounded into her with each thrust. His pace quickened, and with each move, Sarah's moans got higher and higher in pitch. On his next thrust, Sarah arched her back off the rug, the fire's roaring flames reflecting off the light sheen of sweat that coated her taut skin.

As she exhaled long and hard, her body floating back down, Jacob dug his hands under to grip her backside and hammered home his erection. His release came like an enemy fighter jet dropping its large-weight bomb. His seed pulsed out of him in great hot spurts, filling Sarah with the very distilled essence of him. He hadn't realized how high he flew, how high his heart rate had soared, until he crashed in exhaustion on top of Sarah, his head cradled in the crook of her neck. Without another shred of logic or any care for his own emotional well-being, he let his heart have its own release as well.

"God, Sarah. I love you," he whispered directly into her ear so there was no mistaking what he said. With Sarah, he had finally found his peace.

Her silence, however, spoke volumes.

CHAPTER 19

I*love you.*

Amazing how those three little words could mess with a woman's head. Even more amazing when, deep down, if she *really* examined things closely and was honest with herself, she would find that, perhaps, she felt the same way.

She loved Jacob.

And wasn't that just a kick in the pants...or skirts, as it were?

Sarah remained horizontal on Jacob's bearskin rug, panting her last gasps of exertion as her heart rate slowly settled back down to Earth. Her skin was tacky and superheated, the fires from both the hearth and Jacob doing their jobs at pumping out the BTUs. The soft hairs of Jacob's beard tickled her neck as he lay nestled there, his contented smile beaming at her between breaths, like a puppy settling into its master's lap.

This felt like heaven, and Sarah had waited so long for this type of romantic connection, heck, *any* connection. In such a short amount of time, Jacob had made an imprint on her not just in a companionable, show-me-around-town dependable kind of way, but as a vital part of her. If he were no longer a presence in her life, her heart wouldn't just be broken; a fundamental piece of her would be shattered, a link in her DNA destroyed.

And that just friggin' gutted her, because how could she possibly forget about him when she eventually returned back home? And she *would* make it back home.

Her silence in responding to his statement stretched on as the thought of home had her rolling her head to the left side to inspect her Lady Liberty complexion. For those few blissful moments when she was finally able to exist out of her headspace and just *feel*, her problems had been the furthest things from her mind. Jacob did an amazing job of consuming every thought, sensation, and urge that careened through the eight-lane superhighway that was her head. But with Jacob's big "I love you" admission, her world immediately sank back down to her internal time clock.

The color of her skin was so hard to see in the dark cabin, the only light emanating off the fireplace's flickering flames. But when she squinted at her shoulder, it looked as if the green cast had snaked its way down to her elbow.

Shit!

She quickly untangled her sweat-slicked limbs from Jacob's, hopped up off the rug, and crawled over on her hands and knees to the fire. She put her shoulder so close to the flames, her skin felt like it would begin retreating in on itself any second. The almost-searing heat caused her to inch back a bit as she took her fingers and palpated her arm.

"What's wrong?" Jacob joined her in front of the fire, the amber light casting worried shadows across his strong features. He rested his warm palm on the back of her neck and gently massaged the base, trying to ease the tension away. It didn't work.

She elevated her shoulder toward him so he could see what she saw in the full light. "It's growing. I don't feel any different, but I don't know what this means."

The grim line that formed on Jacob's face unsettled her because it echoed his uncertainty as well. They were both clueless.

"My gut tells me that my time is running out," Sarah whispered into the flames before glancing up at him. "I need to find Ramon. I'm not made to be here, clearly, and whatever force threw me back in time is making it damn explicit that this isn't a free pass to shack up with a gorgeous soldier in a cabin in the woods until the cows come home."

At that, Jacob bristled a bit and paused his ministrations at the back of her neck, retreating his hand back to rest on the rug. The hurt she caused him was a direct hit to herself as well.

"Please believe me when I say I care about you deeply." More than he knew. "You've been my lifeline to this place when you had absolutely no reason to stick by my side. But I think this rash or whatever is a sign that I need to focus on my mission. What happens if it spreads more? What if I can't hide it? What if other symptoms start presenting as it grows?" Sarah began to panic when the thoughts ran wildly through her mind, a picture reel of science fiction outcomes she never thought held any truth until now.

"Shhh, come here." Ever the gentleman, despite her rejection, he welcomed her into his arms.

She willingly crawled into his lap and huddled close into the protection of his chest. She knew she had no right to accept his affection, but she was too terrified to turn it down. And didn't that make her feel all the more like a total user? In another amazing testament to Jacob's upstanding character, he continued to hold her, shushing her fears away as if he had the power to fix everything.

They sat there, clustered together in a jumble of naked limbs, for a few more minutes as the fire continued to pop and sizzle. Her breasts were compressed up against his solid chest, and the length of his cock, now soft and sated, bumped into her hip. The two were as intimately close as lovers could be without actually being intimate.

Another minute passed, and Jacob let out a long exhale against the crown of Sarah's head. His breath cascaded down her skin, tickling her nose and causing her to sniffle. She was afraid he'd interpret the sound as a precursor to tears, but who the hell was she kidding? On the inside, she was barely holding it together, and oddly enough, Jacob had been one of the few people who'd seen her cry to begin with. She didn't want to examine what that meant either.

"Tonight, let me care for you in what small ways I can. Tomorrow, I promise to take you back to your great-grandfather. I have my vehicle now, so it's no bother to head back into the city on a whim."

Sarah stilled. "You'd do that for me? Why?"

"Because I love you, stubborn woman," he said with a chuckle. "Nothing you have shown or said to me in the last fifteen minutes has changed that, in spite of what you may feel. And if I'm only to have you in my life for a short while longer, I'll gladly take that in whatever form I'm given."

Sarah looked into Jacob's eyes, the dark brown of his irises penetrating straight to her soul.

"I have felt a great lightness return to my life since you barged into it. I'd be a goddamn fool to cut that short."

How the hell was she ever going to leave this man? Because she couldn't stay here, right? Frustration and confusion flitted through her mind. A subtle glance at her skin reminded her she was on borrowed time and her choices weren't her own. But if she had the choice, if she *could* stay, would she?

Too overwhelmed to examine things further, she settled on showing her love for him the only way she could think to do so. Since she still didn't trust herself with words just yet, Sarah closed the space between them and delivered him the sweetest, most chaste kiss she could before her hand dipped lower between their naked bodies. She couldn't offer much, but she could ensure the good memories she'd leave behind.

Sarah stood in front of the same stone steps of Martinsville University she remembered from a few days ago when she first arrived in Baltimore in 1919. The stone was gray and dingy, but the edges of the steps were still pristinely carved. Amid the noise around her, between the honking and clanging of automobiles and streetcars that volleyed for road space, she was hardly able to hear her own thoughts. Looking down at her gloved hand, she held the image of Ramon sitting on these very steps. She had no idea where her next act would lead her, but she had to do something.

"Are we ready, then?" Jacob asked as he fiddled with his black leather glove, the fabric squeaking as he tried to wrestle his thick fingers into the lining. The poor brute, in his haste, had accidentally shoved his pinky and ring finger both into the same finger slot. The imagery of his struggle, this giant man being bested by a small scrap of fabric, his scowl one of frustration and determination, completely undid her. On a loud snort, Sarah raised her hand to her nose and bent over next to him, doing her best to hide her laughter.

"What, pray tell, is so damned funny?"

"Ow, ow! Okay, sorry, I'll stop..." Sarah let out in between breaths. The side stitches were real, and man, had it been a while since she'd enjoyed a good laugh. Standing upright with her hand over her midsection, the other hovering near her mouth in case of round two happening, she appraised her gentle giant's expression. He was pissssssed.

"Your fingers were having a sleepover, Jacob."

Crickets.

If she had just sprouted a lemon tree from her hat, Jacob's expression just then would have been absolutely what she had expected to see. Alas, there was no lemon tree there.

"I'm afraid I don't follow."

"Your fingers! One decided to sleep over into the other's finger slot."

More crickets from Grumpy.

"It's a classic little kid problem when small children start to learn how to wear gloves instead of mittens, and it's always so adorable to watch them sort out. It's easy entertainment for a solid ten minutes. And, well, watching a grown man having the same difficulty of, say, a three-year-old? That makes for a very enjoyable show. So thank you." The grin stretched across Sarah's face felt damn good.

Jacob's grip finally sorted out, he shoved his hands in the pockets of his overcoat and huffed out his frustration. He was clearly not amused. "Glad you found me good for a laugh, then."

Not wanting him to walk around with an embarrassed ego for too long, Sarah conceded, feeling a wee bit sorry that maybe her twentieth-century funnies didn't translate well at his expense. To offer amends, she sidled up to him and snaked her arm around his elbow.

Still staring straight ahead at the steps, she spoke just loud enough for his ears to pick up. "I find you good for several other things as well."

With that, she led him by the arm up into the hospital, his gait stumbling a bit in trying to keep up with her stride. The smirk on her face gave her the confidence she needed to move forward, even if she had no idea what the hell she would do once she got inside.

CHAPTER 20

Deja vu was an eerie feeling. Jacob had always portended it as a bad omen. So when he found himself in yet another patient room, holding up another hospital room wall, with Sarah on top of yet another examination table, he was over the routine. And he also learned something new about himself: He officially hated hospitals.

The door swung open after a soft knock, and Dr. Mendez walked in again, wearing the same standard-issue doctor attire they last saw him in. Jacob kept his eyes hyperfocused on the man, especially his hands. Under no circumstances would Jacob let the doctor touch Sarah again. No way, no how. Only problem? He hadn't exactly discussed this with Sarah.

"Hello, Miss Johansson." Ramon beamed at his patient, obviously relieved she wasn't still horizontal and vomiting into a waste bin between breaths. "It's good to see you again. How have you been feeling? I had not expected to see you for another three or four days. Is everything all right?" His words rushed out toward the end, clumping together on a rapid string of Latin R's made more prominent by his Puerto Rican accent.

Sarah nervously played with the collar of her blouse. When she had gotten dressed that morning, the green rash on her skin had spread a bit to just underneath her left collarbone. She had spent extra time arranging her attire to conceal her skin, but Jacob knew she was nervous about anything showing unexpectedly. God, how he wished they knew what they were fighting.

No, what *she* fought. And he would do well to remember he would get her back home at the end of this.

"I'm much better than before, thank you." Sarah crossed her ankles and swung her legs nervously, another sign that didn't sit well with Jacob. He began to read her tells, and yet what need did he have for deciphering her body language?

"Good, excellent. I won't lie, your previous episode took me a bit by surprise at the time...That's not to say I don't have the necessary skills to treat you, Miss Johansson. I assure you, I'm very capable..." The man started rambling a bit, more of that accent coming out, his nerves eating away at the tension in the room.

"Don't worry, Dr. Mendez. That thought never entered my mind." A kind smile from Sarah set the man at ease, despite the tense lines that pinched the corners of her mouth.

"Thank you, Miss Johansson." Ramon grabbed a nearby stool and planted himself on it while reaching for a handkerchief from his back pocket to wipe away the newly formed perspiration. Once finished, he returned the cloth and began making notes on a piece of paper in her chart. The fact that Sarah even had a chart at all aggravated Jacob. She shouldn't be in this room or this damn hospital. She should be in his cabin on Lake Roland, away from this doctor and all this nonsense, whether the man was kin or otherwise.

But *she* didn't think it was nonsense. He couldn't solve her problems by keeping her hidden from the world.

Her time here is short, so don't be a selfish bastard.

Jacob ground his molars as he paid attention to more of the conversation.

"Now, have you had any more nausea? Any episodes of vomiting? General unsettledness of the gut...?"

Another rap on the door echoed off the linoleum tiles, but this one was so soft Jacob had to strain to convince himself he'd heard anything at all. Seeing Ramon swivel toward the door and say, "Come in," confirmed his suspicions that, yes, another guest would apparently join them for this game of charades.

Tiny pale fingers gripped the edge of the door as it was pushed open. A young brunette woman with the largest blue eyes Jacob had ever seen inched around the door through its frame. Her hair was half pinned up behind her head, with the rest of it falling softly just past her shoulders. Jacob thought she couldn't have been more than eighteen or nineteen, but judging by the commodity-style frock she and every other non-medical female staffer wore throughout the building, he figured she must be a clerk or something.

"Sorry to intrude, Dr. Mendez, but Dr. Monroe wanted me to make sure you had your schedule for next week. Dr. Monroe will be away for the weekend, so he's just trying to get a jump on the rounds and assignments now." Her slender hands held out the stack of paper toward the doctor, noticeably keeping her eyes down so as not to appear intrusive to the patient's appointment.

"Oh, no intrusion at all, Miss Schneider. Thank you for bringing them to me." Ramon grabbed the opposite ends of the papers from where Miss Schneider gripped the stack. Once Ramon had them secure, Jacob waited for the woman to release the papers and leave so he and Sarah could figure out what the heck to do next, but she just kept standing there with her fingers glued to the doctor's assignments. It also wasn't lost on Jacob that the good doctor didn't seem all that eager to shoo her out of the room just yet. Obviously, these two had a connection.

How adorable.

"Miss Schneider?"

The sound of Sarah's voice took Jacob's eyes off the pair in front of him. The slight woman took her hand back and acknowledged Sarah for the first time. "Yes, miss?"

"Are you Miss Helen Schneider?"

The woman's eyes darted back to the doctor a moment before meeting Sarah's gaze again. "Yes, miss...Is there something I can get for you?" The uncertainty in her voice added to the apprehension in the air.

Jacob noticed Sarah's slack-jawed expression and tried to put the pieces together on his own. Sarah clearly knew this woman from somewhere. But Miss Schneider didn't wear a nurse's uniform or anything. And he doubted Sarah would remember the names of the staff in that short time she was a patient here, as out of it as she had been.

"Oh, no, that's okay. I'm fine. You, uh...you just look like someone I recognize, that's all. Her name was Helen as well, but clearly, you two are different Helens. Sorry." Sarah fiddled with the pleats in her skirt, giving her body an outlet through which to expend her nervous energy while her eyes and brain clearly took in more than they could process.

"Yes, well, it would seem so," Helen forced out, throwing one more glance in Ramon's direction. "If you have any questions about your schedule, Dr. Mendez, I'll be here for a few more hours."

"Yes, Miss Schneider, of course." Ramon stood from the stool in a rush, all too late recalling what basic manners he had, and opened the door wider to allow her to pass through more easily. A coy half-smile graced the corner of her mouth, and she left the room, with Ramon slowly shutting the door behind her.

"Apologies for the intrusion there," Ramon said as he resumed his seat. "Now, where were we? Oh, right. Miss Johansson, have you experienced any loss of appetite, tastes and smells being different than what you know to be true...?"

"Actually, doctor, I'm really feeling much better. I think rest away from the city did me a world of good," Sarah hurried out the words, jumping to her feet. "Honestly, I feel like a new woman. If there isn't anything else you need, I think I may be all set."

For added show, Sarah brought her hands to her stomach and gently rubbed her belly, making like she soothed her unborn babe. Jacob had no doubt that was what she intended to portray in her action, but to him, it looked absurd. She stroked her stomach in the same manner he'd seen town drunks scratch themselves after they've eaten too much and their hairy bellies were bloated with whiskey.

Lovely.

One thing was made clear about her action, though: His spitfire was an absolutely exhilarating—and terrible—liar. He could forgive the lack of talent at deception because, as Sarah did her best to talk them out of the rest of the appointment, a slight flush rose in the apples of her cheeks and a spark brightened her hazel eyes. The sight reminded Jacob of the last time he had seen those attributes on Sarah...when she writhed underneath him back at his cabin, the light from the fire the only thing offering her delicious body any sort of coverage from his roving eyes.

"Jacob, let's go!"

Shit. He missed what she had said, so lost in thought he was about that woman, but he noticed Ramon was no longer in the room with them...and that Jacob also had a very obvious erection to batten down.

"You, my dear," Jacob gritted out through clenched teeth as he tried to discreetly reposition his wooden soldier, "are an absolutely abysmal liar and I feel it is my duty to inform you lest you proceed through life thinking it a great skill of yours. Two Helens? Really? What was that nonsense about anyway?"

"Easy, Grumpy. You can make fun of me all you want later. I promise. But right now, I need to find Helen."

"Why? What's so special about her?"

When he hadn't heard an immediate answer, he quit looking down at his crotch and brought his head up. Sarah stood there, stoic as a statue. He knew this look, loved the hell out of this look, and braced himself.

Sarah shot her arm out toward the door, her index finger pointing at it as if that plank of wood were Exhibit A in a murder trial. "That is Helen Schneider. My great-grandmother. In two years, she will marry Ramon."

Jacob eyed the door as if it held the answers Sarah clearly sought. Answers he didn't understand, but that he would scour this hospital to help her find. "So, you wish to what? Have them marry sooner? It seems they are well on their way to that already without you meddling."

"No. In two years, Helen will marry Ramon. The year after that, Ramon will die. And I have to prevent that from happening."

"How? Jesus Christ, woman. You're even crazier than I am. Do you know that?"

"If I don't change the course of Ramon's fate, I...uh...I think I'm in trouble." After she got the final word out, Sarah grabbed the high-button collar of her blouse and undid the top two buttons to create some slack. Snaking her fingers into the collar, she pulled the left side down, and to Jacob's great horror, the green rash had begun to creep up her neck.

Sarah was right. Time was not on their side.

The examination room door clicked shut behind Sarah. She and Jacob quick-stepped it down the hall. She still couldn't believe her great-grandmother had waltzed into the room like Sarah was any other patient. Of course, to Helen, Sarah *would have been* any other patient. Doing the math quickly in her head, she figured Helen must have been only nineteen or so. The knowledge that Helen only had two and a half more years of happiness made her stomach as uneasy as if she had chugged curdled milk. Well, that and the fact that she would soon have to start using the same foundation color as Kermit the Frog.

They rounded the corner of the hallway and were spat out into the main entranceway of the hospital. Nurses and doctors in white coats and uniforms were flying across her field of vision, reminding Sarah of shooting stars cutting through the dark canvas of the night sky. Amid the sea of white, a hint of dark brown tresses caught the sunlight that peered in through the front entry windows. There Helen stood, facing the front doors and having a conversation with a much taller, physically intimidating man dressed in a khaki suit and matching wide-brimmed hat.

"There she is! I'm just going to..." Before Sarah could run up to Helen and say what she had no Earthly clue, her heels screeched against the tile floor and halted her in her tracks. There was some-thing about the man speaking with Helen that set off warning bells in Sarah's mind. The way he hid his hands in his pockets but leaned over toward Helen so intently. Leaning to the right, as if he could hear better out of his right ear.

"Shit. No, no, no."

"What's wrong?" Jacob scanned where her eyes were looking, and as soon as they landed on Helen's companion, he let out the same curse.

Standing inches apart from Helen, engaged in conversation, Dick Stevens towered over the girl, his hulking shoulders shrugging together and overshadowing the sweet clerk.

Fear and panic crippled Sarah in that moment. Her immediate reaction was to run. Turn right around and run out a back exit somewhere. Run to Jacob's car and leave the city. Run back home. But she'd never get home if she didn't get to Helen first.

Jacob's soft whispers landed in her ear. His warm hands embraced her shoulders from behind and wrapped her in safety. She never did tell Jacob what Dick had tried to do to her, but judging by the protective comfort he was throwing her way, she imagined he already may have sussed things out on his own.

"I've got you, love. He's not getting near you, and just remember that we are in a *very* public place. There is no safer establishment than a hospital, especially the front entryway of one. Let's stand out of sight for a moment. If he's here looking for you—and that bastard will have himself a fight on his hands, I swear to you—best not make it easy for him. Come."

Jacob ushered Sarah into an alcove that offered them some protection from view, but still allowed her to observe Helen and Dick together. Too bad she couldn't make out what they were saying. As she watched the conversation intently, terrible thoughts skidded through her mind about what their potential connection meant for Sarah's family.

God, was Sarah related to him in some sick way? Did he abuse Helen?

While her mind ran off the rails, Helen had a small box in her hands. It was hard to tell from the distance, but it looked like it contained medical supplies. She could make out the rolls of gauze and some darker colored vials, but really couldn't identify much. When Helen handed over the box to Dick, he removed his hat and accepted the box from her. Once the hat was off, Sarah could clearly see the damage to his eyes. He squinted down at the box, already having to hold it only two inches away from his eyes to assess what was in it. His peering and blinking were constant affairs, but from her distance, red scratches and bruising around his eyes were visible. A satisfied smile crept across her face at the memory.

She only wished she could have clawed them out altogether.

Box in hand, Dick brought his arm around Helen and gave her a quick hug before exiting out the main doors. Now *that* threw Sarah for a loop.

"What do you suppose that was all about?" Sarah wondered, her eyes tracking Helen as she walked across the main floor toward the front desk.

"I don't know, but my guess is they know each other already."

"Well, let's find out." Sarah broke out of the alcove and jetted across the main floor until she trailed behind Helen by three feet, making for a very effective shadow of the poor girl. "Miss Schneider?"

Helen whipped around and threw her hand over her chest. "Oh! Sorry, I was a bit startled. Miss Johansson, right? Are you well? Would you like me to get Dr. Mendez for you?"

"No, no, I'm just fine. I actually wanted to make sure *you* were all right. That man you were just speaking with, did he hurt you at all?"

"What? No! No. Why would you say that, miss?"

"I saw him put his arm around you. Um...I wasn't sure whether the gesture was wanted on your part, I guess."

"Miss, of course it was welcome. He's my brother."

CHAPTER 21

"Your brother?" Sarah croaked out when her voice finally decided to make itself known again.

"Yes, my brother. Well, half-brother, technically. My older half-brother. Same mother, you see. He knows I work here so he was just popping in for a few odd bandages and the like." Helen shrugged shyly, and when Sarah didn't say anything else, Helen's eyes darted around at the hospital workers making their rounds. The clicking of heels on hardwood provided the rhythmic percussion to the squeaky melodies of gurney wheels.

"Well, if you have no further need for me, I've got a few more tasks to do for Dr. Monroe." Helen made to leave and began to step around her human roadblock when Sarah abruptly laid her hand on Helen's forearm. Confused, Helen glanced back up. "Um, miss?"

"Has he ever done anything to you, Helen?" Sarah whispered her question, holding the woman's gaze. She needed Helen to take her seriously, and she had no qualms about preying on her tender sensibilities as a hospital worker. In Sarah's EMT days, health care workers were well versed in treating every patient's concern as if it were their own. As the pressure from her fingers gently increased, Sarah gambled the same was true in 1919 and that Helen's compassion for a pregnant woman would win out over hospital errands.

"No, ma'am. But I must say, you sound as if you've met his acquaintance before. Do you know my brother?"

"Yes, we've met before." And that was all Sarah would say on the subject. "But I'd like to talk to you about Dr. Mendez for a moment, if it's possible."

Helen's eyes darted back to the hallway they had all come from, the one that led to the patient exam room where she had left Dr. Mendez. A pale blush painted her complexion at Sarah's mention of the doctor's name.

"Of course. Is there anything you need me to give to him? A message?" Helen offered up eagerly.

After a moment's contemplation, Sarah asked, "Oh, no, no message." Stepping in a bit closer, Sarah steeled her spine and threw out her Hail Mary pass. "Actually, I have such a strong admiration for Dr. Mendez. He really has helped me immensely through my...um...pregnancy. And I couldn't help but notice the strong connection between the two of you. I wanted to know how long it's been since you've taken a liking to him."

"Miss Johansson! I assure you, I feel no such thing! Dr. Mendez is an amazing, talented, proficient..."

"...attractive, doting..."

"Brilliant doctor whom I respect greatly!" The flush in Helen's cheeks began to creep up the thermometer and the poor girl's hands were thrashing wildly about, inadvertently serving as road flares to pinpoint her own enthusiasm for the man.

"Helen—and you're welcome to call me Sarah, by the way—it's as clear as day how you admire him. It's also blatantly clear the man shares the same affection for you."

Helen shook her head. "I'm sorry, what? No, you must be mistaken. Dr. Mendez is not fond of me in that way, I assure you. I'm one of several clerks here, and he's Martinsville's rising star in gynecology."

"But you're the only clerk who Dr. Mendez has managed to fall over his feet trying to impress."

Sarah boldly embraced the poor girl's shaking hands with her own. It was clear she had thrown the blanket off something Helen wasn't prepared to address. But Sarah needed to speed things up, and getting these two on board the Love Train had to happen sooner than later.

"Helen, I've seen how he looks at you, how he was a different person with us in the exam room a moment before you entered. There's a spark there, I promise. And I have a few matchmaking successes under my belt." Jacob would no doubt yell at her for that little lie later. "Please, it would bring me great joy and comfort to facilitate a connection. I've never seen two people light up the way you two just did. Let it be my last good deed before my world gets turned upside down and I'm immersed in new motherhood."

"Um...oh, geez, I don't know what to say, really," Helen breathed out as she took back one of her hands and brought her palm up to cover her bangs.

Sarah stood there chewing the inside of her cheek, nerves of her own settling in the pit of her stomach. When Sarah couldn't take the silence anymore, Helen let out a long exhale and threw her shoulders back. The confidence was clearly not truly felt on her part, but it seemed Helen thought that was the appropriate look to adopt.

"Yes, I do admire Dr. Mendez...in *that* way," Helen leaned over and whispered to Sarah, the girl's eyes darting around the hospital room floor. "If you think he feels similarly, I would like to trust you in that regard."

The loud clap of Sarah's hands together startled the nurse passing by. Sarah threw out a quick apology and then grabbed Helen by the shoulders. "Yes, absolutely! Nothing would make me happier. Let me know what your typical work schedules are and we'll start there."

Sarah's beaming happiness was so great, she darted her head around toward where she had left Jacob to let him know steps were moving in the right direction. But instead of a smiling Jacob, he was leaning his hulking shoulder against the wall, the muscles of his biceps bunched up as his arms crossed over his chest in a standoffish manner. The stern look on his face, with the downward cast eyebrows and the grim line of his lips, told Sarah she'd have some convincing to do.

Apparently, Grumpy didn't trust her leap of faith.

Whatever Jacob just witnessed between Sarah and Miss Schneider, he was sure he didn't like it. He had agreed, reluctantly, to stay back after Dick left, but he wasn't happy with Sarah marching off on her own. The bastard had attacked her once, and if he had seen her again, who knew what Dick may have done? Under normal circumstances, Jacob would say Sarah had a lack of self-preservation, but he knew that not to be true as she was actively seeking out a way to save her life.

Or so he thought.

There was no plan discussed, no explanation of the next steps. Wherever Sarah's feet took her, that was where this caper wound up. Jacob, it seemed, was just tagging along for the ride, and, boy, did that not sit well. He was a farmer-turned-military man. Strategy and logistics were familiar to him. He had never been one to fly by the seat of his pants, even before the war. Whether it was his regiment missions or even managing the farm with Isaac and his family, intel was always shared for the benefit of all. Until now, it seemed.

"Why so grumpy, Grumpy?" Sarah practically skipped back from Helen, the pep in her step was so apparent. Her ear-to-ear smile was at odds with the bubbling skepticism brewing within Jacob.

"You know, I truly hate it when you call me that."

Sarah faltered at that remark, freezing in place. Her smile was erased as quickly as it arrived. "Where did this come from, now?"

"Tell me, what was so important about your conversation with Helen that you would not only willingly risk your life in the process with Dick roaming about, but do so without speaking to me first?"

"Excuse me, but I wasn't aware I had to run anything by you? And if you didn't notice, I'm on borrowed time here. Yes, I saw Dick and waited for him to leave before speaking with Helen. You said so yourself that he wouldn't do anything stupid in a public place like a hospital. Jesus, what's going on, Jacob?"

"Are we not partners here?" Jacob bellowed out the demand so suddenly, a few of the passersby stopped to look back at him. Gritting his teeth, he grabbed Sarah by the arm and escorted her out of the building, his grip on her bicep firm the entire time. If he had room for any other emotion besides rage and betrayal, he may have felt slightly guilty for the mark he no doubt left on her upper arm. Once they were down the stone steps and had crossed the busy street, he urged her into an alleyway where they would have more privacy.

Slightly out of breath, Sarah was finally able to dig her heels in. She spun and reeled at him. "Don't you *ever* strong-arm me again!"

"Answer me, Sarah. What was so goddamn important about talking to Helen that you couldn't wait half a fucking minute to clue me in as to what your plan was?" He was pissed, and the closer Sarah got to him, the farther away they were from the hospital, the more affected he was by the situation.

"I already told you. She and Ramon are going to get married in a few years. Shortly after, he'll die."

"Yes. Get to the point."

"I'm *trying!* Geez," Sarah yelled. She turned her back to him and rested her forearm against the red brick of the alleyway, her head peering down at the ground. After a moment, she did a one-eighty and faced him, determination and anger rising on her face. "Something you said in that examination room gave me an idea."

Jacob stared at her, and even though he was furious, he was sensible enough to appreciate Sarah's poise and tact when embroiled in a heated argument. Compared to her, he was a raging rocket with no feasible course other than to home in on a target and explode.

"When I found out Helen was my great-grandmother, you had jokingly asked whether I wanted them to marry sooner. Well, after I mulled it over for a minute, that idea kind of made a lot of sense to me. What if they *could* marry sooner?" Sarah brought her hands together in a fist and began wringing them out while pacing a small circle in front of Jacob.

"I never told you this, but my Aunt Marie once mentioned to me how it was always Ramon and Helen's intention to move back to Puerto Rico so he could practice gynecology there once he earned his medical degree here and got established as a physician. They never got to that point, unfortunately. He died here before they could go back."

Jacob's blood cooled a bit at the mention of Sarah's family. He had to remind himself of the reason she was here, or so she suspected. He empathized with her grief and recognized the cad-like behavior he exhibited, but that didn't alter the hurt he felt. It only tamped down his outward portrayal of it.

"When I saw how Ramon and Helen looked at each other, it was clear to anyone with eyes that there was a spark there. So I thought, 'What if I could force along that spark? Speed things up a bit?' If I could, maybe that would be enough to speed up the timeline of things and get them to move back to Puerto Rico sooner. If they left earlier…"

"Then you thought Ramon might avoid catching typhoid fever because he would already be out of Baltimore by the time he would have been exposed here," Jacob finished for her, finally unraveling the thread of her scheme.

Sarah stopped her pacing and turned her shoulders to face him, her chin still dipping down toward the patches of ice on the ground. "Yes," she forced out on a whisper. Her gaze never met his.

"Christ! Then why didn't you *tell* me that in the first place? I thought we were a team."

At that, her head shot up. "We are, but I saw the opportunity and I just had to grab it. There was too much at stake for me. Sorry if there wasn't time to form a committee on the subject," she retorted with a hand on her hip.

"And did you not think I had anything at stake either?"

"You're not dying." The coldness of her words lashed through him like an ice shard.

"You don't know you're dying, dammit! And how do you even know what I feel if you don't include me in your journey? Have I not shown you trust? Loyalty? What else must I do to convince you that I'm prepared to be by your side in this?"

"That doesn't have anything to do with it. I respect you greatly and truly appreciate your help."

The panic rose in Jacob again. She talked of him as if he were a hotel bellman who fetched her bags and retrieved her messages. Did she really not know how much he loved her? He would cut down the greatest obstacle in the world if it stood in her way. Even, apparently, if that obstacle was himself.

"When this is all over, though, we both know it's most likely a dead-end road for us." Sarah fumbled over her words, wounding him with haphazard strikes of a blade instead of precision thrusts. The damage, nonetheless, was still quite effective.

"No, we both don't know that. But, clearly, you do." He marched closer to her and dropped his voice lower. "I am no expert in time travel, but I damn well know loyalty. Since the moment you wandered into my life, I have been loyal to you, even in spite of common sense. I don't know why your skin is turning green, I don't know how to stop it, but I trust you. I would have trusted you to do whatever you thought necessary to get back to where you need to be, even knowing that meant leaving me."

Sarah stared at Jacob, as it was now his turn to pace. Grabbing a chunk of hair on the top of his head, he fisted his fingers into his scalp and breathed out a curse before turning back to her.

"I love you. I told you this back at the cabin, and I'll tell it to you again now, even knowing it's not reciprocated. I love you. And I'm the greater fool for it. I have happily clothed you, fed you, and cared for you to the best of my ability, and would eagerly do so again. You brought me to life when all I had known for the last few years was death. I'm sure I would be dead like my family if you hadn't wandered in when you did." The scoff that chortled out of him made Sarah take a step back. "But one cannot pour from an empty cup. So I'll ask you one more time. Why are you shutting me out? What more do I need to do to prove to you that you are not alone in this? Christ, if you won't let me help, then what am I even doing here?"

Sarah stood there with her mouth agape, Jacob having finally said his piece. He needed to be heard, and God, he needed to be heard by *her.* So he waited for what she would say. Waited for any excuse, reaction, apology—not that he expected to hear any of that last bit. But nothing came. She just stood there, her eyes downcast at her boots, tears beginning to well up. And that right there gave him his answer. Though it clearly pained her, she would not waver.

With an exhausted sigh, he stepped closer to her and rested his hands on her slender shoulders. Still, she wouldn't budge.

Jacob slowly brought his lips down to her pale cheek and graced her cold skin with a light kiss. A farewell kiss, as it were.

"Goodbye then. Godspeed."

CHAPTER 22

S arah clenched her fists so tightly at her sides for so long, her nails began to eat into her palms. Fortunately for her, the skin on her extremities was so frozen, she could hardly feel the pain...at least, not the physical pain. Emotional pain, now that was a different story. It wasn't lost on her where she stood. The poetic justice of her coming full circle was laughably ironic.

She still couldn't believe the anger that came off Jacob in torrents. It reminded her of when she was a small child and had visited a water park with a wave pool. She was about five years old when she found herself alone in the pool and had been knocked down by one of the waves. The waves kept coming and pounded her down to the bottom of the pool. Trapped under the water, she hadn't been able to get her legs under her or her head above the water. The terror of being hit with wave after wave of angry water and her lungs never getting the opportunity for a full breath of oxygen was something her body would never forget. Ultimately, she had been pulled out by her mom, who hadn't been that far away, but the memory was there. And this time, there was no one to pull her out from under Jacob's ire.

The most hurtful thing of all was that he was absolutely correct. In all of it. Just like that, with a wave of his hand and a few harsh words, he took her measure. The result was a painful reminder of what she already knew: She was found wanting. But there was more to the circumstance than she had been willing to let on about.

Sarah steeled her spine and pumped her fists a bit, an effort to try and thaw the ice in her veins and bring warmth to her fingertips. The tears, which had been threatening to fall during Jacob's entire tirade, finally overpowered Sarah's will and tumbled down her cheeks like boulders careening down a rocky ledge. She glanced down at the crash site, her tears freezing on contact as soon as they touched the frozen surface of the icy puddle. Not even a satisfying ripple of rings in water. No, the symptoms of her anguish were just swallowed up and absorbed into nothingness like they never existed. Even her tears wouldn't waste their time with her.

The overcoat she wore did little to keep out the chill, but she was grateful for it. Grateful for the extra layer of warmth, even if it was only just a surface bandage. It managed to hide the tremors she had been experiencing as of late.

Sarah huddled the coat around her and began the slow trek back to the hospital. The show must go on and all that. She had never told Jacob, but in the last twenty-four hours, new symptoms had begun to show up. She first noticed them while holding a cup of hot tea back at the cabin. Her left hand, the one holding the handle of the mug, had begun to tremble slightly. At first, it just felt like her hand was on pins and needles and the flow of blood back into the extremity caused all sorts of c'mon-get-happy with her nerve endings. But when the trembling got more frequent and more noticeable (and always on her left side), she began to worry. It became a preoccupation to hide it from Jacob, and her long sleeves and overcoat seemed to conceal the tremors for the time being.

The weakness was another thing altogether. Gradually, over the last several hours, Sarah had begun to experience bouts of fatigue on her left side. It wasn't constant, but it actually got to a point where she wasn't entirely confident her left leg could support her weight reliably. She had been grateful for the car ride and the limited distance she had to traverse since arriving back in the city. When Jacob grabbed her arm and hurried her from the hospital, the fatigue took over and she nearly lost her footing. She let him think her imbalance was due to his manhandling.

The memory of their argument snapped Sarah back to her present predicament.

"God, what an asshole I am," she whispered to herself as she parked her frozen duffer on top of the waist-high retaining wall adjacent to the hospital's main entrance steps.

She was really beginning to hate those steps.

As the chill from the frigid stone began seeping through her coat, she bent down toward her waist and brought out the photo of Ramon she kept close by.

The picture was starting to show more of its age now. Pale creases slashed through Ramon's neck where Sarah had folded it so many times. The edges of the paper had begun to fray a bit more. This photo, like Sarah, had seen better days. For a woman who worked under intense deadlines for a living, she certainly wasn't responding well to the deadlines of her current situation. Then again, she reminded herself of the big interview she missed out on at her job before all this time travel mess. Of all the errors, the missed story opportunities. An intrepid medical reporter she was not.

As Sarah sat there, running her icy fingers along the worn edges of Ramon's photo, she thought of Jacob and tried to analyze the situation as objectively as possible. But was that even really possible when magic was involved? And this had to be magic, right? Because none of the standard rules seemed to apply, and for a woman who worked in such a data-driven world, not having the tangible to analyze turned a bad situation worse.

But with Jacob...God, could she mess things up any more?

Sarah brought her elbows to her knees and grabbed her hair with her fists, nearly crumpling Ramon's photo in the process. The tighter she squeezed her eyes closed, the more she foolishly hoped that would protect her from the repercussions of the last five minutes. Heck, the maneuver didn't work when she was five and her parents were fighting in the hallway. Why would it work now?

Jacob had been nothing but supportive and helpful since she'd crash-landed in his life. He'd literally clothed her, fed her, protected her.

Loved her.

It was the last one that really twisted the knife in her heart and was the true reason she didn't let on to him about the rest of her symptoms. This whole ordeal was temporary.

Originally, "temporary" to Sarah meant she would go back home; however, she began to feel that "temporary" actually meant she wouldn't come out of things alive and well. And she just couldn't do that to Jacob. The poor man had suffered more than most ever should. Even if she loved him back—Who was she kidding? She knew in her heart she absolutely did—she just couldn't bring him any more anguish. No, this last leg of the journey had to be done alone. She certainly wasn't worth his pity or frustration. His anger rang out crystal clear. Once again, she wasn't able to deliver on expectations.

She truly was back to square one.

CHAPTER 23

The salve Helen gave Dick had been an absolute godsend. After smearing the oily balm around his eyes, he relaxed onto the park bench a block down from the hospital and finally exhaled his first sigh of relief in days. The sharp stinging pain in his eyes slowly began to decrease, the medicine his sister supplied lessening the throbbing and irritation that had plagued him the last forty-eight hours.

His sight had slowly returned to him after that bitch's claws did their damage. Not that he blamed her for the counterattack, and in truth, he appreciated the fight. There hadn't been much to get his blood pumping like that in a while. But the regard was fleeting.

Dick leaned his head back over the bench so his chin pointed up toward the sky. He gently placed some clean gauze over his eyes, adding slight pressure to compress the salve farther into his skin and sockets. His eyes were so tender after the abuse they'd suffered, but nothing was permanent, thank God, unlike his hearing loss.

He wouldn't have minded the injury if Bellamy had gotten his ass burned as well. But, once again, the man was like a slippery fucking weasel.

He groaned. The salve burned but in a good way. No pain, no gain, and all that. Throwing the gauze to the ground, he just let his head lay there upside down as the blood slowly began to pool in his head, his eyes and skin tingling. Dick cracked his eyes open, his blurry vision finally sharpening up, though at a snail's pace.

From upside down, two young women walked down the main thoroughfare next to the park, elbows linked. One was a honeyed blond, the other a brunette, and both wore their hair mostly down, though one woman was significantly taller than the other. Dick squinted a bit and tilted his still-upside-down head to the side as the slight threads of recognition began to knit themselves together.

On a rush, he righted himself, and the speed of the change brought on dizziness so strong, he fell horizontal on the bench, the thud of the impact jarring his other dormant senses awake. He stayed that way while the world around him turned like a merry-go-round behind his closed eyes.

Once things began to settle, he sat up straight again and sought out the pair of women he had just seen. Significantly more lucid than a moment ago, he was able to confidently make out the form of his sister in her clerk uniform. Next to her, however, the much taller blond was no other than the feisty Miss Johansson he so earnestly wanted to thank for her lovely handiwork currently causing his eyes to incrementally swell shut again. But what were the two of them doing speaking to each other on the street? How did they know each other?

Dick rose off the bench and crept closer to a copse of trees lining the edge of the park directly across the street from where the two were congregating. They had paused their stroll in front of the local Methodist church's front steps. He couldn't imagine what they were talking about. One thing that did come to mind, however, was where Bellamy was in all this.

As much as Dick wanted to repay Miss Johansson for her bestowed *affections*, if he were being truly honest with himself, deep down, that reward would only be short-lived. And if the woman were somehow a friend to his sister, though he still couldn't figure out how, he wouldn't want to get his sister involved or hurt in any way. No, toying with women could be fun in the moment, but it wasn't a deep satisfaction. More often than not, he was just playing the role society expected of him in that regard.

Dick stood there for another minute, hidden behind a tree, though he was far enough away he felt confident they couldn't really see him. He hated lurking, hated the shadowy life he felt condemned to. When he was drafted into the Army, it was supposed to be his way out. His father had told him once there were only two options that would afford him the particular type of discipline he'd need to succeed in life: the Army or prison. He supposed the Army was the more socially appropriate option and had hoped to work his way up through the ranks.

Until he had been matched with Bellamy, the fucking boy wonder, in the same regiment. Compared to Dick, Bellamy shined like a bright copper penny while Dick stained like congealed engine grease. His commanding officers had never overlooked an opportunity to let Dick know how Bellamy had a faster time on this or a more strategic viewpoint of that. The comparisons were painful and relentless. Bellamy had shined so brightly, he burned everything around him to the ground, including Dick, incinerating any opportunity Dick had to rise again.

His eyes glazed over a bit as he was pulled back into that final offensive in France that started him down this path.

The tat-tat-tat *of German machine guns pierced through the quiet of the Argonne Forest. Dick tucked his head underneath his forearms as shells streaked overhead. The morning's dense fog inhibited his ability to see the enemy clearly, but the howls of oncoming fire were hard to ignore. Mud and mire erupted about twenty feet off to Dick's right. The adrenaline pumped so hard through his body, he couldn't be sure whether the tremors that wracked him were biological in nature or vibrations from the nearby tanks. He supposed it didn't make a difference.*

He and his regiment had been at this for nearly two months, having just seized the town of Ville-devant-Chaumont. There had been some rumblings among the men about the fighting letting up, that maybe this war would end soon. But all that talk of hope was beyond Dick's pay grade. He'd learned not to put stock in hope. Besides, his father had made it perfectly clear: Dodging shells of mustard gas was the best thing a man like Dick could do for God and country.

Through the din of the machine gun onslaught, shouts of soldiers behind him took Dick out of his unpleasant trip down memory lane. When he craned his neck around to see what the commotion was about, he saw Bellamy running through the incoming fire, dodging bullets as he ducked behind a barrier erected near where their brigadier general was situated.

The sight of Bellamy was a welcome vision. His fellow runner had been sent off on a mission a few days ago, and one never knew if or when they'd be back. Both he and Bellamy were the only runners in their regiment, and so far they'd both managed to keep their hearts beating. Not much of a consolation, but hey, he'd take his wins where he could get them.

Bellamy shouted something at their CO, but they were too far back for Dick to make out the words. He squinted into the fog at the pair, hoping his curiosity would magically give him the ability to read lips from dozens of yards away. No such luck.

Off to his right, a nearby unsuspecting oak tree became a riddled target for the wonderful artillery that was no doubt meant for Dick's thick head. The face of the mighty oak's trunk began to peel away under the onslaught, pieces chipping off in all directions, abandoning a sinking ship.

Christ, where was the damn fire coming from? The pea soup fog was so thick he could hardly make out his hands in front of him. If he could take out the German fuckers with the machine guns, Dick would be able to breathe easy for a damn moment. Maybe even take the long-overdue piss behind that blasted tree, which had been more at the forefront of his mind than saving his own hide. Priorities and all.

Another shell streaked across the sky when he thought he heard his name echoing behind him.

"Dick! Dick!"

Bellamy crouched in a low run trying to get to him, pausing in his trek to take occasional cover behind a tree. What the nut was doing, Dick had no idea. But the two of them had long accepted their roles of running into oncoming fire as just another day that ended in Y.

Dick looked back at Bellamy as the man's head peeked out from behind the tree. His mouth was open in a shout, but again, Dick's lipreading skill was paltry.

167

"Dick!...fighting...more gunfire!"

A new barrage of bullets laid waste to the patch of forest between the two. Every other word the man said got lost in the explosions. Dick could barely make out Bellamy's face as the smoke from the shells mixed with the fog to form a noxious cloud on the ground.

"Fighting...gunfire, Dick!" Bellamy pointed in front of Dick toward where the machine gun shells were coming from.

He swung his head around to the left in relation to the tree line. He couldn't see it. Couldn't see anything, dammit.

Bellamy waved his hands over his head and continued pointing toward that area. None of the man's words were reaching Dick, the explosions around them were so great.

Looking back at the trees, he tried to figure out what the hell Bellamy was getting at. Could the man see something Dick couldn't? Thinking quickly, Dick grabbed for his field glasses—his one and only parting gift from his schmuck of a father—and peered into the fog toward the area Bellamy indicated.

Nothing. Fucking nothing. But...wait. There. He could vaguely see the outline of a German helmet. He found it! The damn machine gun nest.

"Dick!...gunfire!"

Bellamy's broken words were barely reaching him, but he got the gist: Take out the gunfire. It was madness to attempt on one's own, and Bellamy knew that. What was Bellamy thinking? But then again, the man never did anything without thorough analysis. There were never any unexamined angles. Christ, the man was so anal Dick had a hard time believing Bellamy would even take a piss without first triangulating the best wind direction for the stream. He must have known something Dick didn't, then. Fuck.

With a final nod at Bellamy, Dick got down on his stomach, hooked his bayonet over his shoulder and into both hands, and Army crawled his way through the muck toward the cell. He managed to make it a dozen or so yards before a shell landed on the ground to his left, mere feet from his head. The blast exploded in his ear and threw him onto his back, knocking the wind from his lungs. Shrapnel rained down on his skin, but it was the left side of his face that burned. As blood seeped into his eyes and mouth, screams rose up out of his throat like an inferno, but the sound never reached his ears.

Nothing. He heard nothing on his left side. On his right side, the faint muffles of men registered from a great distance, but they were overpowered by a constant ringing in his working ear.

Dick closed his eyes and tried to focus on breathing, which proved to be a monumental task. The last thought Dick had as he drifted into unconsciousness was how Bellamy had urged him into the hellfire on his own.

He vividly recalled the vow he made to himself on the battlefield in that moment: If his heart were still ticking on the other side of this, he'd be sure to return the favor to Bellamy.

Dick slammed his back against the trunk of the tree as realization finally dawned on him. He wasted his time with the woman. Wasted his time with the drunks. He would never be able to move on until Bellamy was done and dusted.

A plan was finally forming. He must go to the source. Take out the infection before it could spread further.

Another trip to Lake Roland was in order.

CHAPTER 24

The sun was setting over Lake Roland when Jacob pulled his Chevrolet onto his family's property, the pebbles crunching under the tires an announcement to no one that he had arrived. As if he needed the reminder that he was utterly alone on his family's land. He didn't think there would ever be a time when he'd be able to think of the land as his own, even though he was the only surviving Bellamy to lay claim to it. He didn't think he could lay claim to much anymore, if he were being honest with himself.

Unhinging his gloved fingers from the steering wheel, he hauled his hulking body out of the driver's compartment and launched himself over the edge of the door. He found the added exertion good for his bones, good for his mind. The drive back from the city was way too much time for him to be in such a small, confined space where he was alone with his thoughts with no hope of escape.

He jogged up the short path to the front porch and took the two steps in one leap. The last time he'd come to his childhood home, he'd been so enthusiastic at showing Sarah his family's estate, he stupidly ran ahead of her and left her outside to approach the property alone. Not the most chivalrous of acts, true, but he'd been so eager to share this space with her, share with her glimpses of the life he had before the war. Before everything.

Jacob shut out the cold behind him and stomped into the living room over toward the hearth. He barely had time to squat down before he realized he hadn't yet taken off his boots. His mother, God rest her soul, would be appalled at his manners. Jacob chuckled silently to himself at the memory of his mother's knack for scolding.

In truth, the woman didn't have a mean bone in her body, so whenever she'd attempted to discipline or chastise him and his brother, even his father from time to time, the woman couldn't pull off the ardor. More often than not, he'd do what she wanted just to avoid the pained look on her face because she could never bring herself to really yell. The men of the house obliged her nagging to put their poor mother out of her misery.

After he got the hearth lit, he toed off his boots by the doorway and hung his coat on the adjacent coat rack, but his hand was frozen to the fabric. On the hook next to his coat was Sarah's oversized cardigan, the one he first saw her wearing when she muscled her way into his hospital room...and his heart.

The dark green of the fabric started to catch the light from the blooming fire. Jacob moved his hand away from his own coat and gently brushed his fingertips down the length of one of the cardigan's sleeves. The yarn was so different from what he knew. Heck, everything about that woman was different from what he knew. Why couldn't he get this woman out of his head?

On a frustrated growl, he yanked the duster-length sweater off the hook and dragged it on the floor over to the kitchen, its fine threads sweeping up the grime and mud tracked in by Jacob's boots. With one hand, he reached up into the cabinet above the stove and pulled out his father's old bottle of whiskey. Without even reaching for a glass, he stomped back into the living room, bottle in fist, and sat in the rocking chair facing the flames.

He draped the cardigan across his lap while he uncorked the whiskey bottle. Jacob took four large gulps straight from the spout, dribbles of the amber liquid leaking out the corner of his mouth, before placing it on the floor by the chair. His fingers dangled over the edge of the rail and never strayed too far from his source of courage, like a master who habitually extended his hand out to a loyal canine to ensure the mutt was within reach.

As he waited for the burn to subside and the numbness to settle in, his mind zeroed in on the one thing he tried so hard to forget.

God, he felt like an utter fool. But it was more than that. His infatuation with Sarah had gotten into his head, gotten the better of him. He couldn't understand why she wouldn't trust him. Had he not shown her loyalty? Confidence that he would keep her secrets? He just couldn't get into her head to justify her reasoning. Even if she didn't reciprocate his feelings, why refuse the help?

"Sarah, what were you thinking, foolish woman?"

The flames danced across his vision as the lethargy finally started to creep into his bones. He grabbed the whiskey bottle and took three more swigs, determined to pass out in the chair and forget things altogether. But he doubted he'd be so lucky.

He looked down at the cardigan and ran his fingertips along the edges of its front opening. The action reminded him of Isaac when his younger brother was about three or so. Mother had sewn him a special blanket and the poor boy refused to go to sleep until he ran his tiny fingers along the edges of the entire cloth. When their father would ask him what on Earth he was doing, Isaac always had the same remark: "I'm looking for the softest edge." Whether it was true or not, Jacob didn't know, but that line always bought Isaac an extra half hour or so of his family's time before he'd finally concede and go to sleep.

The pain of loss began to slither back up as he was assaulted by thoughts of his younger brother. Loss of his parents, loss of his brother. Loss of Sarah.

A wet spot formed on the back of Jacob's left hand. When he looked down, he was astonished to see that a teardrop had landed there...even more astonished that he was capable of crying.

Alone in his cabin, with no one to see, he supposed it was harmless. The tears wouldn't last long. He raised the whiskey to his lips once more and set the empty bottle down on the floor, where it rolled around in front of him on the unevenly pitched floor like an arrow directing his future.

He tilted his head back in the rocking chair, draping Sarah's sweater over his chest and tucking it in underneath his beard. It still smelled of her, like fresh rain mixed with a deeper verdant note, the perfume of her hair left lingering in the fibers and tickling his nose, tempting him.

How would she fare out in the city without him tonight? Where would she sleep? How would she look after herself?

He couldn't concern himself with that any longer. She'd made it perfectly clear she was fine on her own. But, damn, the rejection cut deep. The hurt, the emptiness. He couldn't believe he was back here again and feared the thoughts that would begin to creep into his mind if he let the pain of loss consume him wholly again. Hence the whiskey. If he could pass out from finding his solace in the bottom of a bottle, surely that would prevent him from traveling down roads that had landed him in Martinsville in the first place.

The last wisps of consciousness flitted through Jacob's mind, sleep finally pulling him under.

Would he let Sarah go?

Yes, he would.

His spitfire wasn't the only one who was capable of stubbornness to rival a goddess.

"Thank you for the meal, Helen," Sarah said as she lifted the linen napkin to her lips to knock off a crumb from the corner of her mouth, trying to hide the discomfort she felt at the pangs in her stomach.

"Oh, any time! It's the least I could do since..." Helen's voice dropped down to a low whisper as she leaned forward across her sandwich. "...since you offered to help me with Dr. Mendez."

The coyness of her expression struck home to Sarah that Helen was, in fact, a teenager. At nineteen, though she was very much a contributing member of Baltimore's workforce, she was still a girl, green about men, emotions, and the like. The innocence of it cracked a slight smile on Sarah's stern expression.

"Happy to help, like I said," Sarah reiterated as she laid the napkin next to her plate, her fingers hovering over the linen, not quite sure she was ready to place it down yet.

Helen understood Sarah's napkin placement as the universal sign for "I'm finished," but bent her brows down in concern. "You have not eaten much of your supper. Is everything all right?"

Sarah had taken a few nibbles out of her turkey club sandwich, but overall, her appetite wasn't there. The thought of putting anything else into her mouth and having to actually swallow the stuff made the bile slosh around in her stomach. She should be famished, absolutely ravenous. The last time she'd eaten anything had been with Jacob earlier that morning before they'd left the cabin. Their hurried meal of sardines and sweet biscuits seemed like a lifetime ago.

In truth, Sarah could hardly stomach much of anything lately, and hello, she had just eaten sardines for breakfast. Since then, it was all she could do to lift her glass of water to her lips without spilling it all over her plate or her own skirt for that matter, her tremors had become so bad.

The worst, though, was the fatigue. No longer coming in spurts, the lethargy was now constant and worsening. When she first sat down at the table in the small cafe with Helen, there was no graceful deceleration into her chair. Nope, her butt hit that cushion as if her overcoat was a twenty-pound weighted blanket. Her lungs felt like fireplace bellows that needed an external operator just to fully expand and take in some oxygen.

But she wouldn't worry Helen, despite how terrified she was. Geez, just swallowing her food was an Olympic sport. Her meal felt like it shot down her belly at seventy-five miles per hour. There was no resistance anywhere.

Sarah did her best to lean back in her chair and put on an "I'm fine, really" face. She squinted and shook her head quickly back and forth. She hoped it passed as a nonchalant "nothing to worry about," but she suspected she looked more like she just had gas. Lovely.

"I'm fine. It's...uh...the baby and all." That sounded believable, right? Oh, wait. Pregnant women were supposed to be voraciously hungry, weren't they?

"Oh, I completely understand. Believe me. I'm one of seven children, with two younger siblings. My youngest sister, Dorothy, is thirteen years younger than me. I remember when our mother was pregnant with her. Mother couldn't stand the smell of eggs for three whole months! We never saw her at breakfast during that time, and she'd only ever eat with the family herself when she was much further along with Dorothy. The cooking smells got to her, she'd say."

"Ha...yeah, well, I can relate, that's for sure." Sarah should have been focusing on Helen's words, should have been rehearsing in her head how she'd plan to ask Helen for a place to stay that evening, but that all floated out the door.

Breathe, Sarah. In through the nose...out through the mouth.

The air around the cafe felt stuffier, thicker, as if the whole place had been transformed into a hot yoga studio, and Sarah had to shell out the exertion for downward dog while choking back steaming exhaust fumes. Squeezing her eyes shut, she tried to make the pictures spinning behind the back of her eyes still their revolutions. No dice. What the hell was going on?

"Sarah? Are you all right?"

Helen's soprano voice registered faintly in the room, but the echo of her words wasn't quite right. She sounded like she was in a tunnel, the notes reverberating off the arced walls. Sarah slowly pried her eyes open to get her bearings, but that proved less than smart. Helen, or the dark blurry figure she assumed was Helen, hovered in front of her face. There were no discernable features, yet the blob-formerly-known-as-Helen wouldn't stay in one place. This was a damn merry-go-round of torture.

Sarah dropped her head down toward the table and stared at the linen, hoping a stationary target would be less of an affront. Nope, the tablecloth's brightness had no problem assaulting her vision. Too harsh, too much, the light reflecting off the cloth's brightness was like foil to a migraine sufferer.

A nagging feeling, one of several, tickled the back of her mind as the nausea crept higher. She had felt these symptoms before. The dizziness, disorientation, nausea, all of it. Bracing for impact, Sarah grabbed for the linen napkin that still rested under her hand and held the cloth to her mouth, damning what she knew would come up next.

Not five seconds later, stomach bile mixed with whatever Sarah had managed to choke down at dinner came roaring up with a vengeance, coating the napkin and cascading over her spread-wide fingers, landing in vile puddles on the plate.

Helen screamed and clamored out of her chair, knocking its four legs to the carpet. Voices were raised and footsteps on the carpet became louder, but Sarah couldn't pay attention. Her throat was on fire, and her body wouldn't respond to any commands. With no other recourse, she let the weight of her muscles take her over the edge of her seat. Her head and torso landed with a thud on the dark red carpet while her feet and legs still dangled off the chair's cushion. The impact jarred her teeth together, but offered a dulling to the pain in her stomach.

As spittle dribbled down her cheek and began to puddle on the carpet beneath her, the enormity of her situation came crashing down upon her.

She wasn't better off alone. She had flown too close to the sun, the blinding brightness finally making clear to her what should have been apparent all along.

She needed Jacob, and not just as an excuse to help her navigate her terrifying circumstances, but because she didn't recognize herself without him. Somehow, he had woven himself into the fibers of her tapestry. He was as comforting and necessary to her as the thoughts of her family back home, of the legacy she was so consumed to research.

Her eyes drifted closed as more blurry figures shuffled in and out in front of her, but she didn't pay them any mind. Her only thought was of Jacob and how, as she melted into a carpet of a cafe a hundred years before her time, she had lost her final opportunity to tell him she loved him.

CHAPTER 25

The light inside the cabin was barely visible through the small windows in front, but Dick knew he was in the right location going off Bellamy's Chevrolet parked at the end of the trail that led up to the property. Just looking at the automobile got his blood heated.

When the war ended—or, he should say, when his time in active duty had ended—his reintroduction to society had hardly included shiny Chevys and cozy cabins waiting for him. No, as soon as he landed state-side again, he'd had to relearn how to walk without falling over like a baby fawn on shaky, spindly legs. The shell blast had been so close, his left eardrum was ruptured and the bones inside damaged. For weeks after, his equilibrium was shot. And the father who had been so eager to ship him off to Uncle Sam? Dick had learned his old man's apartment had been vacated with no forwarding address. And the mother who'd cast him off in favor of a newer, shinier family? Well, he refused to darken her door with his burden.

Dick stood up off the fallen tree trunk he had been resting on and pressed his hands to his lower back, stretching out the lower vertebrae, his spine cracking as he twisted left then right. The walk from town hadn't been long, about fifteen minutes or so, especially given that Dick still had light to make his trek by. He had been sitting on the log for about two hours, waiting for the cover of darkness to fully descend over the area. Even though the property was remote enough that he didn't really have a concern for bystanders coming upon them, he wasn't up for leaving a chance that someone may see them in the dwindling daylight.

He looked down at his watch and noted the hour was half past eight. "Right. Time to get organized."

It was still freezing outside, the nearby lake having developed more than a skim coat of ice on the top. Dick squinted over at the lake to make sure he had his bearings. The moon's reflection off the ice's surface was dull and muted, not crisp and shiny like if the ice were deeper and thicker. That told him the surface of the water could be broken, but not lightly. That would work. Big splashes weren't his thing, despite his occasional penchant for dramatic flair.

―――――

A soft tap-tap-tap echoed in Jacob's mind, knocking around in his skull like an old copper penny inside an empty coffee can. He couldn't place the noise and honestly didn't care to. He preferred the numbed state of indifference to anything involving concern. He was fresh out of concern, thank you very much.

The rapping sounded again, this time registering as knuckles on hardwood. That much he could figure out. It was the why that had him stumped. What would be so important to make him actually care whether the persistent noise stopped or not?

Another knock.

Sarah.

The thought slammed into his whiskey-laden mind a second too late. She had come back! Of course she had. Where else would she have gone? Like an arrow hurling out of its bow, Jacob flung himself from the rocking chair, tripped over the empty whiskey bottle, and— with all the grace of a humpback whale—landed chin-down on the bearskin rug.

The jarring bite of his tongue didn't faze him as he scrambled to his feet, his hands running through his disheveled hair, as if a quick finger comb through would convince Sarah that, nope, he hadn't been knee-deep in whiskey and depression and he was still an overall upstanding presentable guy.

Jacob took three more strides toward the front door, his palms sweating at the thought of seeing Sarah again. Christ, he missed her, missed who he was with her. This sloppy shell was not him. But they needed to have an earnest conversation. He would be upfront and honest with her and demand she be the same with him. Whatever her hang-ups, they could work through it.

He rubbed his palms down the thighs of his pants a few times and shook out his hands by his head, hoping to stem the tide of nervous perspiration that seemed insistent to flow. On one final exhale, he grabbed the doorknob and yanked open the door wide.

"Sarah—"

"Not quite."

The deep resonance of a male's voice snapped Jacob out of his drunken stupor. He knew that voice, but why was he having trouble placing it? Willing his vision to clear, he squinted into the darkness and tried to make out the form of whoever stood in front of him. The outline of the man's broad shoulders filled out the doorway entirely. He was comparable to Jacob's size, though his hair was cropped much shorter. He wore a long wool trench coat, the top of which dusted his boots. When Jacob brought his eyes back up to his visitor's face, he noticed the man angled his head so his right ear was closer to Jacob.

"Stevens? Is that you?"

The moonlight behind Dick flickered briefly as the man moved so quickly, he became a blur of shadow. On the next instant, Jacob's jaw met with a force so strong, his head whipped around and spun him like a top. He tumbled to the floor in a heap. The slow, heavy footfall of trench boots crossed the doorway into Jacob's cabin and stepped over his stunned body.

"Thought I'd pay you a little visit, repay you for all of your kindness." The last word dripped with disdain.

Pain laced through Jacob's scalp as Dick's meaty fingers grabbed hold of Jacob's hair and pulled him to his knees. Jacob grabbed onto Dick's fists and tried to pry his fingers open, but his strength wasn't where it should be. The damn whiskey hindered his reflexes.

As Dick fisted more hair, he settled down on one knee in front of Jacob. The light from the dying fire was just enough to illuminate the red splotches and puffiness all around Dick's eyes, the deep gouges in his skin, and the whites of his eyes painted with red, blown blood vessels. All he was missing were the horns and pitchfork and he'd make a compelling fill in for Satan.

One side of Dick's lips raised in a sneer while the bastard's fist turned and tightened even more. "Were we really that different?" Dick said on a whisper, his head cocked to the side.

"Fine!" Jacob spat out. "You want to end this? Let's end this!"

Jacob's right leg was in perfect alignment for a swift assault on Dick's crotch, his knee serving as a battering ram for the bastard's not-so-privates. Dick growled out in pain and immediately released Jacob's hair, clutched himself for a moment of self-preservation, and sneered daggers at Jacob.

"So that's how we'll play this, then?" he said through gritted teeth.

"I'll play it any way I need to, Stevens. You're on my property now, my home."

A slight chuckle left Dick's throat as he began to even out his breathing, gearing up for the next round. "Did you also use that line on the lovely Miss Johansson? Funny. I thought you two would be together, but when I saw her by herself outside Martinsville, well...true colors and all that. She couldn't stand the ego, I gather."

The burn of the whiskey began to fade, and in its wake, Jacob rose out of the ashes. As he gained his footing, he anchored his legs, one in front and one in back. Crouching low, he lunged for Dick's midsec-tion, running the man backward and out the door like a gale-force wind pummeling a barn.

The men burst through onto the porch, with Jacob landing on top of Dick. A simultaneous grunt escaped them as the shock of meeting the floor cut short their descent. Jacob threw a punch before Dick registered his surroundings, the man's head whipping sharply into the wooden floorboards. Blood sprayed across Jacob's white linen shirt as he intended to continue his assault. He pulled back his right arm, fingers clenched tightly in a fist, and prepared to let it fly.

Jacob cried out as burning pain sliced across his back. The fire extended from his left shoulder down to his right hip. He gritted his teeth as Dick slowly brought the nine-inch trench blade into Jacob's blurry field of vision. Blood trickled down the steel blade and pooled in the cracks between the brass knuckle guard and Dick's skin.

"Should have come prepared, Bellamy," Dick barked out. "Now, up we go."

Dick hurled Jacob around and grabbed him by the throat, the tip of the blade pressed into the side of his neck. His back was pressed up against Dick. The rough wool of the man's overcoat served as a painful abrasive to his exposed gashes. He fought for balance as Dick dragged him back down the porch steps and out toward the front of the property.

"You see, Bellamy," Dick hocked a blood-filled loogie off to the side as he shimmied his jaw back and forth, "in spite of all those accolades our respectable COs threw your way, you're a terrible soldier. Whatever happened to knowing your landscape?"

Jacob winced as the knife's tip made a shallow slice into his skin. He felt every drop of blood well up, every trickle moving about as the heated liquid met the frozen night's air.

Dick finally slowed his progress, halting Jacob's march in front of the property's old well. Jacob's back was slammed into the retaining wall. He stifled a scream through gritted teeth. Stars danced on his vision's periphery. The stone wall's coarse edges abraded against his bleeding back.

"Why, Stevens? Why have you hated me all this time, even after I saved your fucking life in France?" Jacob spat into Dick's face.

"Liar!" With his knife to Jacob's throat, Dick reached behind Jacob to grab the rope from the pulley and yanked it around Jacob's throat. One solid pull of the rope made Jacob cough and sputter, his air supply diminishing under his windpipe's compression.

Dick leaned closer to Jacob's chest as he was bent back over the retaining wall. "You tried to kill me, remember?" he growled out. "Told me to run into the gunfire. Sound familiar?"

Confused, Jacob tried to breathe under Dick's onslaught. "What?" he rasped. "No. Dammit, I screamed at you to *stop* the fighting. *No more gunfire!* The war was officially ending." A diminished cough bubbled up in Jacob's throat, but he needed to press on. "I had just gotten word from the front that they signed the armistice."

Color began to drain from Dick's face. "Bullshit!" He made to pull the rope tighter, but uneasiness and doubt crept into the action.

"Listen, dammit! The war was ending at eleven a.m. I tried to tell you to stop fighting." Jacob tightened his grasp on the knife at his throat. "A ceasefire was to be called in ten more minutes. Then we would have been home free. *That's* what I tried to tell you."

Hatred was a funny thing. As the dizziness threatened to overtake Jacob's equilibrium, he started to reflect on Stevens' hatred for him. Hatred in general, actually. Did Jacob hate his time in the service, fighting for the Allied troops? He supposed he was mostly indifferent to it all. Motions he had to go through, bullets he had to dodge. He had been a very numb character emotionally, but the rules and orders he appreciated, the drive, the adrenaline. He certainly didn't care about any assassination of an archduke in a European country. And territoriality was not anything he felt strongly toward. The loss of his parents and brother—now, *that* he hated.

Dick, on the other hand, was a different story. Did Jacob truly have hatred toward him? No, not in the same black-hearted, eat-you-alive sense that Dick had been experiencing. The man was arrogant, to be sure. Headstrong, most likely to shoot off at the mouth. Their COs were always trying to get him to work smarter, not harder. He was a brute, a womanizer, and would have won the award for most likely to waste away behind iron bars in a penitentiary, but did Jacob hate him? No, he didn't. In truth, Dick was just another blip on Jacob's radar, another crop in the field to check in on because the well-being of one contributed to the well-being of all.

Jacob stared up at the man who held a blade to his throat and the noose around his neck. This man was content to be labeled an executioner—insisting on the role, even. But the hesitation in Dick's eyes was just the crack in the strong man's facade that Jacob needed.

"I had just returned back from the front in the north of Paris with word that an armistice had been reached," Jacob recalled. As he spoke, the rope around his throat eased up slightly, but not enough to allow for an escape. Still, it was encouraging. He pressed on.

"The Germans wanted to halt the fighting immediately, but the Allied commander wanted to press on until the end as a final show of strength or something, I didn't know the precise reason."

Despite the frigid cold, sweat began to bead on Dick's forehead, his brow furrowing at Jacob's words.

"Our regiment was told to keep fighting until the armistice officially took effect at eleven a.m. Christ, I ran all morning to make it back to our location with the news. When I got to the brigadier general and told him what was decided, he determined it wasn't worth our lives to press on for the final ten minutes of the war. It was finally ending, dammit!"

Jacob took a large swallow of cold air and tried to muster up enough saliva to coat his arid throat. The rope's rough, frayed fibers scratched his Adam's apple as it bobbed up and down.

"When I saw you clutching your rifle and scanning the perimeter for that machine gun cell, knowing we just had to bide our time for a few more minutes and it would all be over, I couldn't let you kill yourself. I tried calling out to you, to tell you to stop the fighting, to end the gunfire. When you looked back at me and nodded your head, I thought you heard me. Thought you knew what I said."

Dick's hold on the knife began to loosen. His hand began to tremble, and the tip of the blade inched a bit farther away from his neck.

"But you ran into the damn hellfire. You hadn't heard a word I said."

Dick leaned down over Jacob, his eyebrows creased in confusion and his gaze set on something on the ground. He had a far-away expression on his face, as if he weren't really present in his own body. On a slight nod so subtle Jacob almost missed it, Dick turned his eyes back toward Jacob and licked his dry lips. Jacob's stomach bottomed out at the malice that reappeared in his old comrade's eyes.

"Bull. Fucking. Shit," Dick ground out through his clenched jaw.

Without letting up on the rope, Dick dropped down to where he had been staring at the ground. He dropped his trench knife and resurfaced with a large rock he managed to awkwardly grip in one hand. Before Jacob could draw the connection, Dick let the rock tumble into the bucket hanging from the rope attached to the well's pulley...and Jacob's neck.

The rope immediately pulled taut around Jacob's throat, his air supply completely cut off as he was jerked back against the wall. At the other end of the rope, the weighted bucket descended down into the two-hundred-foot well.

CHAPTER 26

Muffled voices began to trickle into Sarah's consciousness. The long O's and short A's of words stood out in relief as they were accented with the sharp T's and S's. The rough consonants pricked at her brain, like little acupuncture needles intent on stimulating her nerves and muscles.

Where was she? The firm, slightly lumpy surface beneath her felt familiar. She was prone on her back; that much she could ascertain. But when she tried to lift her fingers or open her eyelids, it was as if she slogged through quicksand. The more she tried, the heavier things sank down.

A soft soprano voice floated across Sarah's ears, enticing her with a hint of recognition. She knew that voice. Wasn't she just having a conversation with that voice not too long ago? Again, she tried to pry her eyelids open. No use. Her lungs were sluggish. She couldn't even draw a large enough breath to exhale her frustration.

She mentally scanned her body again and assessed that all systems were online, even if they weren't necessarily functioning at the moment. Yes, she still had all ten fingers and toes, thank goodness. No phantom limb pain she could detect. Heck, the slight weight of her hair still tickled her shoulders.

Good. At least she could check off those inventory items.

"...only next of kin noted in the chart is a Corporal Jacob Bellamy..."

Wait, that name. That voice. Jacob!

The well of memories came rushing back to her in an onslaught of images. Ramon's spark of connection to Helen in Sarah's exam room, Sarah convincing Helen to let her play matchmaker, Jacob being furious at Sarah and leaving her.

Ah, that last one rang Sarah's bell the loudest.

She winced internally as she recalled his anger, how his ire literally bristled off him like a porcupine extending its spikes. The hurtful things that had been said on both sides.

But what hurt most of all? The anguish on Jacob's face when Sarah's words landed. As long as she lived, she'd never forget the pained and dejected eyes set in the face that had given her the greatest comfort and longing. His lips had been closed tightly, no doubt to spare her more of the vitriol she deserved, the slight crow's feet at the corners of his eyes showing the only cracks of tension in his battle armor.

Armor she had forced him to wear. Shit. She'd messed this one up royally.

"What's Corporal Bellamy's number? Ah, here it is. Marie, can you ring him?"

Helen. That was definitely Helen's voice. Sarah tried to sit up, move her neck, heck, even wiggle her big toe, but nothing came online. This was so frustrating! And a wee bit unnerving. She was just about to try screaming bloody murder when her stomach cramped up so tight, she almost thought she'd ruptured something. A second or two later, the muscles relaxed on their own and a rumble to rival an avalanche off the Rocky Mountains bubbled up out of Sarah's stomach.

Thank God she wasn't mobile. How mortifying! But apparently, the girl could eat.

While Sarah played the human anatomy version of Name That Tune, the door creaked open and the deep timbre of an accented man's voice floated through her ears.

"Oh, my apologies, Miss Schneider! I didn't expect you to still be here."

"That's quite all right, Dr. Mendez. I was just locating Miss Johansson's emergency contact in her file. Marie went on to get in touch with him."

Ramon! Of course!

An awkward silence stretched on for a bit and then Sarah realized she was inadvertently eavesdropping on a rather prime opportunity for Helen and Ramon to get to know each other. A better fly on the wall one could not find.

"How late are you working tonight, Miss Schneider? I thought your shift would have ended at five p.m." A scuffing sound against a wall broke through the silence. Sarah imagined the toe of Ramon's well-polished black loafer streaking black smudges along the white wall in an effort to seem engaged in a room with a whole lot o' nada going on.

Sarah could practically feel the weight of his nervousness in the room. She was surprised at first, but then recalled how young these two were. Ramon was only twenty-three and Helen nineteen, after all.

"It did. But, well, Miss Johansson and I had taken to chatting after her earlier appointment. Turns out, we actually have a lot in common. We had walked down the street to go to Charlie's Cafe for some supper. While we were eating, that was when she had her, um, episode."

Episode? Ah, yes. It all came back to Sarah in gruesome detail. The starkest memory of all was how she wished she had been able to see Jacob again. A deep sob caught in Sarah's chest, held prisoner by her comatose body.

God, she missed him.

"Do you think her baby's all right?" Helen's voice hitched slightly at the prospect of Sarah losing her unborn child.

Oh, right. She was supposed to be pregnant.

More silence.

"Oh, the baby is fine, to be sure. Hyperemesis gravidarum can be excruciating to witness from the reports I've studied, but it will pass.

She just needs to pull through the first trimester and then things will begin to normalize."

"That is certainly good news."

"Yes." Another beat of silence, and then Ramon cleared his throat. "Miss Schneider, may I speak frankly for a moment?"

Sarah could sense the trepidation in Helen's lack of immediate response, but she was dying to look at her face and discern her reactions for real. Not being able to move or open her eyes was such an impediment.

"Yes. And you're welcome to call me Helen. That is, if you'd like to. You, uh, certainly don't have to," Helen quietly responded, uncertainty lacing her words.

A long deep breath was let out on a slow exhale. Sarah figured it was Ramon doing the brace-yourself breathing.

"Helen, first, thank you for your assistance with Miss Johansson. It is always a great pleasure when I get to work with you."

"Of course, Dr. Mendez. I feel similarly."

"Ramon, please. I insist."

"Very well, then. Ramon."

Sarah could make out papers rustling, folders being leafed through and restacked. Distractions for idle hands, in other words.

"I would like to add that I also find it a great pleasure when I happen to pass you in the hall on your way to Dr. Monroe's study. Or when I routinely see you visit Marie at the front desk on her break."

Now this began to get interesting. Was he really going to tell her how he felt? Right now?

"Many times, I have indulged in the pleasure of silently contemplating you, hoping for a glance or a smile to come my way."

"Oh," she said on a whispered giggle.

"To be clear, I admire you greatly and am in awe of how you manage Dr. Monroe's tasks, the manner in which you carry yourself among colleagues, how you interact with patients…"

"Thank you, Ramon. I am very flattered to hear that. Truthfully, um, I have often noticed you as well."

Yes! Sarah could only imagine the deep blush that crept up Helen's cheeks right about now. The girl was so timid, Sarah couldn't honestly believe what she heard.

"Really? Oh, well, that is very good to hear."

The legs of a chair quickly scraped along the hard floor. Sarah imagined Ramon rising in haste to get to the meat of the conversation, the eager beaver.

"I had debated for some time about approaching you, but out of respect for propriety and formality, I had resisted. But now, well, all I can think of is that old adage: Fortune favors the brave," Ramon rushed out on a chuckle. "I guess what I'm trying to say is, would you like to attend one of the theaters in the city with me?"

Oh, man, he did it! If Sarah could pump her fist in the air in celebration, she totally would. After a few silent moments—and, really, Sarah could have sworn she'd heard crickets in that exam room—she held her breath for Helen's response, but Sarah wasn't concerned. The money was in the bag. This was finally the key to her ticket out of here. She could feel it. Her plan had worked.

She heard Helen inhale slightly in preparation for her response. Sarah's own stomach did the butterfly thing along with Helen's, she was sure.

And then the bottom of her victory cup fell out.

"I'm afraid I must decline."

The weather-worn pulley rattled fiercely as the heavy bucket plunged toward the bottom of the well. Teeth clenched, Jacob braced his right foot against the bottom of the well's stone retaining wall as the rope burned his skin, air no longer coming freely.

He'd be damned if he went out like this.

His right foot against the wall became his anchor. Power pumped through his thighs as he counterbalanced the weighted bucket. Strained tendons along his neck rubbed against the rope. His lower back was crushed against the edge of the well. He clenched Dick's shirt sleeves in his fists. Using the man's forward momentum to his advantage, Jacob pushed off the wall. A drop of his left shoulder and a quick duck to the side robbed Dick of his support.

A loud tearing sounded from the pulley over Jacob's head. The rope's fibers split and frayed, its tight coil unraveling. The relief around his neck was instantaneous. As his lungs filled with air, Jacob whipped his right shoulder around. The impact hit Dick square in the upper back. The blow robbed the man of his balance. His bulkier top half fell too far forward over the well. At once, the soles of his boots went airborne. Jacob took advantage. He snatched hold of Dick's ankles, lifted them up like the handles of a wheelbarrow, and let go. Dick slid, headfirst, along the edge of the wall. Gravity took him the rest of the way down the well.

Jacob dropped to the ground and frantically unwrapped the torn rope from around his neck. Dick's screams carried through the night until they were abruptly silenced.

Fits of spasmodic coughing overcame Jacob as his lungs vied for all the oxygen they could pull in. He propped his back straight up against the retaining wall, wincing at the stings from his earlier knife wounds, and sucked in great gulps of air. His broad chest expanded and contracted as he worked to bring his heart rate down.

Dick, that stupid fucking fool!

As he leaned back and rested his head on the rough stone wall, he craned his neck around and raised his eyes toward the pulley. The metal ring through which the rope was pulled showed at least an eighth of an inch of rust all around it, the residue jagged and uneven. No wonder the old rope had snapped. And thank God for it.

Christ, what the hell had he just done? He had just killed a man. No, a countryman. He was sure he'd ended lives in the war during the heat of battle, but never so intentional and intimately.

He dragged his trembling hand down his face, letting it come to rest over his mouth in case he should vomit up all the liquor in his stomach.

No, he wouldn't examine himself as a murderer. Dick had attacked him at his home, tried to end his life on his own goddamn property. The poor fool held a deep hatred in his heart for Jacob, all over a damn miscommunication.

Jacob inched his knees up and rested his forearms along them, caging himself in as tight a ball as he could. He glanced down at his bare feet, filthy and frozen from the elements. The pain in his back was oddly lessened by the frigid air, and judging by the loose scraps of fabric hanging off his shoulders, his shirt was completely lost.

Move. He needed to get up and move. And boy, didn't that seem like the most monumental of tasks at the moment.

Grunting low in his throat, he managed to get his feet back under him and commanded his thighs to somehow get him vertical. It worked, but just barely. Once he was upright, he quickly threw out a hand to steady himself against the well's retaining wall.

Should he look down the well? Would he even be able to see anything if he did? What would he do with the visual information if he *did* see what he was afraid to see?

All questions for another time, he surmised as he trudged back to the cabin. Crossing the threshold, he reached up and over his head to remove the tattered remains of his shirt, his muscles bunching as he contorted at odd angles to do so, and tossed them on the floor. Wincing with each step, he walked over to the hearth to grab the kettle that sat on top of the mantle when the cabin's wall telephone rang.

Who the heck would be calling him? And why did he even have the mental energy to care? But the adrenaline coursing through his veins propelled him forward, his body's movements no longer under his control.

In two great strides, he approached the small back box mounted on the wall next to the kitchen entrance. The phone's two silver bells, which sat atop the box, chimed together harshly. A more grating noise Jacob couldn't determine in that moment. He stepped close to the phone, positioned his mouth in front of the black cone-like receiver in the middle of the box, and lifted the singular earpiece to his left ear.

"Hello?" he barked out, regretting his harsh tone immediately.

"Yes, I have the University of Martinsville Hospital on the line for a Corporal Jacob Bellamy. Shall I patch them through?" the switchboard operator informed him in a tinny tone.

Whatever blood was left in Jacob's head drained straight out of it at the mention of the hospital. Since his discharge, his only connection to the hospital had been Sarah. But she couldn't...no...

"Yes, I'll speak with them," he grounded out, mashing his molars together in angst.

"Yes, sir."

Jacob fisted his hair at his forehead, mussing his locks into a vertical tangle as he waited what felt like years for the operator to make the connection. In actuality, it was only a second or two, but his anxious brain took him through all sorts of terrible scenarios.

"Corporal Bellamy, this is Nurse Macray at Martinsville Hospital. You're listed as the next of kin for a Miss Sarah Johansson. Is that still correct?"

His heart dropped into his stomach at the mention of Sarah's name, the beating thing a great dead weight in his gut. Please, God...please don't let her be...

"Yes, that's correct. What's happened? Is she all right?" he screamed into the receiver, but panic seized a tight grip around his rational thought. Why wouldn't they spit it out already?

"Sir, if you're able to get to the hospital now, I would advise it. She's had another episode brought on by her condition. She's unconscious and has been for some time."

Jacob's world bottomed out upon hearing those words.

"I'll be right there," he stammered and practically ran out of the house.

God, he hoped he wasn't too late.

CHAPTER 27

S he said no. Why on Earth would Helen have said no to Ramon asking her out? The confusion and—yeah, Sarah would admit it —hurt she felt at the girl's refusal cut deep, as if she herself were the one receiving the rejection. A tidal wave of implications rolled over Sarah in that moment, flashing across the backs of her eyelids like a greatest hits reel of horror movies she never wanted to see: Ramon dying of typhoid fever, Helen becoming a young mother and widow, Jacob...What would become of Jacob? Unbidden tears bloomed at the corners of her still-closed eyes at the mention of his name. Oh, Jacob...

"It would be impossible for me to accept your invitation." Helen's soft voice fluttered throughout the room, the weight of the words landing heavily on Sarah and pinning her further to this place and time.

Ramon's deep accented speech followed suit, his words softer and not as confident. "Ah, I see. Well..."

"But my family also thought it would be impossible for me to get this job at the hospital straight out of school."

The tiniest ray of hope inserted itself into Sarah's heart.

"You see, they often thought me too concerned with hair ribbons and high heels to put much more stock in my academic abilities."

On a slightly nervous chuckle, she elaborated more. "Miss Braithwaite, one of my teachers in school, even gave me an A on my sewing for a wide-brimmed hat I made from braided straw as well as a dress. My parents were proud, to be sure, and assumed I'd continue down some safe and frivolous path. But that was not the course for me. So, you see, pursuing a courtship so soon after taking the job at the hospital? Well, I feel it knocks my accomplishments down a peg, in their eyes at least. I worry they'd again see me as the silly girl toying with hair ribbons who was better suited for marriage than business."

Sarah strained to hear more, holding in her breath and hope as tightly as she could.

Ramon hastily took advantage of Helen's hesitation and indecision and cleared his throat. "You know, I, too, had to convince my family that medicine was the path for me. Going against the grain is not an easy thing."

"No, it is not."

"But I admire you greatly for it."

"Yes, well, perhaps carving my own name in the sand isn't such a bad idea," Helen said, a lightness and joviality returning to her voice that lifted Sarah's spirits—and Ramon's, no doubt—higher as well.

"All right, then." Sarah could easily hear Helen's smile through her words, and it was infectious. "Saturday at two p.m. The new moving picture parlor on Frederick Street? I haven't been there yet, but I've heard good things. I can meet you there."

Sarah released the tension she had been holding in every muscle. Oh, man. There was a reason she never cared much for dramatic suspense novels, too taxing on the body.

"I look forward to that greatly, Miss Schneider," Ramon responded, the words tumbling out of his mouth almost before Helen could finish her sentence.

"Helen...please." There was that unmistakable smile in her words again.

"Helen, then. Yes, wonderful."

As Helen and Ramon walked out of the hospital room, they took all of Sarah's tension with them. She finally exhaled a huge sigh of relief as exhaustion overtook her. With no more mental fight left in her, she had no other recourse but to surrender to sleep.

The shuffling of Jacob's boot heels was a gentle rain shower on a roof compared to his escort's heavy step. The night nurse walking them down Martinsville's halls had a march like a hailstorm. The *click-clack click-clack* of her soles on the linoleum floor reminded Jacob of his Army marching drills. Left...left...left-right-left. The audible affront grated on his already threadbare nerves. How many more rooms would they have to pass, dammit?

"Ah, room three zero two." The nurse came up short in front of the door, which led Jacob to overshoot the entrance and walk back a few steps. "Here we are. Now, you should know she's been resting quite comfortably from what we've seen. Her vital signs all seem in order, though she hasn't woken up since she was brought in earlier today. I'll permit you to spend a few minutes with her, though we normally never allow visitors at this hour."

"Of course," Jacob said with a slight nod, impatiently shifting from one foot to the other. Hell, he clasped his wrists so tightly behind his back he was sure he'd soon dislocate a shoulder from the tension. His raging bull was so fired up, he didn't trust himself not to throw a punch at the first obstacle in his way. God, if he could just *see* her already!

"Thank you, nurse."

As the nurse continued her click-clacking back down the hall, it took all Jacob had not to go barreling into that room. He gripped the doorknob with more than a little fear but would never admit to it. His sweaty palm struggled to gain purchase on the cool brass, forcing him to use both fists to corral the thing into submission. One final twist. There!

Sarah's pale and prone sleeping form took up the length of the hospital bed. She reminded him of the lifeless bodies he'd seen sprawled about the French countryside. It had always struck him how a person's final thought could be so precisely etched on their face right before they were taken to meet their maker. Looks of surprise, fear, despair, all of it frozen in time. Though he knew Sarah only slept soundly, the expression on her face was arresting.

The cutely wrinkled V at the apex of her brows was so strenuously furrowed, Jacob wondered what had her attention so rapt that even her stubborn muscles refused to succumb to sleep like their owner.

Grabbing a small three-legged wooden stool, he lugged the thing next to the bed and sat down, inhaling her unique scent. He had only been away from her the better part of a day, but already their time apart was debilitating. For the both of them, it would seem.

Her slender hand rested on top of the cream-colored cotton blanket. Without another thought, Jacob grabbed up her palm in between his two hands and gently kneaded the base of each knuckle. He pressed and squeezed, pulling each digit gently.

"Sarah," he whispered.

Nothing.

His throat tightened at the lack of response. The only thing that calmed his nerves was the gentle rise and fall of her chest through the pale blue-and-white striped convalescent robe the hospital had provided her. Beneath his hands, the steady, strong beat of her pulse thrummed a message of encouragement through her skin.

"Sarah, please wake up," Jacob pleaded. He had been overly harsh with her. He realized that now. By God, the fear had been so crippling, though! The prospect of losing her opened up a giant chasm in his heart, with him on one side and her on the other. Her link to him across that void was a lifeline. He craved being that for her, to be chosen as her equal in whatever battles she may face.

Jacob softly ran the pad of his index finger across the delicate skin of her wrist, her pulse both calming and enticing him. Leaning forward, he gently brushed his lips across the pulse point, rubbing the coarse whiskers of his mustache back and forth over her skin. The warmth of her body insulated by the thick robe radiated up to his senses through her wrist, and a flood of memories came back to him of their time on his bearskin rug back at the cabin.

Of its own accord, the tip of his tongue jutted out and lightly lapped at her wrist before his lips closed in to seal the connection with a proper kiss. The moment his full mouth connected with her, Sarah let out a great gasp.

Jacob's eyes darted to Sarah's face. Her mouth was slightly parted though her eyes were still closed, and her chest rose and fell in a more harried fashion. The movement gently tested the tie of her hospital robe, the measly scrap of fabric the only thing preventing the flaps of her robe from opening more widely.

Jacob stared at her chest, silently hating himself for hoping to see more, more of his spitfire's delectable creamy skin, more of the rich breaths of life pumping in and out of her, just *more*.

He truly was a cad of the first order.

Jacob's breath hitched when a strong, powerful pulse began thrumming more quickly from his charge's hand still cradled in his own. His eyes shot to Sarah's, and to his great surprise and relief, her hazel eyes shone back at him. The smile that graced her face utterly did him in.

The poor stool clattered to the floor as Jacob sprung off the seat and lunged for her, his hands immediately entangling in her hair as his palms cupped the sides of her face. She hadn't yet spoken, but the misty glaze in her eyes was more than enough. Planting himself on the edge of her bed, he used the pads of his thumbs to gently wipe away any errant tears that may have fallen. The fullness he felt at seeing her smile was almost oppressive, but he'd welcome it any day of the week and twice on Sundays.

"Jacob..." Sarah wheezed out. "I'm so sorry, I..."

"Shhh. No need. No need at all," Jacob rushed out, trying to calm her worries.

"No!" she yelled, wincing at the raspy way her words came out as she pinned her arms behind her in an effort to sit up more.

As if she needed a greater position of strength to yell at him.

The corner of Jacob's lips cracked at the attempt. He'd happily sit back and take a million scoldings from her if it meant they were both around to argue at all. To imagine a future together was so tantalizing, but it would have to wait for another time.

Jacob repositioned himself behind her so he had access to her neck. He gently placed his hands on her shoulders and relocated his early finger ministrations from her hands to the tense muscles of her upper body. Sarah immediately calmed and melted back into his hold, her eyes drifting closed slightly.

"You know," she breathed out as his rigid thumbs dug into a knot at the top of her scapula. "I had every intention of apologizing to you. Admitting to you how wrong I was, how you were right and we *are* better as a team." Jacob's deep chuckle bubbled up when Sarah lolled her neck to the side, giving him access to massage more deeply the base of her neck. Even Athena, it seemed, had a weakness. "But I...oh, *man*, does that hit the spot."

Jacob continued his massage as he brought his lips over to her exposed neck and placed a chaste kiss on the taut skin, then rose up, turned around, and did the same to her forehead. "Rest. I promise I will be here when you wake up."

"Rest? But I just woke up! What time is it anyway?" she said, squinting around for a wall clock in the dark room.

"A little after midnight. The nursing staff did me a favor in allowing me to see you this late, but they don't discharge patients at this hour."

The pout that formed on her lips bordered on dangerous, the way he quickly imagined just how much he missed those lips...and where.

Jacob shook the thought away, though the more obvious symptom couldn't be dismissed quite so easily, unfortunately.

An indiscrete forearm across his lap would have to suffice for the time being.

"I'm staying at the hotel for the evening so I'll be close by, I promise. I'll be back for you in the morning and then we can sort this whole thing out," he said as he again gripped her hand in his.

Sarah stared at their clasped hands for a moment before giving a seemingly reluctant nod. "All right. Just promise me one more thing?"

"Anything."

Her gorgeous eyes penetrated his own, and just like that, he was a goner. Totally and completely lost.

"The next time I get on my high horse about some crazy scheme, don't let me jump in the saddle by myself. I was such a damn fool.

Such a fool." She let out a desperate breath, shaking her head back and forth.

Not in a million years did he ever think he'd see his spitfire admit her shortcomings. In the short time he'd known her, she had proved a formidable force to be reckoned with, a relentless wave on the ocean determined to take down a shore structure no matter how hard the tide pulled her back. The strength in that admission was the most awe-inspiring thing about her. Definitely Army general material.

And sexy as hell.

"Don't worry," Jacob said as he rose to head toward the door. "If there's one thing this farm boy knows, it's how to bridle a horse."

CHAPTER 28

The aftereffects of Jacob's whiskey-laden ordeal with first Sarah, then Dick, then Sarah again had finally caught up with him. His body had ultimately given up on burning the midnight oil. When he walked back into his suite's room, he barely made it to the bed before exhaustion claimed him. So when the rough knock sounded at his door several hours later, he wasn't yet sure whether he was still asleep or awake.

He moaned into his pillow as he rolled over. The infernal orange sun shone through the lace gossamer curtain of his suite's bedroom and pooled its rays directly toward the head of the bed. On the back of *his* head more specifically. The damn tapping rang out again despite his pillow fort protection.

God, he really had begun to hate unexpected knocking on doors. Yup, that and hospitals. Both of those things could go right to hell.

Maybe if he ignored the knocking some more, the person would get the hint. Raising his eyes ever so slightly from under the pillow, he peered over at his watch on the nightstand. Was it really seven in the morning?

Shit!

He had wanted to be at the hospital before Sarah woke up. He had overslept. He couldn't remember the last time that had happened.

The knocking persisted at the door. Who the hell could that be at this hour?

Rising from the bed, he padded barefoot over to the corner floor pile where his shirt, pants, and remainder of last night's clothes lay huddled together. Grabbing up a pair of the gray cotton pajama pants he should have already been wearing but was too exhausted to put on last night, he scooted them on his hips and ambled toward the door, too damn tired to give a shit about the rest of his look. Propriety be damned.

By the time he reached the door, the horrible knocking had started up again. His patience hanging on by a thread, Jacob yanked open the door, ready to bite the head off whatever poor messenger was sent to annoy him so early.

"Hi, Grumpy."

Jacob froze in the doorway at the sight of Sarah standing out in the hallway, her lips turned up in a smart smirk. It wasn't lost on him that she stood two feet back from his door, as if she knew he'd come out swinging a punch to whoever insisted on his early morning wake-up call. Always one step ahead, that girl.

She looked exactly the same as when he'd left her the morning after their initial meeting with Ramon, though he could tell she was a bit worse for wear judging by the dark blue bags under her eyes. But...wait. How was she discharged so early?

"Sarah, what are you doing here?" he asked.

"I was discharged," she stated matter-of-factly.

"Well, yes," Jacob went on. "That much I gathered, but how did you get discharged so early? I planned to meet you at the hospital when you woke up."

Her small smile grew larger at that comment, and that was just fine with him. "May I come in?"

Forgetting himself, he stumbled back and out of the way of the door, elongating his arm out to the rest of his room. "Forgive me! Of course. Come right in. I...uh...was..."

"Still sleeping?" She cast her eyes over at the rumpled sheets in the bed and then back to his chest.

Damn, he hadn't put on a shirt yet. At the quick memory of his mostly naked state, he pulled out a sleeveless white cotton undershirt from his laundry pile and hastily threw it on before turning back to look at her.

"No. Well, I was about to get up anyway," he said dismissively, like he hadn't just been caught in a lie. Eager to get back on track, he pressed her again about how she got here.

"I talked to Ramon when he first got on shift at six a.m.," she said as she shuffled over and plopped down on Jacob's bed, her pleated skirt whooshing around her legs before settling above her ankles. There was something about seeing her sitting in his bed that tugged at the primal part of him, reminding him well and fully that he was an animal first, male second, and all other inconsequential things third. His sheets were still warm from his body, and though she was still fully clothed, images of her being wrapped in his warmth came to mind. Surrounding her, protecting her.

"I was up already. Couldn't really sleep anymore. I think I've slept enough for a lifetime, if I'm being honest. Anyway, he didn't see the harm in discharging me before breakfast since I told him I wasn't going far, but he made me swear to rest for the next few weeks."

The thought of a few more weeks churned his gut, especially when he saw the far-off look in Sarah's eyes as she brought up the timeline.

"A few weeks," she said mostly to herself. "That seems like wishful thinking."

The despair in her voice summoned him, instantly awakening him. On a rush, he walked over and dropped to his knees before her, taking her hands in his. "Please. I know it always seems like I'm begging you for things lately, but let's just rest for a moment and regroup. Talk about things."

When Sarah didn't immediately return his sentiment, he got worried again. Worried he'd just said the wrong thing to instigate another fight.

Instead, Sarah removed her hand from his and reached down to grab a fistful of his shirt at the base of his neck. He held back a silent hiss as the shirt inadvertently pulled at his chest hair, and the slightly painful tug sent a pleasurable jolt straight through him. Jesus Christ, what was she on about?

"I'm done resting," she said, her voice huskier than he recalled it a moment ago. "And I don't want to talk anymore."

Sarah's fiery hot mouth stole his next breath.

Who the hell was this woman and what did she do with Sarah? Never in her life had she acted so forward, so forceful, so *wanton*. She felt like a regular type A boardroom babe who would kick ass and take names all day at work and then sexually steamroll through her pick of men at night. None of that was Sarah. She was the introverted quiet type who wouldn't even believe a guy when he'd say she was beautiful unless he would agree to have that statement notarized in front of witnesses. The thought of her initiating sex? Yeah, no way.

But facing one's own mortality head-on did a lot to change a person's tune.

When she got dressed this morning, she'd been so sure that Ramon would be in the clear, that her little attempt to speed along their relationship and get them out of Baltimore before the typhoid fever wave crushed the hospital had worked, she didn't even think twice about the possibility she may be wrong. It wasn't until she took off the hospital robe that she'd noticed the rash had spread more. In the dingy, pitted mirror of her hospital room, the pale green blemish had mushroomed like an all-encompassing tidal wave across her chest and completely engulfed her decolletage.

What did all that mean for her grand plan?

Shit. Didn't. Work.

But what *had* worked this whole time she'd been stuck in this nightmare was Jacob. Every step of the way, he was there. So when she knocked on that hotel door and got an eyeful of his gloriously naked, tanned, rugged torso...well, she only had this one life to live, didn't she?

The flavor that exploded across her tongue when he delved into her mouth was heady. He was her drug and she couldn't imagine a scenario where she'd ever get enough. As his tongue gingerly stroked her palate, her tongue, her teeth, she became intoxicated and was further emboldened.

Slipping her fingers from the top of his sleeveless shirt, she tickled them down the front of his chest. They danced lightly across his left nipple, circling the pert bud through the thin cotton. Her feathered touch skimmed over to the right one and repeated the torture. She was rewarded by the low moan that bubbled up in Jacob's throat. And didn't that just make her feel like a friggin' temptress?

Encouraged, she peppered her fingers more lightly down the rigid muscles of his abdomen, the pads of her digits barely offering the ghost of a caress. His hard muscles immediately contracted at her touch. When her hand reached what she thought was its final destination at the hem of his shirt, another thought came to mind, one that intimidated her and thrilled her. She did a quick gut check to make sure she was certain about her next move. The smile that bubbled up at the thought and spread across her mouth as she kissed Jacob sealed the deal for her. She loved him and needed him to know she loved him in all ways.

Deepening her kiss, she took both hands and dropped them lower to the waistline of his pajama pants. Her determination propelled her forward as she hooked her fingers inside his waistband so the backs of her knuckles could delicately scrape and rub at his delicious patch of dark hair that tempted her down farther. Her fingers solidly hooked in the fabric, she gripped the cotton and pulled them down.

"What are you thinking there, Miss Johansson?" Jacob asked into her mouth, only pausing his own explorations so he could get the words out.

"Relax, Grumpy," she said with a chuckle as he scooted up on his knees to assist her in removing his pants. Once they were completely off and discarded, Sarah pulled away from his mouth and sat back to take in the sight.

Jacob sat up on his knees before her, the broad expanse of his chest rising and falling from the restraint he was clearly trying to exercise. His mouth hung open as he took in great inhales of air. Hidden beneath his mustache and beard, his pink lips bore the evidence of their fervent kisses. Powerful thighs stood squared with his narrowed hips, from which his erect cock stood out bold and commanding.

The sight of this man completely at her mercy was nearly enough to bring her to her own knees. A quick glance up to his face almost knocked the confidence right out of her. His eyes were hungry and homed in on her like she was his only source of succor after starving for so long.

Holding his gaze for fear she'd lose her nerve, she brought her palms to his impressive shoulders—and, boy, were they on fire—and gently pushed her charge backward to the floor. As his back settled down on the hardwood, Sarah climbed on top of him, never letting her touch leave his body. Once they were both settled, she kept his gaze as she slid her hands down his chest and with them her body as well, until her knees were settled on the floor astride his calves.

Farther down, Sarah went until her fingertips were nestled in the dark thatch of curls around his cock. Never taking his eyes off hers, Jacob craned his neck up in rapt attention as Sarah brought her mouth closer to his erection. The tip of her tongue snaked out and captured the bead of liquid that pooled at the head before she took the whole of him in her mouth. Jacob's head fell backward and *thunk*ed on the hard floor, his eyes squinting shut and great exhales bellowing out of his expansive chest.

She couldn't believe she was giving him a blow job. Sure, this wasn't her first time, but this had never particularly been her cup of tea. With previous boyfriends, she'd do it on occasion to keep the spark alive, but only if asked. She had never volunteered, never *needed* to. Until now.

The power and connection she felt spurred her on as she rose up and down along his shaft, chasing each of his moans with a lick or a swirl of her tongue. This man, this frustrating, grumpy, and loving man had somehow called her on all her bluffs, seen through all of her insecurities, and still showed up for her. It had taken some deep soul-searching on her part to connect those dots. The final result ultimately rang clear in her thick-headed skull: She was in love with Jacob, and she'd try her damnedest to live whatever moments she had left with him to the fullest. Starting now.

With her eyes closed, she began to pump faster, the tip of his cock occasionally bumping the roof of her mouth, but she didn't care. She wanted him. All of him. A quick glance his way revealed he had his eyes closed as well, his teeth had bitten into his bottom lip, and his hands were at his sides constantly fisting and unfisting as if he were desperate to touch her but wouldn't dare.

"Sarah," he gasped out. "We have to slow down. I want to be inside you when I come. Oh, God..."

On a rush, he sat up and nearly tackled Sarah to the floor on her back. His lips were on her in an instant, his hands fumbling with the hem of her skirt. She could feel the slickness of his cock still wet from her mouth as it grazed the inside of her leg on its trip northward. That knowledge made her croon inside.

Jacob finally found his target and notched his cock at her entrance. Holding himself up on his forearms, he planted his strong hands on either side of her face and devoured her mouth in the truest form of possession. On the next stroke of his tongue inside her mouth, he thrust into her swollen center. The lack of warning and the intensity of the penetration caused Sarah to throw her head back and cry out. Jacob took advantage of the new angle and peppered the column of her exposed neck with open-mouthed kisses. All the sensations combined led to the most erotic moment of her life. And she hadn't even had an orgasm yet.

The fullness abated as Jacob withdrew from her channel, only to crest again as he reentered with a deeper, more toe-curling angle, if that was even possible. Their breaths mingled, the heavy panting their only source of oxygen. It would have to do.

Jacob picked up his tempo, thrusting into her with such force and speed she began to scoot back along the floor with each push. The tiny spark inside grew more intensity, blossoming into a goddamn supernova. Finally, Sarah's sensations rippled through her body, the explosion one of light, stars, and cosmic energy all wrapped into one. The pinnacle of a time-transcendent love made manifest in the form of an orgasm. As that thought began to register, Jacob's low growl filled her ears, and the hot spurts of his frenzy emptied out of him.

When the final tremors of sensation subsided, he nestled his head in the crook of her shoulder. After another exhale, Jacob rose back on his forearms and took Sarah's flushed cheeks in his hands.

"Sarah, I love you," he said on a gruff exhale. "I fucking love the shit out of you, and you need to know that, dammit."

The glassiness in Sarah's eyes sprung up on its own, but she no longer had a desire to fight. She let the tears fall where they did and circled her own hands around his wrists, holding him firm, both in her physically and emotionally. He was everywhere for her, and she wouldn't have it any other way.

"I love you, too. And no amount of fighting with you or meddling in people's lives will change that. Nor do I want it to. What I mean is, well, I guess I'm claiming you. Grumpiness and all."

The last sentence brought out a great laugh from Jacob, his smile lighting up his entire soul. That happiness was more infectious than any fever she had been misguidedly chasing through history.

CHAPTER 29

"**D**ick's dead? Really? How?"

Sarah's eyebrows went sky high as she bolted upright in the bed. Jacob grimly filled her in on what had transpired during their time apart. God, that seemed like a lifetime ago already. The thought of going back to that farm was even harder knowing Dick's body was laid to rest, as it were, in his family's old well. A quiver rippled through him as he briefly considered what would be involved in having it removed.

The shock on Sarah's face hadn't yet subsided. Jacob let a bubbling laugh die on his lips. Her gorgeous dark blond hair, to put it delicately, was in no neat array, a side effect of their early morning escapades. Tendrils were going every which way at the root, falling where they may despite her normally well-placed side part. The crown of her head saw a much flatter, frizzier depression than the rest of her hair, no doubt a by-product of her preferred positioning. Add to the picture the intense vertical angle of her eyebrows, the wide circles of her eyes, and the cavernous O of her lips, and the image of a surprised blowfish—spikes out—came to mind.

Like hell he would tell her that, though.

Settling his hand on the side of her neck, he took his thumb from the other hand and gently smoothed down the aggressive upside-down V of her brows. A quick kiss to her shocked mouth and she was already melting back into his arms, the desired effect having been achieved. After another moment, Sarah broke away and settled into "her spot," as she liked to call it, tucked in against his side with her head resting on his chest right over his heart.

"I just can't believe it was all over a misunderstanding, that he held such hatred toward you all that time," she said softly, her fingers drawing figure eights in his dark chest hair.

He hugged her closer to his chest and closed his eyes for a brief moment before saying more. "In the end, we all see what we want to see. I can't dwell on it, though. He was, at his core, misunderstood at best and a monster at worst. Regardless of what he thought I did, he carved his own path. Nothing any of us can do about that."

"True. The thought of him lying dead in your family's well, though, bleh," she forced out with a shudder. "Is that why you got the hotel?"

"No. After the fight, I came back into the cabin and got a telephone call from the hospital about your condition. I quickly packed a bag and left for the city. When I arrived, it was very late at night and the only room they had available at that hour was a two-bedroom suite. Honestly, I would have paid for an entire floor of rooms if it kept me close to you."

"Look at you, big spender," Sarah said with a smirk. "Come to think of it, that must have been insanely expensive. I'm not up to the current inflation rates of this time, but how are you able to afford these hotel stays? They can't be cheap, especially in the city."

"Well, I got a salary, of course, for my time in the service, though it was paltry compared to the demands of the job. But still, it was something. Most of my money now, I will say, was left to me through my inheritance and the life insurance policies of my family, as well as the income and investments previously generated by my family's farm. When the developers moved to town, they offered my parents a sizable amount of money for a very small portion of the farm's acreage, all things considered. Needless to say, my parents had invested wisely."

"Clearly so."

"To the townsfolk, they were just owners of the Bellamy farm and one of the main suppliers of crops and produce for the area. But my father was first and foremost a businessman." Jacob took a moment to clear his throat, the memories of his family causing little needles of emotion to tickle down his esophagus.

"As for the life insurance policies, my parents had one, obviously, which listed me and my brother as beneficiaries. When they had passed, Isaac and I were already enlisted. Then, as another benefit of serving our great country, the government offered its soldiers discounted life insurance policies. You see, commercial insurance, more often than not, did not pay benefits should one die in war, or the premiums were cost-prohibitive. When Isaac died, I became the sole benefactor for everything."

The weight of that statement floated around the room for a minute, ebbing and flowing through the air like dust particles before it landed with a great heaviness on his shoulders. But there was another subject he needed to broach with her, one just as delicate and weighty. Steeling himself with a deep breath, he gripped her shoulder more tightly to his chest and peered down at her skin.

The area that drew his concern was mostly concealed from his view by how Sarah was lying on him, but nonetheless, it was very much the elephant in the room. And that fact terrified him. With a gentle but intentional touch, he glided his fingers underneath Sarah's right arm that was draped over his chest and lovingly urged her to lie back so he could re-examine the green rash. She complied reluctantly.

"Where do we go from here?" he whispered, tracing soft lines over the tops of her breasts and dipping down slightly in between. Her skin reminded him of a topographic map with its pale flesh-toned valleys and lush vegetative peaks. He had already memorized the landscape, but he still achingly wished it would change.

Sarah's head lay back against the cushion of his bicep, her eyes staring off into space before him as he continued his petting. "I'm sorry I didn't tell you about my worsening symptoms. I just didn't want to show you how afraid I really was."

Jacob cocked his head at that remark. "Why didn't you want me to know? That's the part I struggle with understanding, I must say."

"Well, I suppose it has to do with my life back home, honestly. In my line of work, interviewing hotshot doctors and writing about the next fad medical treatment, it can be a little intimidating. What if I ask the wrong question? What if I don't ask the *right* question? What if an editor from a competing publication beats me to the story? Or what if I flat-out don't understand what the heck I'm supposed to write about because, at the end of the day, I'm just a worker-bee editor who still Googles how to use a semicolon properly and all that medical mumbo jumbo just goes over my head?"

Jacob blinked a few times as the words sank in. "I'm sorry. Google?"

"A reference source. Never mind about that." She waved her hand dismissively. "Ultimately, what if people realize I'm a fake?"

Her pleading eyes challenged him for an answer, but he suspected she wasn't finished talking so he gave her the floor to speak freely in what, he thought, was the first time in a long time. How honored he felt to be the one she trusted to unburden herself upon. Finally.

"I don't know whether this expression exists in this time but back home people will say, 'Fake it 'til you make it.' Well, I've been faking it a long damn time, Jacob, and I'm not anywhere close to making it. I would have been damned if I let all those vulnerabilities show through to others. But it's only now that I realize how stupid I've been. Hiding your fears and insecurities only makes you weaker, not stronger."

Pride at his spitfire's admission caused his heart to swell well beyond its capacity. God, he loved this woman.

Taking her hands in his again, he gently cupped them into a fist and tucked them inside his own fingers. Once they were one, he brought their united hands to his mouth and planted a chaste kiss for reassurance before bringing them down to settle over his heart.

"Tell me what you need from me," Jacob requested, his voice still a little hoarse from holding back the emotion he wasn't man enough to show. He hoped he came off strong for her.

The sweet smile he had managed to put on her glowing face slowly began to fade. Her eyes stared off into the room again, and her mouth went slightly slack-jawed.

"Sarah?"

"The cemetery," he thought he heard her say, but the ghost of the words were so low he could hardly make them out.

"I'm sorry?"

"The cemetery. Wharton Park Cemetery in Baltimore. I'd like to go there." Sarah's eyes returned to his, and it wasn't a request in the slightest, but clearly their next course of action.

"Of course we can go there. Why the sudden urge, though?"

As a grim expression cast a pall over Sarah's face, Jacob immediately knew he didn't want the answer to his question.

"That's where my family is buried, or will eventually be buried. Gosh, it's so confusing to think of in those terms, but I'd like to go there still." Before Jacob could say anything further, she flung her arms around his neck and burrowed her nose in close near his ear. The warmth of her bare skin seeped into his chest, and the lushness of her body in his hands as he wrapped them around her felt like home. However, from that close proximity, he was also able to clearly make out the one fear his goddess would now freely admit to him.

"I'm not sure how much time I have left," Sarah spoke softly into his ear, her quiet desperation wrapping around his heart.

In that moment, it was all he could do not to scream.

Sarah had no idea what she expected to see at the cemetery, nor where the idea to visit came from. True, she had been researching the Schneider family history for quite some time and thought she had things pretty well mapped out in her head. The entire family was buried at Wharton Park Cemetery, starting with Johannes Schneider who came over from Bavaria in the 1840s and started this whole mess.

The *real* mess before her, she now understood, was her complete lack of comprehension regarding what this cemetery would have looked like in 1919. Namely, all the graves of the family members she wanted to see weren't there yet. In this time, her family was mostly still alive and kicking.

Helen's father, Louis, was still alive, as were most of his nine other siblings. As Sarah rocked back on the heels of her boots, which were buffeted by the frozen Earth, she felt just as lost as before. Arms crossed over her chest for warmth and her frozen breath huffing out before her, she was tempted to stomp her foot in frustration but thought better of it. Knowing her, the only thing she'd gain would be a snapped boot heel.

Warm strong arms wrapped around her from behind, and Jacob's scent, even in the chilly mid-morning air, calmed her frazzled nerves. She leaned back and let him take on her weight, knowing it meant just as much to both of them.

"What's the matter?" he inquired in her ear.

"I honestly don't know. I thought coming here would give me some clarity, some perspective. Back home, I had planned this trip for a year. I had mapped everyone's graves out on the cemetery map, I was going to do grave etchings for posterity, even try to locate some hard-to-find relatives who had their graves relocated. But now they're not here!"

"So, you're upset your relatives aren't dead?"

"Yes! I mean, no. Ugh!"

The light chuckle of amusement grated on her nerves.

"So glad this is funny to you."

"Oh, shush. You know how you're sounding. Now please, help me understand," he said with a comforting kiss to the back of her head.

"I wanted to experience some connection to my family in *this* time. I thought that maybe it would anchor me more. Give me hope or something. I don't know." Sarah began to kick at a rock that was half sticking out of the frozen ground, knowing it wouldn't budge but needing an outlet for her frustration.

Thumping her head back against Jacob's chest, she finally let fly what she had been mulling around in her head for the past hour. Well, as long as she was in the business of laying it all out there, why stop now?

"I guess a part of me was also wondering whether this is where I end up, you know?"

There, she had said it. She was afraid, and that was okay. He needed to know, needed to hear, so he could make the choice to love her anyway, despite what it meant.

The unmistakable sound of a bugle playing "Taps" shook them both from their thoughts as its music rang out through the air off to their left. A gathering of about twenty people or so huddled around an open grave, the casket having already been lowered into its final resting place. The melody was so haunting and all too familiar, those twenty-four notes easily recognized by Sarah as being heard at every military-related wreath-laying ceremony, memorial service, and funeral she could recall.

"We gather here in service to the Lord, for on this day we faithfully usher Private First Class James R. Banwell into the ever-welcoming arms of Jesus Christ so that our James may finally be called home to nestle in the glow of the Lord's light..."

The tension grew at her back when Jacob's body went rigid as the words of the pastor made their way to them.

Turning in his arms, she asked, "What's wrong?"

Jacob silently stewed on his thoughts a moment longer before he opened up, shaking his head in dismissal. "It's nothing. From time to time, when I hear of another soldier who succumbed to their injuries, the guilt is...uh...well, I'm still here and they are not."

Sarah reached up and stroked her gloved index finger along his beard, the underneath of which was buffeted by his favorite emerald green scarf. The cozy fibers of the wool provided the perfect cushion for Jacob's chin, and she couldn't help but smile at how even his clothing chose that moment to wrap him in the warmest hug.

The idea came to her in a flash. It made no sense. Absolutely none. But, oh, did they need this, and it could be healing for the both of them.

"Jacob, take me out on a date," she rushed out.

"A date? I'm sorry, I don't follow your meaning."

"Ugh! Okay. A night on the town. A movie, dinner. You know, a date! Or whatever you may know it as here."

Sarah could see the cogs turning behind Jacob's eyes, and the moment things clicked into place, the corner of that delicious mouth slowly crept higher.

"A date," he reiterated, his gravelly voice rolling over the word and punctuating the T.

"Yes, a date." She hoped the smug expression on her face conveyed her excitement rather than her trepidation.

"Very well then, Miss Johansson. A date we shall have."

He wrapped his arms tightly around her, the slight squeeze powerful enough to turn her insides into jiggly Jell-O. She was so giddy at the prospect of a proper romantic night out with Jacob that, for the first time, she completely gave in and allowed him to feel the worsening tremors that had just begun to wrack her body.

CHAPTER 30

A date! Sarah couldn't believe she would be going out on a real date with her hunky, toe-curling World War I Army corporal in nineteen-friggin'-eighteen. The healing power of having something good to look forward to was truly amazing and not to be undersold by any means.

What was even more exciting was how Jacob had requested—no, insisted—that he go all out. That meant buying her a new dress for the occasion. She wasn't normally one to get excited about new clothes. After all, she had an average body and tended to foster the average look, stemming from the average jeans to the average cotton t-shirts to even the average cotton briefs. There had been very few occasions to get excited about playing dress-up before, and she was okay with that. But with Jacob, she had begun to view herself differently, view herself as *he* saw her.

Standing in front of the mirror in the bathroom at their hotel suite, she assessed the image of the woman staring back at her. The color of her dress was stunning, and never a color she would have picked out for herself normally. The deep burgundy that saturated the long-sleeve velveteen dress enrobed her body and highlighted the light brown flecks in her hazel eyes. The high-waisted matching sash that brought her in at the middle made her feel, for the first time in her life, like she had a shape to her.

Her eyes traced the lines of her new figure as she gently brushed the backs of her fingers down into the curve of the indentation at her waist. The A-line skirt that floated out from her middle reached just above her ankle, exposing her new mid-calf brown leather boots. The fabric felt delicious against her skin.

Sarah's favorite part was the bodice, though. The sumptuous velveteen draped across her torso in a crisscrossing of two separate panels lying flat, one on top of the other. The overlapping effect created a great open collar with a plunging V-neck that drew the eyes to all the right places. To hide her skin, though, she opted for a gold camisole underneath, but even with the extra camouflage, her breasts looked bangin'. Yeah, she had given in at the department store and opted for the front-lace corset. It was a bitch to get into, but damn, the effects were incredible. Jacob was worth it.

She still wasn't really a hat person, but she also wasn't an idiot. The February weather, not to mention the lack of adequate heating in Jacob's highly-exposed-to-the-elements car, made it an exercise in stupidity to be without one. She chose a matching close-fitted velvet hat with a small dropping brim and domed crown. A gold silk ribbon banded around its middle, with a matching rosette appearing front and center above the brim. How she wished she could pull out her phone and take a picture of herself. Her Aunt Marie would love this. But she hoped Jacob would love it even more.

The door to the bathroom creaked open as Sarah walked out. Jacob had been pacing the room, his olive green wool flat cap wrung tight in his hand. The poor thing. *Maybe* she had taken longer to get ready than she originally promised, but she wanted this to be perfect and needed to savor the moment.

The obviously frustrated man turned on his heel at the sound of the door creaking open. The expression on his face lit Sarah up from the inside out. Jacob literally stood there, halted in mid-stride, and just stared at her. His eyes drank her in from head to toe, lingering a heartbeat too long on her breasts (success!), but wouldn't say anything. When the silence dragged on, Sarah started to second-guess herself. Maybe the color had been wrong after all or maybe the hat just made her look frumpy.

She wrung her sweaty hands together and finally mustered up the courage to break the silence. "Well, say something, soldier. I'm getting mixed signals over here. I can lose the hat, if you'd like. I'm not much of a hat person anyway..."

Sarah turned back to the bathroom, her hands already making their way up to the hat to remove it. In the next instant, the room whirled around her as she was spun to face Jacob. The abrupt wall against her back shocked her in the best way. The breath rushed from her lungs, and Jacob's warm mouth found hers. All at once, she felt the warm invasion of his tongue as it slipped between her lips and claimed her mouth. The heady rush of passion made Sarah's brain feel lightheaded, but that was fine by her because thinking wasn't high on her to-do list at that moment anyway.

The kiss went on and on, and Sarah could feel the tension in Jacob's hands at her shoulders as he desperately tried to keep them where they were. She, however, was torn. She wanted a proper, romantic date, but would it be such a bad thing to enjoy dessert before dinner? She'd examine the whole coulda-woulda-shoulda thing later and, instead, decided to follow his lead.

Not a second later, after her brain had come online and *just* convinced the rest of her to go all in, Jacob tore his mouth away, the breaths rushing out of him in great torrents of effort. Taking a moment to do the same, she reflected how she would never get tired of the effect she had over him.

"Miss Johansson," Jacob purred in between inhales. "I do believe I promised you a date. And that is what you will have." Standing upright, Jacob tugged on the end of his coat to eliminate any evidence of their up-against-the-wall escapades and held out his elbow toward her. "Shall we? It would be my great honor to have a goddess such as yourself on my arm tonight."

Goo. Her insides, what were left of them, turned to utter goo at his words. After she quickly composed herself, she nestled her hand into the crook of his elbow and took great delight at having such a deliciously bulging bicep to cling to.

This would be the best date ever.

A luckier bastard there never was, Jacob concluded as he and Sarah walked along the main thoroughfare toward Frederick Street. Christ, when she had emerged from that bathroom, he'd been a moment away from spending himself in his trousers. An ill-advisable start to the evening, for sure.

The color of her dress, the loose falls of her honeyed tresses, and that bust line. Jacob bit down hard on his bottom lip to keep his damn tongue in his mouth. Even covered as she was by the gold camisole she chose to wear—understandably so others wouldn't notice the green hue of her skin—every curve, every swell of her wonderful breasts was obvious to even a blind man. There wasn't a fabric in the world able to cover up her charms. And just thinking about her charms caused him to pick up the pace. Oh, he relished the evening's activities before them, but right then, he was more enticed by the activities that would come later.

"Slow down, Grumpy. You're like a friggin' bull charging down the street. And what's with the scowl? I can tell you right now, I won't tolerate any of that on our date."

Scowl? Well, he supposed he did have a certain amount of *focus* at the moment. He hadn't realized how fast he was headed toward the theater and how Sarah struggled to keep up. A twinge of guilt hit home as he recalled her condition. Halting his pace to allow her to catch up and calm down, not for the first time did he curse himself for his brutish ways. Clearly, his brain below the belt had been calling the shots.

As they resumed their walk and turned the corner, the front of the cinema's building came into view. Though the weather was another brisk offering, the sun had decided to shine down on them. The late afternoon rays kissed the flashy marquis of the theater, brilliant oranges and yellows bouncing off the glass edges lighting their way.

They had decided on a four-p.m. movie showing, with dinner to follow. Sarah had been so anxious for their outing, she wanted to head out as soon as possible. The crowds wouldn't be as abundant before the late evening rush, and that was preferable for him as well. Being comfortable amid large volumes of people was still something he had to work on, but baby steps and all.

"Wow, *Tarzan of the Apes*! Like, the original?" She beamed up at the letters on the marquis announcing the motion picture of the day.

"I'll have you know, Miss Johansson," he said as he leaned down toward her ear, "I am nothing if not original," the corners of his lips rising in a smirk. "But I'm afraid I don't understand your phrasing. This film was just released at the end of last month. Are there others in your time?"

He adored the way she slapped her hand to her forehead beneath her hat, as she had clearly forgotten herself. "You know, there's so much for me to get used to here, I often forget. But yes, by my time, there have been many versions of Tarzan. I'm sure there will be even more in the future. It's a popular story, but I'm excited to see the first one done on screen."

After Jacob purchased their tickets, they waited off to the side and out of the way for the previous patrons to exit the theater. One by one, couples emerged with their arms linked as he scanned the crowd and waited their turn. The gasp at his side turned his head.

"Jacob! There's Ramon and Helen!" Sarah hissed.

She was indiscreetly pointing at the last couple to exit the theater. He quickly cupped his hand over hers, brought it down to her side to avoid drawing any attention, and glanced in the direction she pointed. Sure enough, the happy doctor and hospital clerk walked side by side in the chilly late afternoon air. The coy smiles on each of their faces were a comfort. He sincerely hoped the best for them. Ramon was a good man, and even though Jacob knew what was in store for him based on Sarah's account, he was glad Ramon got to share his final years with the woman he would eventually grow to love.

"Come. I know you want to go over and speak to them, but I think it's best to let them have their moments as well. Let's head inside. The guilt at how cold you must be is already gnawing at me," Jacob said.

As they entered the dark theater, he gently steered her toward two seats in a middle row. Even in such a dark room, he could clearly pick up the light in her eyes as she took in everything for what was, to her, the first time. With every passing minute, he became more enthralled with this woman. How he would manage to behave himself over the course of the next hour he'd never know, but he'd suck it up and give her the evening of her dreams.

They had only been settled in their seats for a few moments before the low lights of the theater dimmed even further down to near darkness. Sarah's hands, still encased in her dark brown gloves, excitedly clung to his arm. He had no wish to remove her touch, but much preferred to have easy access to the satin of her skin than that of the gloves.

"Here," he said as he took her hands in his own and gently pulled each finger to release the gloves' tight holds. "Let's settle in. Get comfortable."

"Oh, this is such an amazing treat," she half whispered, half squealed as the opening credits flashed across the screen, the scratchy black-and-white lettering fading to black as an image of the African Sahara appeared with a family of giraffes meandering across the landscape.

Jacob watched her through the entire movie, not the least bit interested in what the silent moving picture had in store. No, his amazing treat was right beside him, and he never wanted this night to end.

CHAPTER 31

G iddy. Elated. Punch-drunk happy. *In love.*
Those emotions flashed across a marquis banner in Sarah's mind as she and Jacob stumbled up the carpeted steps to the second floor of the hotel. To say they were in a bit of a rush would be an understatement. To put it bluntly, she wanted to jump his bones. Her inner teenager's choice of vernacular caused her to let out the most undistinguished snort. As she ascended the top step and turned the corner, she slammed right into the most perfectly toned booty this side of the Potomac.

The perturbed look on Jacob's face just caused her to giggle even more.

"Geez, lighten up, Grumpy," she said with a laugh. More snorting. More giggling.

It was the champagne. That's what did her in. Oh, the wine with dinner was delicious, but she was a sipper and savorer with the stuff. She relied on it to bring on the initial buzz, but otherwise her glasses of wine—Glasses? Glass? She honestly couldn't remember—were really just the pretty jewelry that accompanied the amazing meal. But when Jacob had asked the waiter to bring over a bottle of champagne with dessert, she'd hit the bubbles hard. And she hadn't cared one bit...until now.

"Miss Johansson," Jacob whispered as another couple passed them in the hallway, "you're worse than a soldier on twenty-four-hour leave. A few more steps and then you can be as lewd as you'd like."

"Yes, sir!" Sarah shouted, bringing her hand palm-side down to her forehead and releasing it in mock salute.

Jacob's eye roll was legendary as he turned and stomped down the hall, his hand digging around in his back pocket for the room key.

"Admit it," Sarah said, clinging to his arm as he fidgeted with the lock. "You can't get enough of me."

"Get inside," he said, the low timbre of his voice doing wonderful melty things to her insides.

Once on the other side of their suite's door, Sarah removed her hat and plunked down on the plush couch. Bending over to undo the laces of her boots, she couldn't get over how magical the night had been...and how magical it was yet to be.

Jacob pocketed his room key and quickly shucked off his coat and hat. He had never been a patient man, but seeing the curve of Sarah's stockinged leg as she freed her feet from her boots did him in. All night the temptress had had him by the balls in the best of ways. Every laugh, smile, or touch stoked his fire. He had been a simmering volcano for hours now and he needed a release.

Stalking over to Sarah on the couch, he swooped in like a fighter plane. His approach was angled just so to elicit the best squeal from his target as he tackled her onto the sofa's cushions. Her neck's silky, smooth skin was under his lips not a second later. All night...all damn night she had been tempting him with this neck. The scent of her skin right behind her ear was intoxicating, and as he nibbled his favorite spot at the base of her ear, her hands climbed up his back and tugged out his shirttails.

"Seems I'm not the only one so eager," he said in between lapping at her skin and teasing her with little biting kisses.

"Quiet, you. I'm trying to focus here," she said as she fumbled with his belt.

"So bossy."

"Hey, I can be sassy when the need arises. Ah, got it!" The poor strap of leather never stood a chance as she ripped it through the belt loops and flung it God knows where.

They carried on like that for a good minute, getting lost in the petting, kissing, stroking. Jacob's hand slid free the sash at Sarah's waist. Immediately, her body jerked, curling in on itself. Reflexively, Sarah's knee lurched upward straight into Jacob's crotch. His poor balls took on the brunt of the onslaught.

A great moan escaped Sarah's lips, and not the kind he had hoped to coax out momentarily. No, this moan took on the ghostly wail of someone's last breath. Even being doubled over in pain himself, he had the foresight to scramble off her as she lunged for the bathroom, the silk of her stockinged feet causing her to struggle with her footing.

The sound of body-wracking heaves reached his ears. He quickly righted himself and rushed to the bathroom, the panic rising in his chest. On the floor was his Sarah, arms flung over the toilet seat with remnants of her dinner swirling in the bowl. Her eyes were pinched shut, and her mouth was an open oval, gulping in great lungfuls of air. Immediately, Jacob crawled over to her and undid the constricting sash around her waist. Next, he squatted down close to lift her out of the tiny bathroom and bring her to the bed.

God, she felt like nothing in his arms. Why had her frailness not registered until just now? Was he so consumed with his own temporary moment of happiness that he had allowed that fever dream to rob him of his reality?

He gently laid her down on the bed, her gasps coming harder and deeper. Christ, she wasn't getting any air!

"Sarah, hang on. Just hang on!"

Turning her over onto her side, he fumbled with the buttons of her dress. Adrenaline raced through him, and a fear took hold like no wartime running mission had ever done before. His thick fingers shook as he slowly worked to pry each button loose. The task took forever, his progress as slow as molasses. As his fingers worked, he took a quick peek over at Sarah's face.

Green. Her whole chest and neck were now green. Only her face shone through with its delicate pale features, but even the charming pallor he was used to seeing in her skin tone took on an ashy gray. Her eyes were closed and her lips, a moment ago rosy pink and lush, hung open in a lifeless imitation of a dead fish.

"No, dammit, no! Sarah, hang on!"

He ripped the top back of her dress open with one hard pull and the fabric relented, with the slack of the dress hanging off her shoulders. He glanced down at the soft curves of her breasts and what he saw froze him solid.

There was no gentle rise and fall of her chest. He laid her down flat on the floor and slammed his head down on top of her chest, resting his right ear straight over her heart.

Nothing.

All he heard was the absence of the heartbeat responsible for restoring his own.

CHAPTER 32

Something mildly abrasive rubbed against Sarah's left cheek. It wasn't so rough as a scrubby sponge used for washing pots and pans, nor was it cotton-ball soft either. It was definitely some kind of fabric. Wool maybe? Or some puffy polyester? Curious, she slowly moved her cheek back and forth along the fibers.

Carpet. Definitely carpet. Of the higher-pile variety, for sure. It kind of reminded her of the carpet in her condo, actually. God, she hated that cream-colored ratty mat, with the ugly flecks of dark gray speckled throughout. It always reminded her of someone taking an ashtray and sprinkling the remnants of their burned-down cancer sticks all over her living room floor. Too bad it'd come with the condo and she hadn't been in a financial place yet to install the full wall-to-wall hardwood floors of her dreams.

Wait.

The hotel room she and Jacob shared didn't have carpet, only accent rugs. And certainly none of this quasi-lush three-ply stuff she got a nose full of right now.

Oh, God.

Dim lamplight started to invade her senses as she slowly pried open her eyelids. Everything had a haze of muted yellow to it and reminded her of the cheap halogen light bulbs she used back home, though she couldn't really discern anything because her vision was still fuzzy.

Floor. She was definitely on the floor. That much she could tell based on the gold coffee table legs staring her in the face.

Her coffee table back home had legs that were gold.

Her eyes sprang open all the way. Though still sideways on the floor, she had definitely created a drool puddle on *her* own carpet in *her* own condo.

Using her shaky newborn giraffe legs, she pulled her knees under her and put all the effort she had into getting on two feet. Her dress hindered the effort, as the skirt got tangled up in her ankles. She had somehow wedged between her couch and coffee table, so her room to maneuver was minimal. But that didn't matter because she was back!

Finally on two feet, she let out the biggest, loudest sigh of relief she could muster. She was home. In her condo, with her furniture, and her...burgundy velveteen period dress that had somehow been ripped open in the back.

Her skin!

Sarah darted around the obstacle course that was her living room furniture setup and raced to her bathroom in the hallway. The mirror over the vanity told her everything she needed to know. Staring back at her was a clear-complexioned image of herself. She hooked her fingers under the open collar of her dress and pulled it down some more until the tops of her breasts and shoulders were completely visible.

No green anywhere.

She ran her fingers up and down her throat, moved her neck left and right, and even pulled down her bottom eyelids to be sure she didn't miss anything.

Nope. It was all gone. The only evidence of her ordeal was the gray bags under her eyes (lovely) and the raspy sore throat she had been trying to spit-swallow soothe since she woke up.

Sarah turned the bathroom light off and meandered back into her condo. Everything was how she'd left it. She peeked over into the kitchen and noticed the corked bottle of red wine on the counter, the dirty dishes in the sink, and even the box of old photo albums she had been rummaging through, which had started this whole mess.

Her toes were back on that tacky three-ply carpet of her living room floor, but she no longer felt the same scratchy-soothing comfort she had before. Realization had finally steamrolled its way into her consciousness.

Jacob.

She'd never see Jacob again. Heck, he wouldn't even be alive anymore.

Her awareness of her situation forced her butt to plop down onto her couch cushions, her come-to-Jesus moment slamming right into her chest. The man of her dreams would always be a man of her dreams.

"Oh, God. Jacob…"

She plunked her head down into her hands and let the tidal wave of emotion sweep her under. This was exactly what she hadn't wanted to happen. Something told her all along that their time together was temporary, but tell that to her stupid heart. The pain felt sharp yet intangible. It called to mind articles she had written on phantom limb pain in amputee patients, where long after the limb had been removed, patients claimed to still feel sensation there.

Yes, she certainly did feel a monumental amount of sensation at the moment.

After she let herself feel what she needed to feel and managed to wipe all manners of snot and tears on her dress, she sat up and collapsed back onto the couch, the corset she still wore making any sort of bend-over-and-sob motion a short-term exercise. Damn, she felt like a tube of toothpaste in this thing and worried she'd have to be squeezed out of it from the bottom.

What did all this mean for Jacob? She ran her fingers down her face, the underside of her fingernails growing wet as they scraped along and collected the tears that were falling.

Had Jacob reverted back to his post-war depression without her there? No, the most likely scenario was that he eventually married someone else…and didn't that thought just suck donkey balls. But it wasn't like she would wish him to live alone forever. She was far from the only fish in the sea, let's be fair there.

The more she thought about things, the more she desperately wished that he'd found someone to make him happy. That was all she ever wished for him and herself: happiness. But, man, did that thought sting deep, though. Sometime from now, once she had relearned how to sleep regularly again and go grocery shopping again and even just read a book again, she would research him. She needed to learn his story, to make sure she hadn't screwed up his life in some irrevocable way.

And if she had? Well, she'd cross that bridge when she came to it. But, God, how would she ever move on from this? And who the heck could she even talk to about her crazy story?

As she ran through all the questions of the moment, her eyes drifted over to the box of photos next to her on the couch. The damn box taunted her, representing everything that made her heart bleed at the moment. The genesis of her disastrous family reunion idea was held up between four sagging cardboard walls. But when she picked up one of the photo albums, the weight of the leather tome felt different. Sure, the surface was still smooth, the engravings still provided little hills that her fingers traveled. What felt different, though, was all internal.

For a reason she'd never know, she was thrust on a remarkable journey. Meeting her great-grandfather, hearing his softly accented English, watching his relationship with Helen bloom amid the backdrop of post-World War I Baltimore. God, she even got to eat club sandwiches with her great-grandmother. Sarah had been closer to her family in a few short weeks than any picture in that album could ever make her feel. And that's when the clarity hit her.

Of course, her family loved her. People show love in different ways. As she thought back over the years, her mother did always call her on her birthday. Not a text or an e-mail, but a phone call. And they'd usually catch up for a good hour before calling it a night. How many of her friends would speak to their mothers for that long, let alone want to? And her nieces and nephews, well, heck, she loved the snot out of those kids. There was no shortage of video calls with them, even to the annoyance of their parents when the calls delayed dinner. But were they truly annoyed, though? Maybe that was their way of showing love: access on demand instead of in person.

More moments began flooding to the surface: walking into her parents' house at Christmas and her dad, without saying a word or making eye contact, slipping her a fifty-dollar bill. Her Aunt Marie making a separate batch of oatmeal cookies without raisins just for her, while the rest of the family had theirs chock full of raisins.

There was love there. She just never saw it.

"Damn," Sarah whispered as she brought the album to her chest, her stupid tears falling once again. It took a trip through time to make her see what was right in front of her. Her throat started to tense as she hugged the album more tightly. She wished she could have thanked Ramon.

As soon as the thought formed, she knew what she had to do.

CHAPTER 33

The bite of the cold hardly bothered Jacob anymore. His skin no longer prickled, and he'd lost track of the last time his teeth chattered. His damn hide had been sitting on the boulder outside his cabin for so long, he was pretty well glued to it.

That was just fine by him. He was content to sit there until the spring thaw. Anything to keep him from his warm bed and the prospect of falling asleep. After a week of tortured nightmares, he was done. Every night since Sarah disappeared, his warped mind had run through the moving picture reel over and over again.

Sarah doubled over in pain on the bathroom floor. Her body laid out on the bed, her lungs not inflating. That damn green rash spreading all over her chest.

No heartbeat.

Then—just dust.

His stomach soured as he recalled the way her frail body had dissolved before his eyes. Like burnt embers wafting up into the air before the particles became so small you lost track of them.

He knew it was coming. She'd warned him. But his head—or was it his heart?—wouldn't budge.

Since she left—and God, how he prayed she just went back to her time and not something worse—he was prepared to spiral down as deep as he needed to. The loss of his parents, his brother, even Dick's death, it all stacked up. But Sarah was the topper that crumbled his whole tower.

So, he came back here. He thought to stay at the hotel for a few more, what, years? But this he couldn't run from.

However, when he came back to the cabin, his spitfire continued to surprise him even after she was gone. By some oddity, he didn't turn to the drink. The whiskey stayed firmly sealed in the cabinet. Sure, there was a moment or two early on in his return where his feet had led him there. But he always halted before even opening the cabinet. When he got into those moods, he could hear her, hear what she'd say to him.

Don't be so grumpy.

He hadn't had a drink since the champagne they shared at dinner together the week before. The night had been the best night of his life...until it wasn't.

The lapping of water against the lake's edge jostled him out of his thoughts. This spot on the boulder beside the lake had become his nightly routine. He figured it was better than being caged in by four walls. At least out there, he could lose control and rage against whatever tree or rock he needed to. The outbursts were always brief, but Christ, he couldn't go on like this.

He focused on the sound of the water again. Closing his eyes, he gave himself over to his senses. In his hands, he cradled the same item he always brought with him to his boulder every night: Sarah's sweater. The softness of the fibers calmed his beast, though he never quite understood why. At first, he thought the association would only crush him more. Her smells on the fabric, the memory of her wearing it. But it was a cool drink of water in his eternal hell. As he continued to stroke the sweater, he could feel his pulse evening out, beating in time to the lap-lap-lap of the water.

When his body finally relaxed, he cracked his eyes open and glanced out over the lake. The moon was bright enough to see the reflection clearly on the water's surface, though the imagery was distorted somewhat by the wind. His eyelids were heavy, but open wide enough to notice the increase in the ripples on the water. To his surprise, the ripples kept moving though his hair remained still against his neck. No breeze had reached him.

Odd.

The uneasiness didn't sit well with him. Out of habit, he clutched Sarah's sweater more tightly in his fists. His thumbs rubbed over the fabric in a harsher, more insistent manner. Across the water, the ripples began to take on a shape. The moonlight danced and mingled with the water, creating an illusion of a shape along its surface.

Strange, the tricks his addled mind played on him.

But the image sharpened when his mind expected it to fade. As he squinted harder, the shape of a man came into view. The dark hair and tanned complexion looked familiar, but appeared fuzzy as if he were in an oil painting that had already been splashed with a solvent. The harder Jacob stared at the shape, the more the man looked like Ramon.

No sooner did Jacob think it than the biggest smile appeared across the water man's face.

Yes, that man looked just like Ramon. Jacob's brain must have been well and truly fried. He slammed his eyes shut. A pounding took over in his skull. He gritted his teeth at the onslaught. The pain shot down his jaw. Quick exhales left his lungs as his hand flew to his forehead. Dizziness toppled his equilibrium. His hand fell away, and Jacob's limp body slid down the boulder to the forest floor. His face was buried beneath his hair, vertigo forcing his eyes to stay shut. When Jacob's hands finally went lax, Sarah's balled-up sweater tumbled from his grasp, and settled next to a rotted-out log.

Light green dust coated the edge of the collar and Jacob's fingertips.

The coffee on Sarah's tongue was lukewarm, but she couldn't be bothered to reheat it for a third time. At least she remembered to take it out of the microwave after her second trip over there.

It might as well have been dirty bathwater.

Her enthusiasm for even the little things had gone down the

crapper over the past week. When she landed back in her living room, she had initially been sad, confused, anxious, but oddly determined. Heck, she knew it was coming. Even tried to hammer it into Jacob's grumpy head that there was a looming expiration date.

But in practice, well, wasn't it always different in practice? Like how it was easy to talk about a wonderful weight loss program, but actually shedding the pounds was a whole other ball of wax.

She was knee-deep in that other ball of wax now. And it just suuuuucked.

Though she was gone for what felt like a few weeks, Sarah was surprised to learn no time at all had passed back home. She still found herself smack dab in the middle of her previously uneventful weekend. Nikki had been understanding when Sarah called out of work, only because Sarah made arrangements with Tracy to cover her stories for the week if anything came up. There weren't any other conferences or meetings lined up for a few weeks yet, so Sarah hoped things would be relatively quiet for Tracy's sake.

From her own perspective, she hardly cared. Most days she rarely left her bedroom, let alone bothered to get dressed. Her leggings had a few questionable stains on them, but doing a load of laundry felt too much like work, so she kept her hobo chic look going strong.

Rest was seldom peaceful. She usually woke several times in the night, her legs tangled in the annoying flat sheet she didn't know why she still used. Thoughts of Jacob always kept her up. At first, they were just memories of their times together: stolen glances and simple touches. But by the next night, they morphed into bone-deep longings and never-to-be what-ifs.

She had been so determined to plow through the pain, but determination and dedication were two different things. In the end, she let herself lean into it. When she was jettisoned back home, a part of her had literally been ripped out and left behind. The mornings, she decided, were for Jacob. In those newly sacred hours, she wrote down her memories, terrified she'd forget one detail. The afternoons and evenings, however, had slowly taken a different shape.

As she set her coffee cup down next to her laptop, she scrolled through her recent notes. In the absence of Jacob, Ramon's story had started to grip her again. All she had seen, all she knew began bubbling up to the surface. Dates stood out, scenes formed, relationships bloomed. As they came to her, she wrote furiously. Her research of her family's history, especially Ramon's, had turned into a spark of an idea. In the lazy hours of the afternoon, that idea grew wings. So she typed and Googled and flipped through photos and typed some more.

She scanned the latest paragraph she had just written, about Ramon's draft card for World War I. He had originally been listed as an immigrant, but the words had been crossed out and replaced with "naturalized citizen." Puerto Rico had just become a U.S. territory. And just like that, Ramon was an immigrant no more. She was caught up in the imagery of it when a loud thud came from her bedroom.

"What the...?"

The sound made her jolt out of her chair. Her bedroom was on the second floor, so an intruder was unlikely...but random thuds in a party-of-one condo were also very unlikely. Hopping from foot to foot, she was unsure which way to go. Should she run to her bedroom to investigate and potentially be killed by a criminal? Or should she run to the kitchen and find a weapon *before* running to her bedroom to potentially be killed by a criminal? She wasn't awake enough to deal with this paranoia.

Decision made, she dashed to the kitchen and grabbed the nearest thing of weight she could find: her forty-eight-ounce tub of mostly full ground coffee. On silent feet, she padded down the hallway, the coffee raised above her head like a cavewoman about to hurl a boulder at a predator. Her heart was in her throat as her toes crossed the ray of light on the floor from her bedside lamp. When her eyes peeked around the door flame, she froze.

On the carpet at the foot of the bed was a man with shaggy dark brown hair and shoulders the width of a sedan dry heaving on his hands and knees. The sounds that came out of him vacillated between a seal's bark and strings of curses commonly found in a satellite radio show host's monologue. But he wore the same navy-blue slacks, dark gray vest, and white long-sleeved shirt Sarah recognized from over a week ago.

"Jacob!" She dropped the coffee, its lid popping open and spilling grounds everywhere. Like hell she cared. She crossed her bedroom's floor in a fourth of a second and tackled Jacob around the middle, but not so hard as to cause him to fall backward. The man, after all, was clearly trying to hurl up the entire contents of his stomach.

At the abrupt onslaught, Jacob fell back on his legs and finally looked up at the woman in his arms. His face was red from all the strain. Even the whites of his eyes were starting to show red veins snaking their way to his pupils. Those eyes, though, had just registered her face and the questioning smile that reflected back at Sarah took her breath away.

"You're alive? Is this real?" Jacob rasped out. Hands, both hers and Jacob's, ran down each other's faces in concert. Every single feature had to be assessed as real lest they lose each other again. Jacob gently held Sarah's head in his hands and used his thumbs to caress everything: her eyebrows, the slope of her nose, the shape of her lips. He left nothing out of his attention. She felt like the most cherished artifact in a museum.

"I should be asking you the same thing," she said as she took his hand and slowly led him to the side of the bed. Her hands gently nudged him to sit.

"But how? You were dead. You collapsed on the bathroom floor in the hotel suite. The rash had completely covered your chest."

"I don't know. After I collapsed in the bathroom of the hotel, I woke up here, back home. But how are *you* here?"

At the mention of time travel, Jacob froze. Well, the parts of him he could control froze. His hands were still trembling from the dry heaves. "Where is *here*?"

Sarah grasped his wrists with her hands and held him steady. This part, she knew from experience, would be hard. "We're in my condo, my home, and the year is twenty twenty-one. We're in my bedroom right now."

At that, Jacob glanced around and took in the salmon pink walls with her shelves of books and battery-powered flameless candles. The black cylinder of her digital assistant stood watch over her knick-knacks and trinkets.

"I'm in the future?" Jacob asked, that last word rolling off his tongue with extreme trepidation.

"Yes."

Crickets.

Jacob squeezed the ever-loving crap out of her hands as his eyes settled back on hers. His silence spoke volumes, the look on his face one she was all too familiar with.

Disbelief. Fear.

And what did she expect to happen, really? That her miraculous traumatized World War I Army corporal would move right in with her and they'd live happily ever after? How would he live here? What would he do for work? Oh, God, how could she be so stupid? But she didn't know how to send him back, if that was what he wanted.

"Jacob, I'm so sorry..." Sarah choked out. This was the last thing she would have ever wished for him.

Before a single tear could fall, Jacob's warm hand grabbed her sweaty one and pulled her toward him. The look on his face was incredulous, determined, as he got down on his knees before her.

"Listen to me clearly." His tone was not one to brook any arguments, so she promptly buttoned up her yap. "There is not a thing in this world that would make me happier than living out my remaining days with you on this Earth. What I have back home is a family buried in the ground and an old comrade rotting dead in my well. Every step I took on that property brought back some measure of heartache, even when fond memories also joined the bad. I had no hope, no future prospects, until you stumbled along and lit a long-dead fire inside me."

Wow. She was capable of lighting a man's fire. Cool.

"This past week had been sheer agony. I never thought I'd get to lay eyes on you again. The weight of that knowledge was more soul-crushing than facing the loss of my family a thousandfold. I can't explain the why of it...but I'm content to trust that things happen for a reason. That I'm *here* for a reason."

There was nothing for it now. She couldn't keep her lower jaw hinged close if she tried. His words were so profound and powerful, the tears came unbidden at the thought of him staying with her. When those traitorous drops began to pool on her lashes and fell one by one, Jacob rose and soothingly swiped them away with the back of his knuckles.

"I love you. Then, now, and for as many tomorrows as we have."

The giddy laughter that rolled out of her sent more happy tears streaking down her face, but she didn't care. There wasn't much that could ruffle her in that moment.

"It's a done deal, then, soldier. I'm afraid we're stuck with each other."

"Perfect." Jacob beamed.

Ramon peered down at Sarah's glowing computer screen, content to give the happy couple their moment together. The corner of his lips rose as he scanned the names she had catalogued.

Ramon Mendez, MD

Helen Schneider Mendez (Gigi)

Ramona Mendez Hoffburg (Mumsy)

Seeing the affectionate nicknames of his family caused his throat to constrict a tad. A silent throat clearing got him through the moment as he rose to his full height, chin held high in pride.

The text ran on, the page overflowing with paragraphs upon paragraphs of anecdotes, vital records, and pasted photos. He didn't need to look further to be content in his decision to send Sarah back. The woman had talent, compassion, and a drive to rival the most stubborn doctor. She just needed a nudge in the right direction. And judging by the abrupt silence from Sarah's bedroom, Jacob had no qualms about guiding her way.

As the white tendrils of his spirit form began to dissipate from Sarah's condo, Ramon basked in his newfound sense of peace. The sensation was so rewarding, he was struck with the hope that others would search out the light as well. Ramon wouldn't be surprised if another soul's journey loomed on the horizon.

There was no breath anymore, no air available for Dick's lungs to inhale. The hard blow from behind, coupled with the retaining wall's assault to his midsection, left Dick like an empty bellow. The absence of air terrified him. What should have terrified him more in that moment, however, was the immediate promise of death. But, no, it didn't.

Truth be told, he was kind of grateful it was all ending. Finally. But, boy, he never would have come up with "plunging to his death in a well" as to how his card got punched. Hell, it always surprised him that he even made it out of the war as intact as he had. And while others would have seen his honorable discharge as a sign from the Almighty to get on the straight-and-narrow, Dick chose to take it in a different direction.

He drank like a fish because the numbness did a great job at evening him out in all regards. His senses were dulled all over, as opposed to just on his left side. For a few short hours, he could pretend he was a full man, albeit a boorish asshole. For those small windows of time, Dick was just another drunk in a bar who would gamble, fight, and fuck his way through the hours.

Come morning, though, when the sun's rays beat down on him and highlighted all his flaws and shortcomings again, the depression returned in full force. He was like a nocturnal animal, only living for the dark with all the other misfit nightcrawlers. He avoided the light like a street dog avoids rancid meat; he accepted the sun's place in the world, sure, but he in no way sought it out.

So when the bright moonlight angled down into the well, the contrast added to his terror. As the tops of his legs scraped along the edge of the well's rough stones, his vision had already started to get disoriented. He knew that because the oddest thing stood out to him, even as he was upside down. As the threat of descending into darkness loomed, a flash of something reflected off his pants. The fabric had picked up some loose powder from the well's stone edge. In the moonlight, it almost took on a pale green hue.

When Dick's body had finally broken free of the wall, he flung his hands out any which way he could send them. The diameter of the tunnel was small for a man of his bulk. All manner of muck and grime painted his hands. As terror settled in his stomach, his hand unintentionally brushed the spot on his pants where that powder had been.

The dizziness hit him like a tornado, his body convulsing from the coughing spasms. All at once, the manic sounds in the well ceased.

The surface of the water had never been broken.

EPILOGUE

Two years later

Sarah topped off her red pail with more wet sand and tamped it down as best she could with her dollar-store shovel. The pail was so heavy with the weight of the sand, she was worried she'd snap off the shovel's head if she loaded any more "cement," as her five-year-old nephew called it, in there.

"All right, she's packed to the brim here. Where's this one going?" Sarah asked.

"Over here on the left. We need to make a barricade so the evil army doesn't get through," her nephew said, walking on his knees toward the area he wanted Sarah to fortify.

"You got it."

As she dumped and dug and dumped some more, the sun beat down on her shoulders. A quick peek revealed a little too much red for her liking, so she needed to take a break to reapply her sunscreen. "Hey, Joey, I'll be back in a sec, all right? I need a quick break."

"Okay, Aunt Sarah," Joey said, knee-deep in digging out the moat that would loop all the way around his castle.

Sarah crawled over to her beach chair, nestled beneath her giant watermelon umbrella, and took a load off to rummage through her tote bag. Against all the odds, she and her family had finally been able to have their long-awaited family reunion, though two years later than Sarah originally planned. The weather was gorgeous and fore-casted to remain so throughout their long weekend at the Jersey Shore. The house they rented was three houses in from the beach and couldn't have been a better choice for the family. The big seller, of course, was the roof-top hot tub that was made available during their stay.

Not too shabby.

The smooth plastic of her sunscreen bottle graced her fingertips at the bottom of her bag. She pulled it out and sat back while she drew little happy faces on her legs with the lotion before rubbing it in thor-oughly. As she worked in the sunscreen, she looked out to the water where her brother and other nephews and nieces were playing.

A flash of perfectly bronzed skin caught her eye. Jacob had just come up out of the waves, the water sluicing off his back as he flung his wet hair back out of his face. He swam a few feet toward her seven-year-old niece, Carly, and ducked under her legs. Then he rose out of the water with her sitting astride his strong shoulders and flipped her backward into the water. The laughs and giggles of her family enjoying their time traveled all the way to her ears, and the joy that brought her was beyond immense.

She was afraid to say it, afraid to admit it out loud, but her life was pretty damn perfect. She and Jacob had been living together for the last two years. After a few tense weeks post-time travel where they worried he might be whisked back to 1919, they managed to breathe a sigh of relief. Whatever magic brought Jacob to her had graciously left him there. No green rash appeared whatsoever. So, despite a few challenging early months of adjustment on Jacob's part, they'd finally reached a point where being together was as effortless as breathing.

One of the biggest challenges had been Jacob's insistence that he financially support Sarah, despite her explaining to him again and again that gender roles were different in this time. They still had many obstacles to face as a couple, but hopefully, one such obstacle was close to being resolved.

A few towns over from where they lived, an abandoned orchard and farm had been put up for auction. Apparently, the previous owners had fallen on some hard times and stopped making the payments to the bank for the mortgage. When the bank repossessed the property and the notice of auction was put out by the town, Jacob had asked Sarah what would be involved in putting in a bid.

After much discussion, evaluation of assets, and a business plan jotted down on the fly (thank you, Internet), the two of them had placed a bid on a farm...and won the auction. Ever since then, Jacob had thrown himself into the land and turned it around. Several of the townsfolk came out and offered start-up capital for the farm as well, as it was such a beloved part of the community.

Together, they had turned the orchard into a pick-your-own attraction and worked out several arrangements with local bakers to sell fresh-baked pies (using the farm's bounty), as well as produce delivery systems for homebound residents. It had all been a massive undertaking, with Sarah not seeing Jacob for days sometimes during those early harvest time periods. He had taken to sleeping on the couch in the office above the farm's general store when four a.m. wake-ups were called for.

But the gamble paid off. Already, they had managed to pay down close to half of Sarah's initial business loan, and they were on track to pay it off completely within the next two years. Watching Jacob shine in such a role made all the struggles worth it, especially when he brought her home some of the first nibbles of sweet peaches or strawberries.

Oh, and then there had been that little side project Sarah had finished six months ago.

Peering over the rim of her sunglasses, she spotted her Uncle Gary sitting in a beach chair nearby reading a book.

Her book.

The bold lettering of the gold embossed title, *A Biography of an Immigrant Doctor from Puerto Rico*, glistened under the sun. It shone like the crowning achievement it was. The past year and a half had brought a lot of growth, but the most rewarding for Sarah was finally being able to write Ramon's story. The thrill of being able to fill in details only she would know brought her telling of his years at Martinsville to life. She had thrown herself into research, examined records, interviewed what family she could, and even scoured old medical school yearbooks. The end result was a manuscript she was beyond proud of...until Jacob encouraged her to reach out to Martinsville and see whether they'd be willing to publish it under their University Press arm. She still smiled every time she recalled the letter she received from the publisher accepting her manuscript for print. And she never would have pushed herself if it weren't for Jacob believing in her.

Lost in her daydreaming, she didn't even notice when her sopping-wet boyfriend meandered up to her and began toweling off right at her feet.

"How's the water?" Sarah asked, grateful for the view and, most especially, that he blocked out the harsh sun from further baking her.

"Great! Even though it's the end of June, the lifeguard over there said the water was already sixty-eight degrees. Once you're in for a few minutes, it's wonderful."

"I'm glad you're enjoying it," she said, tracking him as he sprawled out next to her on his back, one hand resting on his muscled bare chest while he used his other forearm to cushion his head.

"You know, I always find those aerial advertisements so intriguing," Jacob mused as he looked up at the sky. "Who came up with that idea anyway?"

Sarah glanced up, and sure enough, there was another plane meandering through the blue expanse toting a banner behind its wings that said, "Half-price wings and beer at Buster's 4-7pm every day that ends in Y!"

"I don't know, but they are highly effective. If you think about it, you have an entire shoreline of saturated customers with nothing better to do than to look up and see what's tempting them today."

"Exactly! Oh, look, there's another one." Jacob pointed off to Sarah's right this time, though the plane was still a bit far out.

The banner was different from the one they had just seen, though.

This one was all white and had two pictures of trees. From each tree, a single branch extended out diagonally until the two branches came together in the middle to wrap around each other at the apex of the V. At the top was a single red apple. That much Sarah could make out, but it looked to her like the apple was in the shape of a heart. Her eyes dropped to the bottom of the banner, and she read the words, "Sarah, marry me? - Jacob."

As the plane floated directly in front of her and the banner appeared front and center, her head shot to Jacob. He was still lying on his back in the same carefree position, but in the middle of his chest was a tiny black velvet jewelry box that hadn't been there before. His eyes were closed, but his left one opened just a crack to peek in her direction, his ever-present smirk betraying his casualness.

The smug bastard.

"Jacob, is this for real?" Sarah asked as she hesitantly palmed the black velvet. Once her hand held the box, he covered her hand and captured her to his heart.

"For all my tomorrows, Sarah. I promise you."

The ring was absolutely stunning, a single solitaire diamond on a platinum band. But she was curious about something.

"Before I give my answer, how many apples did you have to sell to buy this, corporal?"

"What would be the sufficient number I'd have to tell you in order to accept my marriage proposal, Miss Johansson?"

"Hmm...Let's see. You charge $1.99 per pound, with roughly three medium-sized apples in a pound. But if you're talking about those newer varieties you just began to harvest, those are much smaller. You could easily get four to a pound at least..."

"Is this what the rest of our days will be like, then?" Jacob said through a chuckle.

"Oh, yes." Sarah smiled back at him with a nod.

"A yes! That's a yes, then?"

"Yes."

"She said yes!" Jacob hollered before he wrapped Sarah up in a great bear hug and rolled her onto the beach towel. Catcalls, clapping, and hoots could be heard from her family behind her, but she didn't care.

She was in heaven, and as far as she was concerned, she had all the time in the world.

Thank you, wonderful readers, for diving into *Charmed by the Past!* I hope you enjoyed the first novel in my Spirits Through Time series. The next story explores Dick's journey. Do you think he deserves a chance at redemption? Find out in *Sirens of the Past,* due out in November 2021.

To join my mailing list and learn about upcoming releases, visit aimeerobinsonromance.com/newsletter.

ABOUT THE AUTHOR

Aimee Robinson is a lover of romance novels in all forms. Her absolute favorites, though, are the ones that offer a little bit of something extra: time travel, guardian angels, good old-fashioned meddlesome grandmothers with a supernatural secret to hide, you name it.

She believes romance novels should transport you from the humdrum to the swoon-worthy, preferably while being curled up on the couch with chocolate and tea (or wine...or both!). Aimee's overactive imagination lends itself to fun tales with emotional adventures, sexy snark, and happily ever afters.

When not writing or reading, Aimee enjoys spending time with her husband and keeping up with her two young sons.

Printed in Great Britain
by Amazon

65394702R00151